SEE LOVE

~

KNOW YOURSELF

A Love Game Adventure
Book Two

ALSO BY DAVID MONTGOMERY, M.D.

Loving to Heal: Easing the Way to Wellness

*See Love ~ Know God: A Transformational
Adventure Beyond Belief*

SEE LOVE

~

KNOW YOURSELF

A Love Game Adventure
Book Two

David Montgomery, M.D.

See Love ~ Know Yourself
The Love Game Adventure: Book Two
©2025 David Montgomery, M.D.

Edited by Diane Sova, Global Spirit Publishing

ISBN: 979-8-9920738-3-6

Website: www.thelovegame.love
Contact the author: david@thelovegame.love

Published by David Montgomery, LLC

Dedication and Acknowledgements

I dedicate this book

- ♥ To those who haven't awakened yet to their own Divine Loveself.

- ♥ To those who find it challenging to open their hearts to see life through the non-judgmental eyes of Love.

- ♥ To those who are immersed in playing the survival game unaware there is another game in town.

Acknowledgement ~ Appreciation

- ♥ To Diane Sova's Loveself for supporting me in completing this project.

- ♥ To my Loveself for repeatedly reminding me not to try to control the story. Let it arise out of uncertainty.

- ♥ To those who have challenged me with anger, criticism, rejection, and blame. They have helped me see the north star.

Table of Contents

Introduction

In the first book of The Love Game Adventure series, *See Love ~ Know God*, the transformative power of seeing divine love as the path to truly knowing God was explored. It was a journey into faith, connection, and a sacred invitation to experience love that transcends fear and judgment. With Book Two, *See Love ~ Know Yourself*, that journey continues - this time turning inward. If knowing God begins with seeing love, then knowing yourself is the natural next step. This book is an invitation to meet yourself with the same compassion, clarity, and truth that divine love offers; to discover that your worth, identity, and healing are found not in striving, but in seeing yourself as already known and already loved.

In *See Love ~ Know God,* the summer that changed everything had drawn to a close, though the ripples of transformation continued to expand through the hearts of everyone touched by a precocious eleven-year-old boy's simple discovery.

It began when David, lonely and bullied, received a verbal invitation that would seem impossible to most adults, "Play the Love Game with Me." That voice identified itself as I AM that I AM, known by many names such as God or Love - all one and the same.

To start, David was instructed to go to a park and see how many places he could find God. After some frustration, he realized it was easier to recognize God as Love rather than trying to find the distant, fearsome deity his conditioning had taught him to expect. David was told that it was important to clear judgments and expectations from his thinking in order to open his heart - because only an open heart would be able to see or hear God. He discovered that open hearts could communicate with each other through dreams, intuitions, and non-ordinary ways of knowing.

What started as one boy's quest to find God became an ever-widening circle of transformation. David taught the Love Game to

Angela, an eleven-year-old African American girl fighting cancer, who had been abandoned by her mother Rachel and then cared for by her grandmother Nana. Together, David and Angela discovered that playing the Love Game in partnership amplified their ability to find Love in the most unlikely places – in hospital rooms, during moments of fear, even in the face of death itself.

The natural world became their greatest teacher. Crystals pulsed with divine energy, the serene waters of Peace Pond reflected deeper truths, and encounters with the living world around them revealed profound wisdom. Animals like Chickadee and Deer played important roles in helping them see Love through their timeless presence. These creatures approached them without fear, recognizing the Love that radiated from David and Angela's hearts.

As the Love Game progressed, David and Angela discovered three levels of difficulty, each one more challenging:

Level One was to find Love in what or who they liked - during easy moments, with beloved people, through beautiful experiences. Level one was finding Love in the presence of joy.

Level Two was to find Love in what was disliked or unwanted, including parts of themselves they'd rejected. David and Angela practiced this with a bully and a homeless man but, more importantly, they practiced the Love Game with the shame and guilt they placed on themselves through fears and judgments.

Level Three was to find Love in uncertainty and unwanted situations beyond control - Angela's illness, Rachel's addiction, moments when life seemed to be happening to them rather than for them.

Their loving energy proved contagious. Mrs. Amma Deera, an eighty-year-old widow drowning in loneliness and the physical challenges of aging, joined their adventure and rediscovered wonder. Her son, Dr. Mark Deera, a psychiatrist trained to diagnose and treat problems, found himself questioning everything he thought he knew about healing after witnessing the transformative power of Love in action.

Dr. Crystal Welling, Angela's pediatric oncologist, reconnected with the Love she thought was gone forever. Most miraculously, Rachel - lost in the survival game of addiction and depression - found her way back to reunite with Angela through Dr. Deera's compassionate intervention and David's guidance. Angela's pure, unconditional Divine Love became the medicine that transformed Rachel's heart, teaching her that opening to Love was always possible, even from the depths of despair.

Together they learned that Love exists only in the present moment, that appreciation opens the heart like a key, and that recognizing their unity - their oneness - dissolved the illusion of separation that fueled so much suffering. They discovered they were not victims of their circumstances but creators of their reality, able to transform any situation through the choice to see with Love's eyes. Even when Angela's physical form could no longer contain her radiant spirit, she continued to touch hearts as the Angel she had always been, proving that Love transcends every boundary the survival game insists is real.

The survival game - the ancient pattern of fear, competition, and scarcity - had served its purpose by providing contrast. It helped them recognize the Love Game by showing them what it was *not*. But then a deeper understanding emerged; opening to Love was only the beginning. Learning to live from Love while navigating the persistent voices of fear, depression, anxiety, anger, shame, guilt, and unworthiness - this was the next invitation.

They had not mastered the Love Game, and perhaps they never would. But they were choosing to play it more and more often, turning suffering into joy, peace, compassion, and kindness. In *See Love ~ Know Yourself*, the Love Game beckons them deeper, asking:

> Can you find Love even in unwanted thoughts and feelings that arise within you?

> Can you create the experience of your desires being fulfilled now, rather than waiting for some future time?

> Can you know yourself as Love, even when fear whispers that you are something less?

May your adventures in Love continue.

See Love ~ Know Yourself

Chapter 1: Compassion

Thursday, August 21

"Come quick, Dr. Deera, someone has fallen into a deep hole," Karen's voice cut through Mark's routine morning rounds on the Behavioral Health Unit.

"Who fell in, Karen?"

"It's too dark to tell for sure."

I follow her toward a growing crowd surrounding a dark hole. The cacophony of voices is overwhelming. People are screaming, "Do something! You must save her!" Others turn away, muttering, "Thank God it's not anyone I know."

I recognize the familiar dance of helpers and observers, each playing their part. The empaths crowd closer, their own pain visible in their desperate need to help both the victim and themselves. Some ask God for a miracle. Survivors who've climbed out of their own holes shout advice. Questions pepper the air like artillery: "Why did you fall?" "What triggered this?" "Why does God let this happen?" as if understanding alone could save someone.

I watch as they rain down their solutions into the darkness - self-help books thudding uselessly into the void, colorful rope ladders dangling with promises of escape, drugs rattling down like hollow hope. Snake oil salesmen hover at the edges, promising miracle cures with money-back guarantees.

"Please stop!" The cry from below pierces through the chaos.

The crowd turns to me. "You are the expert, why isn't she following our advice? Why doesn't she want help? What are you going to do?"

I step close to the edge and peer into the darkness. My training tells me to maintain professional distance. Stay at the edge. Observe.

Diagnose. Plan treatment. All the do-gooders are offering helpful advice to the distressed person. But something feels different today.

Then Angela appears beside me, looking like her healthy self before she died. No longer the frail child wearing a turban to hide her chemotherapy baldness, she's a beautiful eleven-year-old black girl with a perfect afro and that unmistakable sparkle in her eyes that would light up any room. She says *"Compassion is offering the presence of your Divine Loveself to another being. Not your fixing-self, not you fear-self nor your ego-self that needs them to be different so you can feel better. Your Divine Loveself it that part of you that sees through the eyes of Love, that recognizes the wholeness in another even when they are suffering."* Angela then takes my hand and together we descend into the darkness.

"Thanks for coming," a young female voice says.

The words leave my mouth before I can think: "Angela and I have not come down to fix you. We just want to be with you."

"That's good," the voice responds. "I don't need to be fixed. I'm here for you."

I reach into the darkness to find the girl's fragile hand. She doesn't pull away. We sit in silence as the distant voices of those above calling out fade away. I am surprised to find myself unusually calm, my breathing steady, despite my uncertainty.

"I don't understand. What do you mean, you're here for me?" I ask.

Angela interrupts gently: *"You don't need to understand, just be open to receive. Just allow your expectations about how this should go fall aside so your heart can open to what she wants to give you."*

The darkness begins to lift, allowing the image of a girl to emerge. "Maggie, it's you!"

*****

Mark bolted upright in bed with an immediate pang of regret - Maggie was right there, finally ready to tell him something, and he'd awakened too soon. The dream clung to him as he tried to understand. "Why now, Maggie? After all these years, what are you trying to tell me?"

The questions lingered as he showered and got ready for his day. He looked in the mirror, noticing the goatee he'd been sporting since starting his practice more than twenty years ago. At fifty, his dark brown hair was beginning to gray at the temples, but still meticulously styled with that precise part on the left side. Even though he wasn't a psychoanalyst, Mark carried the look of Freud.

He couldn't help but think about how much has changed in the psychiatric field since he started his training, when he really wanted to make a difference for those suffering with mental health issues. Now he wasn't so sure about the value he adds or what difference he makes. He needs a change – and decides that if he wants a change, he's going to start by shaving off his goatee.

Without giving himself time to reconsider, he reached for his electric razor. The familiar buzz filled the bathroom as twenty years of carefully maintained facial hair fell into the sink. When he looked up, a stranger stared back - younger somehow, more open. It was a small thing, but it felt like letting go of a piece of armor he no longer needed.

He dressed in his customary crisply ironed white shirt, grey suit pants, and bright blue tie, each crease sharp, each detail considered. His six-foot height and careful attention to his appearance gave him a commanding presence. Sometimes he wished he could let go of the conservative professional appearance that has served as a shield protecting him from others getting too close. The one time he let his facade down was after the death of Angela, when he went to the hospital to make rounds wearing khakis and a Hawaiian flowered shirt. He felt free that day.

When he arrived at his office, he completed his professional uniform by donning his signature white thigh-length lab coat, the embroidered letters over the pocket reading "Dr. Mark Deera, Chief of Psychiatry."

He thinks that too many of the practices today are fear-focused and leave him wanting something more. Much of the actual counseling is done by psychologists, social workers, and nurses, leaving him with pill prescribing - and that was often done over the phone. His administrative duties separate him further from front-line patient care. The conventional approaches to psychiatric care don't excite him the way they did when he first started. Although he acknowledges their value, he's seen too many times where the system failed patients. This is burnout.

Looking back, he was feeling burnt out even before he met David and Angela. The effect those kids had on him made him question his life and his approach to serving the mental health needs of others.

Maybe it was time to allow his heart to be his love-focused guide instead of relying on his fear-focused training.

*****

Rachel glanced at her watch as she hung up her cleaning smock, stepped out of her blue housekeeping scrubs, and hurried to change into street clothes before her session with Dr. Deera.

She took a moment to look in the small locker room mirror, ran her hand over her short-cropped, easy-to-manage hair, and applied a touch of lip gloss. At thirty, her dark brown complexion radiated health. Her final times with Angela had shown her a new way of seeing herself - as well as the world. This translated into her appearance, her posture, and her personal hygiene, revealing the glow of a woman who was finally enjoying life rather than running away from it.

She'd barely make it to Dr. Deera's office on time, but she would never miss her sessions with him. As she hurried down the corridor, her eyes caught those of a troubled-looking visitor. Rachel heard Angela's voice, "*Stop, momma!*"

She stopped and asked the woman, "Are you okay?"

"Not really. My husband is having open heart surgery and I'm waiting to hear how he's doing."

"May I hold your hand for a moment?" Rachel asked as she extended her hand. The distressed woman looked into Rachel's deep brown eyes, wondering why this stranger stopped. She was surprised to find her own hand reaching out to Rachel. Without any words, they continued looking into each other's eyes. Rachel noticed the woman's face softening and her hunched shoulders relaxing in response.

"I have a feeling your husband is going to be fine," Rachel said gently. "The surgeons are taking good care of him." The woman thanked Rachel with a smile, not questioning her statement. "I have to go now, but I'm leaving my Angel to be with you. You're not alone." Small moments of connection like these have become Rachel's favorite part of her job.

"*You're getting good at that,*" Angela's voice whispered in her heart. "*Remember when you couldn't even look people in the eyes?*"

"I remember, my dear Angel. Thank you for being with me."

Dr. Deera's waiting room was empty when she arrived. His secretary must have already gone for the day, leaving the office unusually quiet. His door opened before she could sit down, and she noticed an unfamiliar expression on his face - something between weariness and anticipation.

"It's a new you," Rachel said, noting his clean-shaven face, "but still with Love at your core."

"Good afternoon, Rachel. You look happy."

"Yes, I am. How about you, Dr. Deera?"

"I have a lot on my mind today, Rachel."

Usually, their sessions followed a comfortable pattern in this familiar office with its diplomas and medical journals: her progress with sobriety, her work as a housekeeper at the hospital, her growing relationship with her son Sammy and her mother Nana. Rachel sensed a heavy energy with Dr. Deera today; even the space itself felt different somehow.

"How was your shift, Rachel?" he asked as she settled into her usual chair.

"Good." Rachel smiled. "I was in the psych unit today to clean up a mess. The usual housecleaning person was sick. While there, I noticed a patient who had lost control. He was angry, yelling and throwing things. The nurse called security. I heard Love tell me to go up to him, look into his eyes, and see him as Love. Everyone was surprised when the man turned to the staff, said he was sorry, and quietly returned to his room. Sometimes I feel like I am meant to be doing more than just cleaning, you know?"

Dr. Deera leaned forward, his professional demeanor slipping. "That's actually something I've been thinking about lately. The way you connect with patients without even using words, Rachel - it's not something they taught us in medical school. I'm jealous."

Rachel noticed his change in tone. "What do you mean?"

"The conventional methods..." Dr. Deera stood and walked to his window, something he had never done before during sessions. "Prescribing medications, following protocols, professional distancing - they're helpful, but lately I feel like I'm missing something essential." He turned back to face her. "David and Angela changed everything for me. Now I'm questioning everything I thought I knew about healing."

Rachel sat quietly, sensing there was more. This was the first time she'd seen her psychiatrist so...human. "I think you're selling yourself short, Dr. Deera. Do you really think you didn't connect with me when I was transferred to this hospital? I felt our connection immediately."

"By then Angela and David had already touched my life. I wonder if you would have felt the same way about me before then."

"Who knows, and it doesn't really matter anyway because when we did meet, it was the perfect time."

"It's wonderful that you had an appointment today because I had a dream last night that I would like to share with you. I know I'm supposed to be counseling you, not the other way around, but I feel your presence as Love is the perfect witness for my experience."

"I am here for you," said Rachel.

"Someone had fallen into a deep hole. A crowd of people were standing at the edge peering into the darkness. Many were throwing down advice for how to get out - through books, ropes, medication. Angela was there and together we descended into the hole - the kind of leap into uncertainty I've spent my career avoiding - not to fix or attach a diagnostic label to the person at the bottom, but just to be. The girl at the bottom was Maggie, my sister who committed suicide when she was fifteen years old. She said she was there for me. But damn, I woke up before she could reveal what she meant by being here for me."

Rachel leaned forward in her chair. "Dr. Deera, what if your dream about Maggie isn't just about the past? What if it's showing you a new direction, allowing you to create a different life?"

He considered this, nodding slowly. "David and Angela showed us both how healing happens when we open our hearts to Love."

Rachel added, "Angela told me that Love says, '*What is seen as Me is what unites, nourishes, and transforms both the seer and the seen.*' Imagine when you see yourself as Love, you become both the seer and the seen. The effects are glorious."

Dr. Deera paused, uncertainty crossing his face. "But how do I even begin? Twenty years of training and conditioning about right and wrong ways to help patients is the ground I've built my practice on. I've learned to hide behind the inflexibility of the professional mask as protection, putting distance between me and others. It kept me objective, avoiding unwanted feelings."

"It sounds like you haven't been focusing on what you really want because you're tied up playing the survival game," Rachel said gently.

"I can see it in your eyes. Maybe the place to begin is in this moment. Do you really need to know what comes next?"

Dr. Deera ran his hand through his hair, a rare gesture of vulnerability. "You're right. I'm already trying to live in a future that hasn't happened, imagining all the ways this could go wrong. As a lifelong fixer, I've been focused on doing, doing something or anything. That's where I found value...but now I'm being asked to just be. Even imagining unproductive time makes me uncomfortable."

"Not only to just be, but to be your Loveself. Do you have the courage to open your heart to the present moment without the shroud of fear?"

"We'll see," Dr. Deera said, looking up.

"Are you open to a suggestion?" asked Rachel.

"Yes, of course."

"If you feel stuck, you might take a trip to the Peace Pond. Ask Maggie to sit with you. Put your feet in the water and let it take care of your questions and concerns."

After a long pause, he looked into Rachel's eyes. "I see the Love you are, and I feel...perfect. Thank you so much for being here for me today, Rachel. I think it's time that our roles as doctor-therapist and patient end. I consider you family and a friend now. I will always be here for you in that way to support you. You're doing well, but I might suggest going back to Dr. Bill Shapiro. Talk to him about weaning off your antidepressant medication."

Rachel nodded, feeling a mix of gratitude and bittersweetness wash over her.

"I also suggest that you continue with your AA meetings. I have a feeling that your presence there will be a source of inspiration and healing for you as well as others as you continue finding your way in this life."

Mark smiled. "I can't predict the future, but I'm having a very satisfying feeling right now imagining us working together as colleagues. And please, Rachel, call me Mark."

Rachel felt tears welling up as she moved toward him. Without words, they embraced - a hug that felt like both an ending and a beginning.

Chapter 2: Intimacy

Thursday evening, August 21

Mark sat in Crystal's driveway for a moment before getting out, still processing his transformative session with Rachel. This condo really reflects Crystal's busy lifestyle, he thought - the well-maintained landscaping, simple lines, and inside almost too clean and uncluttered. *Maybe that's why we get along,* he mused. *We both have a compulsion for orderliness.*

He contemplated the word obsessive-compulsive, a label he often used in his practice. There was a coldness about it. He had been thinking all day about changing his life and his practice. Maybe being more human would bring the feeling of warmth that he has been longing for. *Maybe I could put more attention on accepting and appreciating rather than trying to control everything.*

The dream about Maggie continued to occupy his thoughts as he walked to Crystal's door and knocked.

She hesitated a moment before opening it, checking her hair. At forty-eight, she still took care to look nice even after exhausting days, her shoulder-length blonde hair swept back, a delicate necklace catching the light. She opened the door with a tired smile that quickly transformed into surprise. "Oh my God, Mark!" She reached up to run her hands along his newly clean-shaven cheeks and chin, her touch gentle and exploratory. "I can't believe how different you look." She leaned in and kissed him softly. "I like it. What made you do that?" she asked.

Mark smiled. "I'm creating a new me, a more aligned-with-my-heart Me."

"I like that," Crystal responded.

They'd both had demanding days, but something felt different tonight. Since neither had the energy to cook, they decided on their favorite Mexican restaurant, hoping the familiar setting might help them navigate whatever this shift between them might bring.

*****

At Casa Miguel, they settled into their usual booth in the dimly lit corner, surrounded by warm terracotta walls and the soft murmur of other conversations. The familiar scent of cilantro and lime should have been comforting, but tonight even their usual comfort felt somehow charged with possibility. They ordered margaritas and studied their menus, both sensing that something needed to be said but uncertain of how to begin.

When the server asked for their order, Mark chose the enchiladas verdes, and Crystal, too tired to decide, simply said, "I'll have the same."

After the server left, they sat looking at each other across the table. Finally, Crystal broke the silence. "What's going on with us, Mark?"

Mark took a sip from the salt-rimmed glass and considered her question. "I think we might be having some unmet needs in our relationship, or different ways that we approach our stresses that don't align and don't support these needs."

Crystal raised an eyebrow. "Mark, you're talking to me like I'm one of your patients. Can you just tell me what you're actually feeling?"

Mark paused, caught off guard. "You're right. I'm sorry." Taking a deep breath, he admitted, "The truth is, I fear displeasing you, and that fear weighs heavy on me. I know you want to be with me, and I want that too, but I also find myself wanting to hide because I'm afraid I won't be enough for you."

She set her glass down and looked directly at him, her expression softening.

He took another sip of his drink. "For years now, I've come home to an empty house. I appreciate the silence that allows me to recover from the constant interactions with others. On the other hand, I do get lonely and wish I could find some balance." He paused, looking at her carefully. "I enjoy being with you, but I don't know how to alter my fixing and problem-solving habits to fully be present with you and still recharge."

Another pause, his voice growing softer. "Today something shifted for me. I felt a pull or a calling to show up differently for my patients, myself, and for you. Uncertainty and change scare me." He looked up at her. "How are you feeling about what I've just told you?"

"I'm the opposite, Mark. For a long time now, I've been alone, longing for someone to talk to about my day. It helps me when someone can be present without offering advice."

Mark nodded slowly, considering her words. "I think I've trained myself to always be in solution mode. Twenty years of patients expecting answers has made it hard to just..." He stopped mid-sentence, looking at Crystal. "See? I just did it again. You shared something important about what you need, and I immediately made it about my problem instead of really hearing you. I'm sorry, Crystal. Please go on."

Crystal's eyes reflected deep emotion. She touched her necklace as if to soothe the uncertainty of what she is about to say. "Thank you for catching that, Mark. You have no idea how much I needed to hear that. It gives me hope for our relationship." Her voice softened. "What I need is someone who can sit with me as I cry, without resisting my feelings or trying to talk me out of them or fix my pain. What I need is someone who can hold space for the weight of what I carry."

Mark shifted his chair, resisting his habit of responding before he truly heard and understood everything she was saying.

She took a shaky breath. "Today I lost a seven-year-old who'd been fighting leukemia for two years. Yesterday I had to tell the parents their child's cancer had spread. There are days I come home carrying all of that grief, and sitting alone with it feels unbearable sometimes."

Mark sat quietly for a moment, feeling the weight of what she'd shared. "Crystal, I had no idea you were holding all of that alone. I can see how much pain you carry, and I realize now that when I try to make your sadness go away, I'm actually making you feel more alone." He looked directly into her eyes with deep compassion. "I want to be here for you."

Crystal's eyes filled with tears. "That's all I ever wanted, Mark. Just knowing you want to try makes such a difference." She stretched her hand across the table. "Something's different about you today. I can feel it. Like you're really here with me in a way you haven't been before."

She smiled through her tears, squeezing his hand. "We're both so careful, aren't we? Always walking on eggshells."

"I suppose it might be a professional hazard," Mark responded, returning the squeeze. "Though I think it's more than that for both of us."

Her eyes met his. "You mean our marriages?"

"Yes." Mark leaned back slightly. "Sixteen years I was married to Ellen, and in the end, she said she felt like I was married to the hospital instead of her, that I was more present for my patients than I ever was for her. Even with joint custody, Sarah chose to live with Ellen. I think she knew where my real attention was."

"Tom said almost the same thing," Crystal sighed. "Eight years, and all he got was whatever energy I had left after giving everything to my patients and their families. He was a dermatologist - he had no trouble leaving his patients and practice behind at the end of the day. He remarried within six months of our divorce, and I think that relationship started long before we separated." She looked down at her hands. "When our son Eric was fifteen, Tom got an offer from a medical school in Southern California to teach and build a practice there. I didn't fight him on that, but I was heartbroken that I couldn't see Eric as often. Eric was interested in filmmaking, so he was happy to go with his father. I still carry a lot of guilt about not being present for him and not being a good mother.

Her voice grew quieter. "The weight of pediatric oncology follows me everywhere, even when I try to leave it behind."

They sat in silent understanding for a moment.

"I'm afraid of making the same mistakes," Mark admitted.

"And I worry that I'll always put others before my relationship," Crystal responded. "It's why I've been taking things so slowly with us."

He nodded. "I appreciate that. I think we both need the space to figure out whether we can do things differently this time."

"And can we?" Crystal asked softly. "Do you think we can learn to be present for each other in ways we couldn't be for Ellen or Tom?"

The waiter arrived with their food, creating a momentary pause in their conversation. As he set the plates down, both Mark and

Crystal seemed to exhale, the weight of their sharing settling between them.

As they began to eat, they continued talking about ways to support each other, their conversation flowing more easily now. The vulnerability they'd shared seemed to have opened something between them.

Mark paused mid-bite and looked at Crystal with a soft expression. "This is what I want."

"What? Your enchilada?" she asked, smiling.

Mark laughed. "No, what we have right now, the way I feel with you right now. I don't have to think about the future, our future, when I feel the way I do now. I don't have to worry about repeating the past. I'm not the same man I was."

Walking to the car after dinner, Crystal slipped her hand into his. "Would you like to come over for some after-dinner coffee?" she asked with a small smile and a glint in her eyes.

"I'd like that," Mark said, feeling something shift within him.

*****

At Crystal's house, they sat close together on her back porch swing beneath a waning crescent moon. The warm evening air was rich with the scent of jasmine drifting from her garden. Mark smiled as Crystal gazed up at the night sky and let out a delighted squeal when a shooting star streaked across the sky.

She turned and leaned in toward him. "This is perfect," she whispered against his lips.

In the quiet that followed, she pulled back slightly, softly sighing, "Thank you."

"For what?" he asked.

"For trusting me enough to allow your true Loveself to be with me tonight. This is what intimacy is all about."

In silence, they watched the night deepen. No promises were made, no problems solved. Yet something had undeniably changed between them.

And for tonight, that was enough.

Chapter 3: Awakening

Friday Morning, August 22

Mark and Crystal woke almost simultaneously, as if choreographed by some unseen hand. In that liminal space between sleep and consciousness, Mark caught a glimpse of Maggie standing at the foot of the bed, her face radiant with peace.

"Awakening is the first step to knowing your true nature as a healer," she whispered, and then she was gone.

Mark turned to find Crystal's eyes already open, watching him with a gentle smile. The morning light filtered through the bedroom curtains, casting a warm glow across her face.

"Wow, what an amazing night," he said softly, his heart still full from their deep connection.

Crystal's smile deepened, love reflecting in her eyes like light on water. "It was perfect."

They lay there for a moment in comfortable silence, neither wanting to break the spell of the night before. Finally, Crystal stretched and sat up. "Coffee?"

"I'd love some." Mark reached for her hand. "I should probably grab a clean shirt from my car first."

"Always prepared, Dr. Deera," she teased gently.

"Old habits," he grinned. "Though I have a feeling some of my old habits are about to change."

*****

Mark retrieved his spare clothes and showered as Crystal moved through her morning routine, making coffee and toasting bagels. The domesticity felt natural and unforced - as if they'd been sharing mornings for years rather than taking their first tentative steps toward deeper intimacy.

When Mark joined her in the kitchen, hair still damp from the shower, Crystal handed him a steaming mug. They settled at her small breakfast table, spreading jalapeño hummus on their bagels, but their focus entirely on each other.

"You have that look again," Crystal observed, sipping her coffee.

"What look?"

"The same one you had last night when you said something shifted for you yesterday." She set her mug down, her eyes fixed on his. "You mentioned it briefly at dinner, but then we got caught up in...us. Could you tell me more about what happened?"

Mark took a sip of his coffee, gathering his thoughts. "I had another dream this morning, Crystal. About Maggie, my sister who died by suicide when she was fifteen. It's a continuation of a dream I had the night before - that's what caused the shift I mentioned."

Crystal's eyes widened in surprise. "Mark, you've never talked about Maggie before. How old were you when she died? It must have been terrible."

"I was thirteen." Mark's voice grew quieter. "My parents were so caught up in their own grief they couldn't be present to support me. I found ways to survive, but I still carry this guilt that I could have done something to save her."

He paused, looking down at his coffee. "I think that's what drew me to psychiatry - to help others in ways I couldn't help Maggie."

Crystal reached across the table and took his hand. "Oh Mark, you were just a child yourself. And to lose your parent's support when you needed them most..." She shook her head. "I can see now why letting people into your heart feels so dangerous for you. You learned so young that love can disappear in an instant."

Mark nodded, grateful for her understanding. "In the first dream, I saw people standing around a deep hole, throwing down solutions, trying to help someone who had fallen in. Angela was there, and together we climbed down into the darkness, not to fix the person, but just to be present."

His eyes met Crystal's. "When the light came, I saw it was Maggie at the bottom. She told me she was there for me, not the other way around."

Crystal leaned in, listening intently, her free hand wrapped around her coffee mug.

"This morning, she appeared again and said that awakening is the first step to knowing my true nature as a healer." Mark ran his hand through his hair. "It's making me question everything about how I practice psychiatry, how I connect with people. How I've protected myself by never allowing others to get too close."

He looked directly at Crystal. "I'm burnt out, Crystal. I want to change, but my entire identity has been so connected to my role and prestige as Chief of Psychiatry. I receive value by doing things the way I always have."

His voice dropped almost to a whisper. "The fear of change, of losing that identity - it's stagnating me. I feel like Maggie might be offering another way forward, but I'm terrified of what that means."

Crystal's voice was gentle but certain. "Your false identity is terrified, not you, Love." She paused, her eyes soft with understanding. "As Maggie suggested, now is the time to awaken to your true nature as a healer. I AM here for you."

Tears flowed down Mark's face as he saw himself reflected in Crystal's eyes - not as the Chief of Psychiatry or a controlled medical professional, but as the man he truly was beneath all the armor.

In that moment, sitting in Crystal's kitchen with morning light streaming through the windows, he felt something he hadn't experienced since he was thirteen years old: the possibility of being completely known and completely loved.

Chapter 4: Connecting

Friday Evening, August 22

Two months had passed since Angela's transition on June 22nd, and life had gradually settled into new rhythms for everyone touched by her love. For eleven-year-old David, joining the Boy Scouts became part of his new normal - a way to channel his adventurous spirit while his heart continued healing.

David still had the size and appearance of a nine-year-old, which continued to be a source of distress. His blond hair was long enough to cover his ears and collar, with a distinctive cowlick that refused to be tamed. His crystal blue eyes seemed to radiate an inner light that drew both curiosity and connection from those who met him.

This weekend is David's first real camping experience - he doesn't count nights sleeping outside in his backyard as camping. His excitement had been building over the past couple of weeks since joining the Boy Scout troop. After arriving at the campground, while the boys set up their tents, Larry Lucas, the scoutmaster, and John Williams, Jeremy's father and assistant scoutmaster, prepared dinner. Jeremy is the fifteen-year-old in David's Sunday school class who invited David to join the scouts.

By the time dinner cleanup was finished, darkness had settled over their campsite. It was a cool evening, the sky just starting to speckle with stars. The scouts gathered around a fire that Jeremy had built and was tending. The experienced boys knew to grab logs to sit on and how to find the best spot away from the smoke. Despite their efforts, the shifting breeze guided the smoke to them anyway. No one completely escaped it, which would find its way into their clothes and eventually to their mothers' noses. David sat on the ground, soaking up the warmth of the fire.

The sound of tree leaves singing in the breeze and the crackling fire muffled the approach of a fox walking up to the edge of the campfire clearing. No one but David noticed the stealthy animal standing so close.

"Hey guys," David whispered. "There's a fox over there watching us."

The boys turned, saw the fox, and jumped up, quickly putting distance between themselves and the animal. David turned toward where the boys were heading. "Where are you all going?"

"Get away from the fox - it might have rabies!" Jeremy yelled.

David turned to the fox and asked quietly, "Do you have rabies?"

"No, I need some help," the fox responded.

Mr. Lucas clapped his hands and yelled at the fox to leave, but instead the animal walked over to David and sat beside him.

"David," Mr. Lucas called out urgently. "Get up and slowly walk away."

"Why?" David asked. "I'm not afraid. The fox told me he doesn't have rabies." He turned back toward the fox and extended his hand. The animal nuzzled against David's palm. David looked into the fox's eyes and felt the perfect presence of Love. "Hi, I'm David. Thanks for visiting me."

"I am Fox. I saw your light and thought you might help me."

"What can I do for you, Fox?"

"I have a friend that is trapped and hurting."

"Show me."

The fox walked toward the woods, turning his head to see if David was following. David got up and ran after the fox into the darkness.

Mr. Lucas yelled, "What are you doing?" as he hurried to catch up to David. They stopped suddenly when they saw another fox caught in a metal trap. The animal appeared exhausted, and David could see blood where the trap had cut into its leg. The trapped fox lifted his head and growled when he saw David approaching but then lay back down when he heard David's calming voice.

"David, don't get too close," Mr. Lucas warned. "Damn, it's against the law to trap animals in this area. Poachers think they can get away with anything out here."

"*I AM here, David. The fox won't hurt you.*"

"Thank you, Love." David ignored Mr. Lucas's warning and extended his hand, telling the fox that everything would be fine. The first fox walked up beside David to offer silent reassurance. The trapped fox relaxed, allowing David to touch him behind the ear.

Mr. Lucas, stunned by the animal's response, came close, released the trap, and quickly jumped back. The fox struggled to get up.

"It looks like his leg might be broken," Mr. Lucas observed.

"We have to do something," David pled.

"We will. We can take him to the animal hospital emergency room."

David calmed the hurt fox, telling him that he and Mr. Lucas wanted to help, not hurt him. He said to the other fox, "We'll bring your friend back once he's feeling better."

Mr. Lucas took off the flannel shirt he was wearing over his T-shirt and carefully wrapped the injured fox in it. He picked him up and carried him out of the woods. The other scouts stood in shock with eyes wide and mouths open as Mr. Lucas laid the fox in the back seat of his truck. David got in and placed his hand on the fox's back for reassurance.

After a thirty-minute drive to the emergency veterinary clinic, Mr. Lucas carried the fox in, to the surprise of the night staff.

"It's unusual to see an injured fox so calm," noted Dr. Madigan, the veterinarian on duty. "How did you keep him from biting?"

"David talked to him the whole time," Mr. Lucas responded.

"I'll treat the fox's leg, and someone from the animal rescue sanctuary will pick him up tomorrow. You should feel good about what you did - without your help, this fox would have died a slow, painful death."

When Mr. Lucas and David returned to camp, everyone crowded around, excited to hear what happened. Hank, another one of David's Sunday School classmates, asked, "David, why weren't you afraid?"

"The fox said he needed my help, and Love told me the fox didn't want to hurt me. I always believe what Love says."

That statement caused a stir among the scouts.

"You said Love talked to you! Are you crazy?" Jeremy asked. "Love doesn't talk."

"Sometimes I might be crazy, but not now," David said calmly. "And yes, Love does talk. What you call God, I call Love. Angels also talk to me."

David didn't realize he'd just opened a can of worms. Everyone except Charlie started laughing.

With a sneer, Hank said, "If I had any doubt before, I don't have any now. You really are psycho."

David responded with a silent stare. He had no intention of defending himself. He thought, "*Hank is just trying to rise above his own insecurities by putting me down. I don't have to feed him or any of the others with an emotional response. Dad warned me to be careful about who I tell, for fear that I would be ridiculed or rejected. I felt so good after my encounter with the fox that I forgot.*"

Silently, David asked, "Love, what is your view of this situation?"

"*Perfect. Look for the gifts.*"

Hank became uncomfortable with David's penetrating gaze and silent response. "Hey guys, campfire time is over. Let's get settled in our tents."

"I'll take care of the fire," Mr. Lucas offered. The boys retreated to their tents, but David could still hear them laughing and making comments about him.

Charlie, who had been picked as David's tent mate, didn't go with the group, but instead moved over to sit by David. At thirteen, Charlie was often bullied, not only for being overweight and awkward but because he stuttered. His short-cropped red hair, cut like his father's, contrasted sharply with his green eyes. His clothes were always a little oversized, giving him a disheveled appearance that only added to the target on his back. Early signs of acne dotted his face, another source of teenage insecurity. He preferred to be called Charlie, but one of the boys overheard Charlie's father call him "Ch-Chubby," and that became the bullies' favorite name for him.

"D-David, c-could you t-tell me m-more about how G-God talks to you?"

Mr. Lucas, sitting across from them as he tended the fire, leaned forward to hear better.

"Sure, Charlie. I first heard God's voice in a dream, but I didn't know it was a dream at the time. The voice came through my open heart. I learned it's easier to see and talk to God if I focus on Love, since God and Love are one and the same."

"Y-You see G-God too?"

"Yes, I do."

"Wh-What does G-God look like?"

"I could tell you, Charlie, but I think it's better if you find out for yourself. I can help, though." David went on to explain how to play the Love Game. "Charlie, if you practice this game, you'll come face to face with God as Love. It's all about opening your heart by letting go of your judgments and expectations. This can be hard because our beliefs can be very insistent about the right way and wrong way to see the world." David continued, "The good news is, you don't have to do it alone. We can meet at the city park and play the Game together. I'll also tell you more about the Survival Game that you've been playing most of your life and how you have the power to choose what game you play in any moment."

"I-I would re-really like that."

"Let's go back to the tent, Charlie. We can talk more there if you like."

Mr. Lucas extinguished the fire and went to his tent, which he shared with John, who was organizing his gear and laying out his sleeping bag.

"What do you think about David's experience tonight, John?"

John stopped what he was doing and looked up. "I'm not surprised. I heard that David had a near-death experience a couple of months ago, and he hasn't been the same since. It doesn't matter whether I believe God talks to him or not. He believes it's true, and that belief seemed to contribute to saving a fox's life. He's certainly more connected and comfortable in nature than the average eleven-year-old."

"I agree. He's so excited to be in scouts and especially about camping. You know he was ready to pass the tests for his tenderfoot badge the week after he joined."

"He was talking to Charlie about playing a Love Game that helps him not only talk to God but to see Him, too. David said that to play the Love Game, all you need to do is open your heart to the present moment, let your judgments go, and keep your eyes open. It sounds like David is going to be getting a lot of attention, but I fear it's not going to be the positive kind."

"You're probably right, Larry. Maybe David and Charlie will be good for each other."

"Let's hope so."

Chapter 5: Crisis

Friday Evening, August 22

Rachel finished her shift at the hospital, went home, gave Nana and Sammy a hug, then took a quick shower. This was a ritual she started since beginning work at the hospital – taking a few moments alone to let go of any unwanted energies she may have carried home with her. She had come to value the meals she shared with her family more than ever since being discharged as a patient, a stark contrast from the time when alcohol and drugs took priority over food or company.

"Sammy, I don't have to work tomorrow so we can spend the day together. Tonight, I'm going to my AA meeting."

"OK, Momma."

*****

Rachel parked her car and walked past two men smoking outside the entrance of the Methodist church's activity center. Inside, folding chairs were lined up in rows facing a small pedestal at the front. A table was set up at the back with paper cups and a coffee maker, the scent of fresh coffee filling the air. A couple of individuals stood in quiet conversation near the coffee station.

Rachel stayed quiet, observing everything around her as she found a seat. She reflected on her journey - it had been less than four months since she stopped drinking. That was when she was hospitalized after an overdose of alcohol and drugs. She started coming to these AA meetings the week after Angela passed. Many people had supported her transformation and now she wanted to pay it forward.

Individuals started filing in, finding their seats. The moderator began the meeting in the usual way, and tonight a woman named

Sharon was receiving her six-month sobriety chip. She was called to the front of the room to say a few words about her journey.

"I can't believe 'one day at a time' has added up to six months. I thought it might have gotten easier over time, but it didn't for me." She paused, looking at the chip in her hand. "What has made it work for me is persistence. I didn't give up the first few times I fell off the wagon."

She took a deep breath, her voice growing stronger. "The first time I stopped drinking, it was only for a week. I stopped drinking again and that lasted a couple of weeks. I was embarrassed each time I failed to stay sober and wanted to give up. I thank Betty, my sponsor, for her support."

After the meeting, some of the members gathered in the back of the room for coffee and to congratulate Sharon. Betty was the first to hug her. Rachel waited for the crowd to thin before approaching.

Sharon was a petite, slightly overweight woman with shoulder-length dark hair pulled back into a ponytail. Her dark brown eyes sat above puffy circles that spoke of sleepless nights and constant worry. Her delicate features reflected a classical beauty of years past, but alcohol and stress created a weathered look that made her appear much older than her thirty-nine years. She wore a simple summer dress - her husband didn't like it when she wore pants. "A woman should dress like a woman," he would say.

Rachel looked deep into Sharon's eyes. "How are you really feeling?"

"I'm fine, Rachel."

"Sharon, I see that your mouth is smiling but your eyes aren't."

Sharon's facade crumbled. "Nothing seems to be going well, Rachel. I am so stressed that I don't know which way to turn. I am six months sober, yet every day I'm a whisker away from taking a drink."

She glanced around, then lowered her voice. "It doesn't help that my husband insists on having alcohol in the house. In his words, 'there's no way in hell I'm giving up drinking.' My oldest son has been severely depressed, but my husband won't allow him to go to counseling. He says he's not giving his hard-earned money to any shrink."

Rachel listened quietly, her hand gently touching Sharon's arm.

"Instead, he finds fault with just about everything my son does. He treats me and my youngest son the same way." Sharon's voice broke. "I don't know how I would support myself, otherwise I would leave him." She paused, suddenly self-conscious. "I'm sorry, Rachel, I didn't mean to dump this on you. I usually don't share that kind of information. For some reason, I feel safe with you."

"Sharon, do you know that when I look into your eyes, I see the Love you are at the center of your being? This is your Divine Nature."

"How can you know that, Rachel? I'm so flawed."

"That is just a story you have been told and continue to tell yourself." Rachel's voice was gentle but certain. "The perfect feeling I have when I see you tells the truth of who you really are behind your stories of suffering, abuse, and feelings of unworthiness."

Sharon looked at her with confusion - and hope.

"No matter what situations you face in your life, God - what I call Love - is always present. Learning to open your heart to allow that Divine Nature to shine lets you thrive through any adverse experience."

"*I AM here.*"

"Who said that?" Sharon asked, turning to see if someone was behind her.

Rachel smiled. "That was Love speaking through our hearts."

"What?" Sharon shook her head, brows furrowed. "Am I losing it? I don't understand."

"The only thing you are losing is your belief about who you think you are."

"I would really like to talk to you about this more. Can we meet sometime?" Sharon glanced at her watch. "I have to get home now. My son is alone."

"Sharon, we don't have to schedule anything right now. I know it will happen at the perfect time."

They embraced, and time seemed to pause as Sharon experienced a connection she'd never felt in a simple hug before. When they finally separated, all she could say was "WOW. Wow!" The feeling remained with both of them as they turned toward their respective homes.

*****

Sharon arrived home to find her seventeen-year-old son unconscious on the couch. She noticed a drained bottle of gin and her empty lorazepam pill container next to him. Her heart lurched and her hands shook as she immediately dialed 911.

"911, what's your emergency?"

"My son...he's unconscious. Pills and alcohol. Please hurry."

"Is he breathing?"

"Yes, but barely. Oh God, I should have seen this coming..."

"Paramedics are on their way. What kind of pills did he take?"

"Lorazepam."

"Let me know if he stops breathing. I'll stay on the line until paramedics arrive."

The next few minutes felt like hours. Sharon knelt beside Chris, holding his hand, whispering prayers and apologies. When the paramedics arrived, they worked quickly, checking vital signs and preparing him for transport.

He was still unconscious when they arrived at the ER. The doctors pumped his stomach, but all they could do was provide supportive care until the drugs wore off. He was moved to the ICU.

Sharon called her husband, but he didn't pick up. *Why doesn't he keep his phone on for emergencies when he's working late?* She texted him: "Chris is in the ICU at Wellco General. He tried to kill himself."

Fifteen minutes later, he texted back: "Damn him, I didn't need this right now. I'm on my way."

*****

Les Sullivan stormed into the ICU twenty minutes later. At forty-three, he was a tall man in good shape, his time spent at the gym evident in his broad shoulders and confident posture. His short-cropped ginger hair was meticulously styled, and the texture of his skin showed the healed remnants of teenage acne. His well-tailored suit spoke to his attention to professional appearance. His green eyes quickly scanned the room before settling on Sharon.

Holding a box of tissues, her eyes red and swollen, Sharon sat, her face streaked with tears. He immediately pointed his finger at her.

"This is your fault," he snarled. "Were they your drugs that he took? Why weren't you with him? You and your precious AA meetings."

"Les..."

"Don't you dare call me Leslie," he cut her off, glancing anxiously at the nurses' station. "You know I hate that."

"Well, Les," Sharon continued, her voice shaking but growing steadier, "it was my drugs and your alcohol. So don't just blame me."

She took a deep breath, something shifting in her posture. "Maybe if you hadn't spent most of his life finding fault with him, he wouldn't be in this state. How could he not feel worthless?"

Les's face reddened. For a moment, something vulnerable flickered across his features - fear, perhaps, or recognition - but was quickly replaced by familiar anger. "He needs discipline, not your coddling. It's a tough world. I was just preparing him for what's to come."

"Are you ashamed of him, Les?" Sharon's voice carried a new strength. "Is that why you won't let him get counseling? Afraid of what he might say about you? Since everything is always about you."

Les straightened his tie, his jaw tight. The accusation hit closer to home than he would admit. "That's ridiculous. I just don't believe in paying strangers to tell us what we already know."

A nurse approached. "I need to ask you both to step outside if you can't maintain a reasonable volume. This is an ICU."

Les nodded curtly, attempting to regain his composure. "Fine by me. I have actual work to do. Call me when he stops being dramatic." He turned and walked away, his stride stiff and controlled.

Sharon watched him go, clenching her fists. Part of her wanted to scream after him, but exhaustion suddenly hit her like a wave. She slumped into a chair by Chris's bed, looking at her son's still form.

She thinks about Les's words, "preparing him for the world," and wonders if instead he'd been preparing them both for this moment. The weight of it all threatened to crush her.

Through her weariness, she remembered Rachel's words about Love speaking through their hearts. As if in response to the memory, she heard it again, clear and gentle: "*I AM here.*"

The presence brought an unexpected calm, as if those three words could somehow hold both her and Chris in this moment, even in the midst of everything falling apart.

Chapter 6: A Shared Dream

Saturday Morning, August 23

Charlie woke in the middle of the night and saw that David was awake.

"David, I had the weirdest dream," Charlie whispered, not wanting to wake the other scouts. "We were walking in the park and a chickadee flew down, landed on your shoulder and looked directly into my eyes. I had a wonderful feeling that's hard to describe. Then I heard that voice again: 'I AM here.'"

David smiled at the excitement in Charlie's green eyes as he told him about the dream. "Did you notice, Charlie, that when you were telling me this dream you weren't stuttering?"

Charlie's mouth opened in surprise. "I wasn't? I wasn't, was I? How is that possible? I always stutter."

"Charlie, what did you think when Chickadee asked you if you wanted help seeing Love?"

"How could you possibly know about that?"

"Remember, I was in the dream, too."

"But I thought it was my dream."

"It was actually our dream, Charlie." David shifted in his sleeping bag, his voice gentle but certain. "When someone connects with another person and both have an open heart, aligned to their Loveselves, they can share a dream at the same time. We are One and a part of the collective Divine consciousness."

David paused, letting that concept settle. "The feeling you had when Chickadee looked into your eyes is the presence of Divine Love. I call that feeling 'Perfect,' because no other single word describes the experience. Some might say that the feeling is a combination of happiness, joy, peace, unity, connection, appreciation, and love. In that moment your thoughts are free of judgment."

Charlie nodded eagerly. "At first, I was stunned hearing Chickadee speak. I appreciated your invitation to talk to her. You know all this, right?"

"Yes, I do, Charlie. Talking about it is a way to make it real. It wasn't just a dream; it was you creating reality." David's voice grew softer. "What was your experience at the Peace Pond? Sometimes Love will talk to your heart and I won't know what it tells you unless it's speaking through my heart at the same time."

"Oh yes, the Peace Pond." Charlie's voice grew quieter with wonder. "I remember you leading me there. The Pond asked me to throw my expectations and judgments about God into the water and then look for an image to appear." He paused, his eyes wide with memory. "I was confused when I saw myself reflected, followed by the voice saying 'I AM here.' You told me that it was my Divine Loveself I was seeing and hearing. Again, I was blown away by the same indescribable feeling you call Perfect."

"With that, Charlie, I'm going back to sleep. We can talk more in the morning."

"I don't know if I can, David. I have so much energy."

Charlie did stay awake for a while, replaying everything he'd witnessed on this camping trip, before drifting off to sleep.

*****

After breakfast, the troop set out on a two-mile hike through the forest to a waterfall. Mr. Lucas, who usually led from the front with the older boys, asked Mr. Williams to take point while he brought up the rear - ostensibly to ensure no stragglers were left behind, though his real motivation was to stay near David and Charlie. The previous night's conversation about Love and God had piqued his curiosity, and he hoped to hear more of David's unique perspectives.

The two boys naturally drifted to the back of the pack, more interested in looking for signs of Love in nature than keeping pace with the group. A canopy of maple trees filtered the morning sunlight, creating a painting of dappled light on the winding trail. An earthy scent rose from decomposing leaves that nourished wildflowers scattered across the forest floor. Bird calls echoed through the trees, creating nature's symphony.

"Charlie, what do you appreciate about this moment?" David asked, his small frame moving easily along the trail. "Appreciation is really helpful in playing the Love Game."

"I appreciate the presence of you and Mr. Lucas." Charlie looked around the forest surrounding them, his oversized camping clothes making him appear even younger than his thirteen years. "I have such a peaceful feeling walking with the two of you." He paused, wonder crossing his face. "For the first time in my life I feel that I belong and am being hugged by the nature around me."

Mr. Lucas walked quietly behind them, listening intently to their conversation.

The boys ahead had just moved out of sight around a curve in the path when David said, "Hey Charlie, look up."

Charlie and Mr. Lucas followed his gaze to see a chickadee sitting on a branch directly above them.

"What do you say, Charlie? Why don't you call it down and have a talk with it, kind of like an old friend?"

Charlie extended his hand upward. "Hi, Chickadee. Would you like to come and visit with us?" A moment later, the little bird flew down, landing delicately on the tips of Charlie's fingers. "Nice to see you again, Chickadee."

"Nice to see you again too, Charlie. I see you and David are playing the Love Game together. Who's your friend?"

Charlie turned his hand toward Mr. Lucas so Chickadee could look into his eyes. "This is Mr. Lucas, our scout leader."

Mr. Lucas stared at the small bird, his mouth slightly open. "Wow, wow, wow," he repeated.

"I am glad you are open to learning more about the joy of playing the Love Game. David is a true way-shower," Chickadee said.

"What...?" Mr. Lucas's brows furrowed, crinkling his forehead. He squinted at the chickadee, then held his palms up and turned to David. "I don't understand what just happened."

"Did Chickadee talk to you?" David asked.

"I don't know. I suddenly had a thought that the chickadee was glad I was open to playing the Love Game. Where did that come from?" Mr. Lucas chuckled nervously. "Maybe your imagination is rubbing off on me."

"I've learned that when I get messages from beings that I don't think can talk, it comes from the Loveself part of my heart." David's voice remained patient and kind. "Whether it's your imagination or not, what was your experience in that moment, Mr. Lucas?"

Mr. Lucas considered this for a moment. "I have no words that perfectly reflect my experience, David. I do feel like my whole body is smiling."

"When playing the Love Game, a good sign that God, or Love, is present is when you have that kind of experience. Sometimes you'll get a clear message: 'I AM here.'" David paused, watching Mr. Lucas's face carefully. "If your heart is open - that means without judgment or expectations - what you see with your eyes is Love in physical form."

"I'm curious, Charlie," Mr. Lucas said, still processing what he'd experienced. "When did you first meet Chickadee?"

"I met Chickadee last night in a dream David and I shared."

"What do you mean, a dream you shared?"

"David, would you tell Mr. Lucas what dream-sharing is?" Charlie asked.

"I could, Charlie, but I have a feeling you'll do just fine. I'm interested in what you took away from our talk about dream-sharing."

Charlie straightened up, his confidence growing. "Well, Mr. Lucas, David told me that when two people connect with open hearts and are aligned to their Loveselves, they can share the same dream at the same time. We're all One and part of the collective Divine consciousness."

He continued without stuttering, his words flowing naturally. "In our dream, we walked to the Peace Pond where I learned to see my Divine Loveself. That's when I met Chickadee, who helped me understand the Love Game better."

Mr. Lucas blinked in surprise. "Charlie, I've never known you not to stutter, but you've been speaking normally with David and now with me. What happened?"

"I don't know why I'm not stuttering, Mr. Lucas," Charlie responded, his voice clear and steady. "What I do know is that I'm feeling very happy and calm right now playing the Love Game." He looked straight into Mr. Lucas's eyes. "I see the Love you are and I feel Perfect, and my words seem to flow out.

David smiled at what Charlie has done. He knows Charlie is getting the hang of playing the Love Game when he can see Mr. Lucas as Love. David hadn't used the phrase "I see the Love you are" with

Charlie before, so he knows Charlie's heart is wide open and Love is speaking through him.

Mr. Lucas's eyes filled with tears, not knowing how to handle the surge of emotion he was feeling. For a moment, he experienced something he's never felt before - complete acceptance and unconditional love from this thirteen-year-old boy who's usually the target of bullies.

"Thank you, Chickadee," David said softly. "We appreciate you sharing this moment with us."

Charlie nodded. "Will we see you again?"

"*Whenever your hearts are open to Love, I AM here,*" Chickadee responded, then spread her wings and flew back to the maple branches above.

The three of them walked in silence for several minutes, each reflecting on what they'd experienced as they caught up to the rest of the group. The forest around them seemed to pulse with the same love that was awakening in their hearts.

Chapter 7: Intensive Care

Saturday Morning: August 23

Sharon spent the day with Chris in the ICU. She had been at the hospital all night and it showed - her dark hair had escaped its ponytail, her clothes were wrinkled, and her eyes were red and swollen from crying, dark shadows bruising the skin beneath them. The nurses told her she should go home and rest, but she couldn't begin to quiet her mind. Her anger toward herself and Les was an emotion she just couldn't control.

Chris came out of the coma early in the morning but wouldn't speak to anyone. Sharon panicked. "Come on, Chris. Why won't you talk to me?" She turned to the nurse. "What's wrong? Why won't he say anything?"

"I don't know why," said Nurse Lenus, the ICU nurse on duty. "We put in a consult to Dr. Amara, a neurologist. She will evaluate him for any brain damage that he may have suffered from low oxygen when he wasn't breathing well. The good news is, his vital signs are all normal at this time." She paused. "She said it's also mandatory for any suicide attempt that we call the psychiatric department for their assessment and plan recommendations. He will most likely be discharged from the ICU later today."

The psychiatric resident physician, Dr. Taft, was called as soon as Chris regained consciousness. His neurological exam and CAT scan were normal. Dr. Amara told Sharon that she had no explanation for Chris not talking. She hoped that Dr. Taft could shed some light on the state of Chris's emotional health.

After his evaluation, Dr. Taft talked to Sharon in a small conference room adjacent to the ICU. "Mrs. Sullivan, since Chris is not talking, I can't adequately evaluate his mental status. We take the fact that he attempted suicide seriously. He will be transferred to the Behavioral Health Unit later today. We can keep him safe there."

Sharon asked, "How long will he be there?"

"He will be there at least three days. That will give us time to evaluate him and give you our recommendation for care from that point. Dr. Deera is the medical director of the unit and has a special interest in young people who have attempted suicide."

Sharon felt her shoulders drop, releasing tension she didn't realize she was holding. The Behavioral Health Unit. The words should frighten her, but instead they offered an unexpected comfort. Three days where Chris would be safe - safe from himself, safe from Les's cutting remarks, safe from her own uncertain ability to protect him. She thought of Les's text: 'Damn him, I didn't need this right now.' No, the hospital was exactly where Chris needed to be.

"Yes," she told Dr. Taft, her voice steadier than before. "I'm comforted knowing he will be getting the attention he needs to recover. Why do you think he's not talking?"

"Let me ask you some questions about Chris first. Did he talk freely before the overdose?"

"Chris has never been much of a talker. He is shy and careful about his words for fear that he might say the wrong thing. He talks to me more than his dad. If you ask him questions, he usually responds with only a few words."

"Has he had counseling or treatment for his depression previously?"

"No. Les, his father, doesn't believe in counseling. He thinks Chris should 'man-up' to his fears and control his emotions." Sharon's voice grew heavier. "Les never compliments Chris about anything. He's always finding fault, calling him stupid or an idiot. He tells Chris how disappointed he is in him. Chris is so sensitive - he cowers when Les yells at him."

She paused, gathering her thoughts. "Les often threatens the boys if they don't do what he says, but he's never hit them or me. He's away a lot on business, and when he does come home, he closes himself up in his office. The boys barely see him, and when they do..."

Sharon paused.

Dr. Taft repeated, "When they do?"

"They hide in their rooms," Sharon responded.

Dr. Taft set down his pen. "What is your relationship with Chris like?"

Tears came to Sharon's eyes. "I get the same crap from Les as the boys do, and I found my salvation in a bottle and taking anti-anxiety pills. To answer your question, I've neglected my boys." Her voice broke. "Six months ago, I thought I could always handle my liquor, but I woke up to find out something terrible had happened..."

She took a shaky breath. "I woke up one morning on the couch, wearing the same clothes I had the previous day. I couldn't remember anything about the last twelve hours. Chris came in and asked what happened to the car. I told him I didn't know. He said the side was scraped like I had hit something, and that I'd gone out the night before, though I couldn't remember why. When he went out for the paper that morning, he'd found the garage door open and the car parked half on the lawn, half on the driveway."

Dr. Taft leaned forward slightly. "That must have been terrifying for you."

"That's when I knew I couldn't pretend anymore that I had everything under control. I wasn't just hurting myself." Her voice dropped to almost a whisper. "I realized my boys were watching me fall apart, and I was becoming just as dangerous to them as Les was, in a different way."

Sharon wiped her eyes. "That's the day I stopped drinking. I started going to AA. I have been more of a presence for both the boys, but they've kept to themselves mostly. I have been struggling with so much guilt. I'm such a bad mother."

"Sharon, thank you for sharing something so difficult. What you're describing sounds like a blackout episode, which is a serious sign of alcohol use disorder - a medical condition, not a character flaw," Dr. Taft said. "The fact that you stopped drinking that day and have maintained sobriety for six months while attending AA shows tremendous strength."

He paused, his voice gentle but firm. "Recovery is a process, and it's understandable that the boys are still guarded. Trust rebuilds slowly after family trauma. You're not a bad mother - you're a mother who was struggling with addiction and is now actively working on recovery. That takes courage."

Sharon looked up at him, surprised by his compassion.

"It sounds like you haven't heard that from many people. Now, help me understand how Chris is handling things - how has he been doing in school?" Dr. Taft continued.

"His grades have dropped this past year from mostly As to Cs and Ds. His teachers say he's withdrawn and doesn't participate in class discussions. He used to love reading and writing, but lately he just sits in his room staring at nothing."

"What about friendships? Social relationships?"

Sharon's face grew sadder. "He doesn't really have any close friends. The kids at school either ignore him or...well, some of them can be cruel. He gets picked on for being quiet and different. He spends most of his time alone."

"Has anyone ever suggested he might be on the autism spectrum? Sometimes highly sensitive, intelligent children can struggle socially."

"A teacher mentioned it once, but Les shut that down immediately. Said there was nothing wrong with Chris that couldn't be fixed with more discipline."

"Tell me about his relationship with his brother."

"Charlie is four years younger, and they're very different. Charlie gets bullied too, but he's more...I don't know, resilient somehow. Chris tries to protect Charlie when he can, but mostly they stay out of each other's way. I think Chris worries about being a burden to everyone, including Charlie."

Dr. Taft continued taking notes. "What about sleep patterns? Has he been having trouble sleeping?"

"For months now. He stays up all night and sleeps during the day when he can. I hear him pacing in his room at 2 or 3 in the morning. When I ask if he's okay, he just says he's fine."

"And what brings him joy? What does he enjoy doing?"

Sharon's face brightened. "He likes to watch TV shows and movies about animals. He also reads books about animals - I can't believe how much he knows. Sometimes he'll sit for hours in our backyard listening to and watching birds. He really got into biology when he was a sophomore in school." Her voice grew sadder again. "But lately, even those things don't seem to interest him as much. It's like he's given up on everything that used to make him happy."

Dr. Taft put down his pen and looked at Sharon with compassion. "Based on what you've told me and what I observed, I suspect his silence is a reflection of severe anxiety and trauma, not under his control at this time. The suicide attempt itself was traumatic, and it sounds like he's been carrying emotional burdens for a long time."

He shifted his focus. "How are you doing, Mrs. Sullivan?"

"Really crappy," Sharon admitted, twisting the tissue in her hands. "I knew that Chris was depressed, but I never imagined he would try to kill himself. I left him alone last night for a couple of hours to go to my AA meeting. His father was at a business meeting, or so he said, and our thirteen-year-old was on a camping trip."

She took a shaky breath. "I asked Chris if he was okay being by himself. He said, 'Go, I'll be fine.' I should have sensed he wasn't fine. A good mother wouldn't have left him."

"I'm sorry you are feeling such regret. It would be nice for any of us if we could predict the future and always know the 'right' thing to do. Your emotional health is important too, and going to AA is a really positive step."

Dr. Taft paused, then continued. "I would encourage you to consider family counseling for Chris's sake. If your husband is resistant, then go yourself. It will be important for Chris's mental wellness if he can come home to an accepting family environment. I invite you to go home and rest. I'm sure you've had a long night. The nurse will give you information about the Behavioral Health Unit and how to contact us."

"Thanks for your help, Dr. Taft. I'll stay here a little longer to see if Chris will talk to me, then I will go home."

After Dr. Taft left, Sharon sat quietly for a moment. For the first time since finding Chris unconscious, she felt something other than panic and guilt. Maybe, just maybe, this crisis could become the beginning of getting the help her son needed all along.

Chapter 8: Coming Home

Sunday, August 24

The scouts broke camp with less care than they had taken setting up. Sleeping bags were rolled loosely and clothes were stuffed into packs without the careful organization of Friday night. They just wanted to get everything loaded into the converted school bus quickly. However, they did take extra time to scan the campground for trash or anything that didn't belong in nature, following the scout principle of leaving no trace.

The ride back to the church was mostly quiet except for a few whispered remarks about David being a "psycho." David sat with Charlie, and they replayed their favorite parts of the weekend - the shared dream, the chickadee encounter, and Charlie's discovery that he didn't stutter when his heart was open. Their quiet laughter occasionally bubbled up from the back of the bus, a sharp contrast to the whispered cruelty from other seats.

The bus arrived at the Methodist church parking lot at exactly 1 p.m. Most parents were already waiting, eager to hear about their sons' adventures.

David spotted his dad Jesse immediately and broke into a run. "Dad!" He launched himself into his father's arms, squeezing tight.

"Hey there, camper," he laughed, lifting David off the ground. "Looks like you had quite a weekend."

"The best weekend ever, Dad! I have so much to tell you." David's eyes were bright with excitement as he pulled back. "But first, I want you to meet my new friend." He turned and called out, "Hey, Charlie! Come meet my dad!"

Charlie approached shyly, his camping gear slung over his shoulder.

"Dad, this is Charlie. Charlie, this is my dad."

David's father extended his arms with a warm smile. "Charlie, I'm glad to meet you."

Charlie hesitated, not used to being hugged by men. Something in the genuine warmth of the gesture drew him forward, and he stepped into the embrace. When they broke apart, both were smiling.

"Sounds like you boys had quite an adventure," Jesse said, ruffling Charlie's red hair gently.

He started to load David's pack into the back seat but immediately reconsidered when the smoky essence hit him. "Whoa, that's going in the trunk," he chuckled, making David laugh.

As they drove away, David waved enthusiastically at Charlie through the rear window. One by one, the other parents collected their sons until only Charlie remained in the empty parking lot, sitting on a bench with Mr. Lucas.

"Your dad running late?" Mr. Lucas asked.

"He's always late," Charlie said, without his usual stutter. "He doesn't really like picking me up from things."

For thirty minutes, they sat together in the quiet afternoon sun. Mr. Lucas found himself wanting to hear more about Charlie's transformation.

"Charlie, can you tell me more about what happened to you this weekend? You seem...different. More confident."

Charlie's face lit up. "Mr. Lucas, I learned to play the Love Game. I talked to a chickadee and it talked back to me. I saw God in the Peace Pond - it was my own reflection, but it was God, too." He paused, looking directly at Mr. Lucas. "And I see the Love you are, Mr. Lucas. I really do."

Mr. Lucas felt his throat tighten with emotion. "Charlie, this weekend...what David showed us...it's changed something in me too."

A BMW screeched into the parking lot, engine purring despite the aggressive driving. Jolting to a stop, a man jumped out, clearly agitated and in a hurry.

Charlie's excitement bubbled over as his father approached. "Dad! You won't believe what happened! A chickadee flew down and sat right on my hand, and..."

"Ch-chubby, get in the car," his father snapped, interrupting him. He grabbed Charlie's pack and threw it into the trunk. "I don't have time for your stories."

"Oh, oh okay, d-dad," Charlie stammered, his stutter returning immediately.

Charlie's face fell, his joy extinguished like a blown candle. He glanced back at Mr. Lucas, who stood frozen in shock at the harsh treatment.

Without a word of thanks to Mr. Lucas for waiting with his son, Charlie's father slammed his door and gunned the engine. As they pulled away, Mr. Lucas heard the man's voice through the open window, "Your idiot brother tried to kill himself Friday night."

Mr. Lucas stood alone in the empty parking lot, tears welling up in his eyes, stunned by the cruelty he just witnessed and the devastating news about Charlie's brother. The boy who had discovered Love and found his voice was heading back into a world that seemed determined to silence him.

As a high school counselor, he recognized the abuse - he'd seen it many times before, and it always tore him up inside. The verbal cruelty, the public humiliation, the complete dismissal of a child's joy. But witnessing it happen to Charlie, a boy he'd just watched bloom with spiritual confidence, made it feel personal in a way that surprised him. His professional training told him to document, to report, to follow protocols. His heart wanted to chase down that BMW and confront Les Sullivan face to face.

*****

In their car, David bounced with excitement, struggling to fasten his seatbelt as words tumbled out of him. "Dad, you won't believe what happened! There was this fox, and he was caught in a trap, and Love told me he wouldn't hurt me, and we saved him!"

Jesse glanced in the rearview mirror, smiling at his son's enthusiasm. "Slow down there, buddy. Tell me everything."

David took a deep breath and launched into the story of the injured fox, Mr. Lucas's amazement, and the trip to the animal hospital. "Dad, I don't know if I should tell Mom or not. You know how she worries when I'm around wild animals."

"It'll be okay, David. Your mom will understand once she hears how you helped that fox. She'll be proud of you."

David's excitement dimmed slightly. "Dad, there's something else. I got so excited about the fox that I told the other boys about

Love talking to me." He looked down at his hands. "Some of the kids started calling me psycho."

His father pulled over and turned to face David fully. "I was afraid something like that might happen, son. I can see that hurt your feelings, and I'm sorry you had to experience it." He paused, his voice gentle. "Do you think this might be another opportunity to practice your Love Game - to see Love even in the bullies?"

*****

Charlie's ride home in Les's BMW stood in stark contrast to David's loving conversation. He sat pressed against the passenger door, trying to make himself as small as possible as his father ranted on.

"Your brother is a complete idiot, you know that? Trying to kill himself over what - having to grow up and face reality? I don't understand how I ended up with such weak children. Both of you, nothing but disappointments."

Charlie stared out the window through watery eyes, watching Mr. Lucas fade in the distance. He tried to remember the feeling of the chickadee on his hand, the perfect moment when he saw Love in Mr. Lucas's eyes, but his father's voice drowned out the memory.

At home, Les didn't slow down his verbal assault. "Get your gear out of the trunk and put it away properly. I don't want to see any of that camping junk lying around."

"W-where is m-mom?" Charlie asked quietly, his stutter returning full force.

"At the hospital babying your pathetic brother instead of being home where she belongs. Just my luck." Les grabbed his keys and headed for the door. "Your mother doesn't know when she'll be back, and neither do I. I've got things to do." He paused at the door. "Don't mess up the house while I'm gone."

The door slammed, leaving Charlie alone in the sudden silence. Despite everything, there was a small blessing in his father's absence - at least now he wouldn't have to listen to the constant criticism.

Charlie sat on the couch where Chris had lain unconscious just two nights ago, trying to hold onto the love he'd found in the forest, but feeling it slip away like smoke. He had never felt this alone in his whole life. One of the best weekends of his life had ended with one of the worst days. Charlie sobbed, "What's going to happen to me?"

He didn't want to eat. He didn't want to clean up or change his clothes. All he wanted to do was sleep.

*****

Larry Lucas drove toward his empty house, his mind churning with everything he'd witnessed. As a high school counselor, he'd seen his share of troubled kids and dysfunctional families, but watching Les treat Charlie with such cruelty sparked something dark in him - the urge to grab that man by the collar and show him what real fear looked like. The intensity of his anger surprised him; despite his gentle nature, he'd actually wanted to punch Les.

He forced himself to take deep breaths, thinking about the weekend's extraordinary events. Just three days ago, he'd been Larry Lucas, forty-one, divorced, living alone in a house that echoed with memories of betrayal. Three years since his wife ran off with his best friend, now married to the man who'd sat at Larry's dinner table countless times. He'd gotten involved in scouting to connect with his son, found it rewarding, and stayed on as an antidote to loneliness after his son left for college. Trust didn't come easily anymore.

This weekend had changed something fundamental in him. He remembered his initial fear when that fox appeared, his concern for David's safety, then the profound gratitude he felt helping save an injured animal. Learning about the Love Game from an eleven-year-old boy. Looking into that chickadee's eyes and feeling a connection he'd longed for but never found - not even in his marriage. The elation of watching Charlie's stutter disappear when his heart opened. The compassion he felt seeing both boys bullied for their spiritual gifts.

And now this rage at Les's cruelty.

As he pulled into his driveway, Larry realized he wasn't the same man who left for camping on Friday. The Love Game awakened something in him - both a capacity for deeper love and a fierce protectiveness he'd forgotten he possessed. Now he had to remember to play the Game, especially when he thinks about Charlie's father.

*****

Earlier that afternoon, Rachel had been cleaning the psychiatric unit when she spotted someone familiar in the hallway. "Sharon?"

Sharon turned, her face lighting up despite her exhaustion. "Rachel! What are you doing here?"

"I work here now - housekeeping." Rachel set down her cleaning supplies and opened her arms. They shared a long hug, and Rachel could feel the weight Sharon was carrying. Something felt different about her — she seemed heavier, more fragile than at the AA meetings.

"I've been thinking about you since Friday night," Rachel said gently, her voice barely above a whisper. "I know Chris is here on the unit."

Sharon's composure cracked. "I found him unconscious on our couch Friday night with pills and alcohol." Her voice shook. "I should have seen it coming, Rachel. I left him alone to go to my AA meeting, and when I got home..."

She stopped, unable to finish the sentence. Rachel placed a gentle hand on her arm.

"And now he won't talk to anyone. The doctors say he's physically fine, but emotionally..." She wiped her eyes. "I feel like I'm failing both my boys. My husband..." Sharon's voice dropped even lower. "He's making everything worse. The things he says to them, to me..."

Rachel's heart ached hearing the pain in Sharon's voice. She could sense there was so much more Sharon wasn't saying - years of accumulated damage beneath the surface.

"Rachel!" Karen, the head nurse, called sharply from down the hall. "You're here to clean, not socialize. Get back to work."

Rachel quickly slipped a piece of paper with her phone number into Sharon's hand, pressing it firmly into her palm. "If you need anything - anything at all - I AM here. Do you understand me?"

Sharon looked into Rachel's eyes and saw something there - a depth of understanding that went beyond words. "I think I can handle it, but thanks for asking," she replied, trying to muster strength she didn't feel.

As Rachel watched Sharon walk away, she noticed the defeated slope of her shoulders, the careful way she moved as if afraid to take up too much space. Rachel heard Angela's gentle voice in her heart, *"She will call, and you will be ready."*

"I will be ready," Rachel whispered back.

*****

At 4:00, Sharon returned home to find Charlie curled up on the couch in the darkened living room. She touched his shoulder to wake him up.

"Charlie? Honey, I'm home."

Charlie stirred and looked up at her with sleepy, confused eyes.

"Are you alone?" She looked around. "Where's your dad?"

"H-he left. I d-don't know w-where he went or when he'll be b-back. H-he didn't say. H-he was really m-mad."

She sat down next to Charlie and embraced him. "I'm sorry I wasn't here when you got home, honey. How was your camping trip, sweetheart?"

"I d-don't want to t-talk about it now," Charlie responded, his voice barely a whisper.

"Okay, then," Sharon said softly. "Did your dad tell you what's happening with Chris?"

"N-not r-really. He s-said Chris tr-tried to k-kill himself and he's v-very disappointed in b-both of us." Charlie looked up at his mother with frightened eyes. "Is C-Chris okay now?"

"Physically he's okay, honey, but emotionally he isn't well. He's getting help at the hospital." Sharon smoothed Charlie's red hair gently. "Are you hungry?"

"No, m-my st-stomach aches."

"How about some tea to soothe your stomach?"

Charlie nodded.

As Sharon moved to the kitchen to make tea, one thought echoed in her mind, *I have to do something to protect my kids.* Protecting herself and her children was the priority now. But how? she wondered. Do I have the strength to do what is necessary?

Charlie drank his chamomile tea and fell back asleep on the couch. Sharon gently covered him with a blanket, watching his peaceful face - so different from the frightened, stuttering boy who came home just hours ago.

She went into the bathroom, one of the few places in the house without security cameras. She called her new friend.

"Rachel, I need help."

"Are you safe right now?" Rachel asked immediately.

"Yes, for the moment. I need to get myself and the boys away from Les - he is destroying us."

"I have the day off tomorrow. Let's meet and make plans."

"I don't want to leave Charlie at home alone."

"I have the perfect solution. Let's meet at my house - I'll text you the directions. I'll ask my friend David to come over and keep Charlie company while we talk."

"Rachel, you are a godsend."

Chapter 9: A Moment with Love

Monday Morning, August 25

In his dream the night before, Charlie found himself back at the Peace Pond, sitting at the edge with his feet dangling in the cool water. The familiar serenity of the place immediately began to soothe his wounded heart.

"Why doesn't my dad love me?" he asked the pond, his voice carrying across the still surface. "Why does he have to be so mean? Am I so bad he can't find anything good to say? I want him to love me, but I'm afraid to be around him. I would like him to hug me the way David's dad did."

He paused, his voice growing quieter as deeper fears surfaced. "I can't seem to please him. I'm worried about Chris and Mom too. I knew Chris was really sad, but I didn't know he wanted to die. We don't talk much." His voice broke. "What if Chris tries again? What if something happens to Mom when Dad gets really mad?"

The pond remained calm and silent, its surface like a mirror reflecting the soft light filtering through the trees.

Charlie heard footsteps coming up behind him and turned quickly to see David and Mr. Lucas approaching. They sat down on each side of him, shoulder to shoulder, their presence immediately comforting.

"We came to keep you company," Mr. Lucas said gently. "I've never been here before. It feels really peaceful."

David smiled. "This is the perfect place to find Love."

All three of them heard the words, "*I AM here,*" as Angela's image appeared above the water, shimmering with golden light.

David introduced Charlie and Mr. Lucas to her. "She is the Love of my heart. She is always present even though I don't always see her."

"How can she be the Love of your heart when she is just a reflection in the water?" Charlie asked, still trying to understand.

"*I can answer that,*" Angela said. Her reflection began to rise from the water's surface, transforming into a luminous three-dimensional form before them, radiant and peaceful. "*Love just is, in all its forms, and is present in every heart, everywhere. You will see Love when you let go of expectations and judgments to appreciate the moment.*"

"Like playing the Love Game," Mr. Lucas said, his voice filled with wonder.

"*Precisely,*" Angela responded, her smile warming them all. "*I AM here is a reminder that you are never alone. Love is here.*"

Angela's gaze settled on Charlie with infinite compassion. "*Charlie, would you like to share your experience during your ride home after the camping trip and the questions you later threw into the pond?*"

The three of them listened as Charlie related the story and his questions. He ended with a sigh, "The pond hasn't answered yet."

Angela's voice was gentle but clear. "*Charlie, Love focuses on the present moment - even the thoughts we have in the present moment. 'Why' questions keep us focused on the past, trying to understand what happened so we can predict the future. Understanding is just another story about the past - a survival game strategy that has value, but it's not Love's way.*"

She paused, her image shimmering with compassion. "*Instead, you could ask the Pond to help you see this situation in a way that serves your highest good - in other words, in a way that aligns with Love. Ask how your experience can benefit you, or how you might see things through the eyes of Love.*"

Mr. Lucas nodded slowly, letting out a quiet "Wow." He sat in contemplative silence, clearly moved by Angela's wisdom.

"*The Love Game isn't about changing others, Charlie,*" Angela continued. "*It's about remembering who you are even when others forget who they are. When you see your father as Love - even when he's being unloving - you stay connected to your own heart.*"

Charlie's voice trembled. "But how can I see Love in someone who calls me Ch-Chubby and says I'm a disappointment?"

Angela's image shimmered with deep compassion. "*Charlie, I can feel the shame and worthlessness you're carrying. It's so challenging to change your story in the midst of an upsetting or terrifying situation. Love sees value in even the worst situations, but it takes practice and a conscious desire to feel better.*"

Her voice grew even more tender. "*Eventually, you might see your dad not as the angry man hurting you, but as a little boy who has forgotten his true nature. There is a time to resist and a time to accept - that is the wonder of living."*

Charlie wiped his eyes. "What about Chris? I'm scared he might try to hurt himself again. How can I help him when I can barely help myself?"

Angela's expression filled with understanding. *"Your love for your brother is a gift, Charlie. Sometimes the most powerful thing you can do is simply hold someone in your heart as Love, especially when they can't see it in themselves. Chris is struggling to remember his worth, just like you are. When you play the Love Game, you create a space of peace that others can feel, even if they don't understand it."*

"And my mom?" Charlie asked. "She tries so hard, but Dad makes her sad, too."

"Your mother is stronger than she knows," Angela said, her voice carrying a note of certainty. *"She is learning to protect what she loves most. Trust that Love is working through her, even when it doesn't look like it."*

They all sat in silence, reflecting on Angela's words. Charlie felt something shifting inside him - not the heavy despair he carried to sleep, but a gentle strength he didn't know he possessed.

David stood up saying, "It's time for me to go. I want some hugs."

Charlie and Mr. Lucas stood up, each taking turns embracing the others. Mr. Lucas felt Charlie melt into his arms - hearts merging timelessly, a connection that transcended the boundaries of the dream.

David whispered to Charlie, "I'll see you later at Rachel's house."

"Who's Rachel?" Charlie asked.

"That's my momma," Angela said with a warm smile.

As David and Mr. Lucas began to fade, walking away into the soft light of the dream landscape, Charlie sat back down at the edge of the pond. The water seemed to pulse gently with life.

"Pond, I appreciate how you have given me just what I need today," he said, his voice stronger now. "One more question. How can I best help my mom?"

As the dream began to dissolve around him, Charlie heard Angela's voice one last time, *"I am Love, you are Love, we are Love, and together we will see your mother as the Love she is. That is the best way to help her."*

Chapter 10: Unconventional Breakthrough

Monday, August 25

Dr. Deera arrived at the psychiatric unit Monday morning, making his usual rounds and gathering weekend updates from the nursing staff. He glanced around the unit, looking for a familiar face.

"Karen, have you seen Rachel this morning?" he asked the head nurse.

Karen's expression hardened. "This is her day off. Why are you so interested in her anyway?"

Dr. Deera paused, noting the edge in her voice. "Your tone suggests you don't like her."

Karen hesitated, trying to cover her true feelings. "I don't dislike her. I just think she should know her place and not get involved with patient care."

"Rachel has shown remarkable compassion and insight for mental health challenges. She has a gift for connecting with people who are struggling," Dr. Deera responded. "Plus, she is my friend."

"Isn't she your patient?"

"Not anymore. Respectfully, our relationship is not your business."

Karen lowered her gaze, clearly uncomfortable. *Why does he defend her so much?* she wonders. *What happened when she calmed down that agitated patient last week, going against everything I learned in nursing school?*

Her awkwardness was interrupted when Dr. Taft approached with a clipboard.

"Dr. Deera, there was only one admission over the weekend," Dr. Taft said, glancing at his notes. He presented Chris Sullivan's case file. "Seventeen-year-old male, suicide attempt via alcohol and benzodiazepine overdose. Comatose. He's now been medically cleared but hasn't spoken since waking from the coma."

Dr. Deera's attention sharpened. "Any background?"

"His mother provided extensive history, including ongoing verbal abuse from the father throughout Chris's life. The family dynamic appears quite toxic."

"Other than not speaking, how has he been behaving?"

"He stays in his room, resisting any invitation to come out into the common area. He sits in a chair and stares ahead when his bed is being changed. He doesn't watch TV or read."

This piqued Dr. Deera's interest, just as Dr. Taft expected. Mark's recent insights about heart-centered healing made Chris's situation a perfect opportunity to practice a love-focused approach.

"What have you done so far to help Chris?"

"We've kept him safe on suicide watch. I've tried to talk to him, but without any verbal response. He will nod. Maybe starting him on antidepressants will help him open up."

Dr. Deera, accompanied by Dr. Taft, Karen, and Dr. Lewis, a first-year intern, entered Chris's room.

"Good morning, Chris. This is Dr. Deera - he's the chief of psychiatry in this unit," Dr. Taft announced.

Dr. Deera noticed Chris clench his jaw and tighten his hands. He sensed that Chris might be overwhelmed by all the attention. "Hi Chris, I'd like to sit with you for a while. Just the two of us. Would it be okay if we move to a counseling room where there are more comfortable chairs?"

Chris nodded.

The counseling room had three chairs and a small table. Photos of calming nature scenes adorned the walls. There was a one-way mirror on one wall where others could observe sessions from the adjacent room.

They sat down facing each other, with Chris positioned so he faced the mirror, allowing the observers to focus on his reactions. "Chris, you don't have to talk to me if you don't want to," Dr. Deera said gently.

The silence stretched between them. Dr. Deera found himself more uncomfortable with the quiet than Chris appeared to be. He took a deep breath, reminding himself of his commitment to being present without the need to fix or force progress.

Meanwhile, behind the one-way mirror, the observers shifted restlessly.

"Why isn't he asking any questions?" Dr. Lewis whispered.

"Just wait," Dr. Taft replied, though his own patience was wearing thin.

Dr. Deera closed his eyes briefly, imagining himself at the Peace Pond, dropping his expectations and judgments. He silently asked for guidance, then simply sat in the moment with Chris.

Twenty minutes passed. Then thirty.

The observers' attention began to drift. Karen checked her watch, and Dr. Lewis glanced at his phone.

Then Chris lifted his hand and pointed at the empty third chair.

Dr. Deera looked over but saw nothing. He turned back to Chris. "What do you see?"

For the first time since his admission, Chris spoke, his voice barely above a whisper. "I see a teenage girl."

Behind the mirror, the observers exchanged surprised glances. "He speaks," Dr. Taft whispered.

"What's her name, Chris?" Dr. Deera asked gently.

"I don't know."

"Why don't you introduce yourself to her and ask her name?"

Chris hesitated, then nodded. "Okay." He turned to face the empty chair. "I'm Chris. What is your name?"

A moment passed in silence, then Chris's eyes widened. "She says her name is Maggie."

Dr. Deera focused intently on the chair, opening his heart the way he learned at Peace Pond. As he did, the image of Maggie slowly appeared - first as a shimmer, then solidifying into the familiar face he remembered from childhood.

"That is my sister," Dr. Deera said to Chris, his voice filled with wonder and recognition. "And she's here to help us."

Chris gave the slightest nod toward Maggie, and something that might be the ghost of a smile touched his lips.

Behind the mirror, the observers leaned forward in confusion.

"What just happened?" Dr. Lewis muttered.

Dr. Taft shook his head, his mouth a tight line. "Let's wait and see."

"Are they both experiencing some kind of shared delusion?" Karen asked.

"Unlikely," Dr. Taft replied, though uncertainty flickered in his voice. "Maybe Dr. Deera is using some kind of therapeutic technique to help Chris open up."

Back in the room, Dr. Deera watched as Chris's hunched shoulders began to relax and his clenched fists slowly unfurled. Whatever was happening - whether real, imagined, or something beyond his understanding - was reaching Chris in a way that conventional approaches would not have.

"Maggie understands what you're feeling," Dr. Deera said carefully, unsure how much to reveal but trusting the moment. "She knows what it's like when the pain feels too heavy to carry."

For the first time since his admission, Chris looked directly into Dr. Deera's eyes. The connection was brief but unmistakable - a flicker of recognition, of being truly seen.

Maggie's voice was soft, like a gentle breeze carrying warmth. *"Chris, I see you. Not the labels they've put on you, not the mistake they think you made, but you - the soul who has carried so much pain for so long."*

Chris's eyes widened again, and he turned toward her presence in the chair.

"You try to stop the hurting the only way you can think of," Maggie continued, her voice free of judgment. *"That doesn't make you weak or broken or wrong. It makes you human. It makes you someone who has been surviving something that no child should have to survive."*

Dr. Deera watched as tears began forming in Chris's eyes - the first emotional response anyone had witnessed since his admission. His breathing deepened, as if he was allowing himself to truly breathe for the first time in days.

"You are not your father's words about you," Maggie said. *"You are not the shame he has tried to make you carry. You are Love itself, Chris, even when you can't feel it. Especially when you can't feel it."*

Behind the mirror, the observers leaned forward again. Dr. Lewis whispered urgently, "Look at the change in his posture - his shoulders are dropping and his hands are completely open now. Even his facial muscles are relaxing."

Chris slowly lifted his head, looking between Dr. Deera and the chair where Maggie sat. His lips parted slightly, and in a voice barely above a whisper, he asked "She...she really sees me?"

Dr. Deera's voice was warm and reassuring. "Yes, Chris. She sees you completely. And so do I." He paused, letting the words settle.

"It's a gift to be seen and accepted for who you are, not for what you do or say or how you perform for others."

Chris nodded slowly, a single tear rolling down his cheek.

"There's no pressure here," Dr. Deera continued gently. "We can sit in silence, or if something comes to you that you'd like to share - about yourself, about what you hope for...for you, your brother, your mom...I'm here to listen. But only when you feel ready."

Chris looked toward Maggie again, then back at Dr. Deera. He took a shaky breath and seemed to consider speaking, but then simply closed his eyes and leaned back in his chair. The tension in his body continued to release as he settled into a peaceful quiet.

They sat together in comfortable silence for another ten minutes. Chris occasionally glanced at Maggie, and each time he did, his breathing seemed to deepen further.

Finally, Dr. Deera said, "Chris, I'm going to step out for a few minutes to speak with my colleagues. You can stay here as long as you like. Maggie will remain with you."

Chris opened his eyes and gave a small nod of understanding.

Dr. Deera quietly left the counseling room and joined the observers in the adjacent space. The room buzzed with barely contained energy and confusion.

"You're going to start him on antidepressants, maybe antipsychotic medication, aren't you?" Dr. Taft asked.

"Not yet. Let's see how he does in the next day or two."

"What exactly did we just witness?" Dr. Taft continued, his professional composure clearly shaken.

Dr. Lewis was pacing. "I've never seen anything like that. The physical transformation was remarkable - he went from practically catatonic to responsive in under an hour."

Karen stood with her arms crossed, skepticism written across her face. "Are we supposed to believe in invisible spirits now? This is a psychiatric unit, not a...a spiritual woo-woo healing center."

Dr. Deera took a moment before responding. "What we witnessed was a breakthrough with a suicidal teenager who hasn't spoken in three days. The method may be unconventional, but the results speak for themselves."

Just then, they saw Chris through the mirror, speaking softly and leaning toward the chair, his face more animated than it had been since his arrival.

"Look at him now," Karen said sharply. "He's talking to an empty chair. Doesn't this concern anyone else?"

Dr. Deera looked through the mirror at Chris, then back at his colleagues. "Who says it's empty? It isn't empty to him. Just because you can't see or hear telephone signals flying through the air doesn't mean they aren't there. You have to tap into the right frequency. That's what Chris is doing - he's talking to Love, or what you may call God. Are you denying the existence of God because you can't see Him?"

The room fell silent.

"The point is, we think we know what reality is, yet we can all agree that we don't know everything," Dr. Deera continued. "If seeing Love and healing where others see pathology makes me unconventional, then I'm willing to be unconventional."

Dr. Deera, Dr. Taft, and Karen left the observation room to continue their rounds. Dr. Lewis chose to stay behind, wanting to observe Chris's continued interaction.

As the the three approached the common area, they noticed Carlos, an artist who had been admitted in a crisis after stopping his medications for paranoid schizophrenia. He was in the midst of creating a new drawing that caught Dr. Deera's attention.

"That's a remarkable likeness of the person Chris has been talking to," Dr. Deera said matter-of-factly, then walked on with a slight smile.

Karen and Dr. Taft exchanged glances, both frowning. "I need some coffee," Karen muttered.

"I'll take mine with a shot of whiskey," Dr. Taft added, shaking his head.

Chapter 11: Friends

Monday, August 25

Sharon gently shook Charlie awake. "You need to get cleaned up. You still smell like campfire and outdoors from the camping trip. Why don't you go take a shower and I'll bring you clean clothes."

She followed Charlie to the upstairs bathroom and closed the door behind them. "I want to tell you something beyond the view of the security cameras. We're going to visit my friend, Rachel. I don't want your father to know where we're going. We can talk more in the car. I'll get us something to eat in the meantime."

"Rachel, that's Angela's momma."

"How do you know that?"

"She told me."

Sharon paused, processing this. "She's also my friend from AA. She works at the hospital where Chris is staying."

"Great, I'm going to meet David there."

"Who's David?"

"He's my friend from Boy Scout camp who must also be a friend of Rachel's."

"Charlie!" Sharon's eyes widened. "You're not stuttering."

"I don't seem to stutter when I play the Love Game that David taught me."

"I don't understand. And how do you know he'll be there?"

"He told me last night in a dream."

Sharon paused, studying her son's face. There was something different about him - a calmness she hasn't seen in years. "A dream? Charlie, that seems...well, it seems a little unusual. But I'm really glad you found this game. You'll have to tell me more about it later. I really want to know more, but right now we have to get ready to go."

While Charlie was taking his shower, Sharon put some cereal and milk on the table and poured him a glass of orange juice. She toasted a bagel for herself, spread some hummus on it, and sat down with a cup of coffee.

As she sipped her coffee, a strange feeling washed over her - an anticipation that something major was going to happen with her and her children's lives. She couldn't shake the sense that this visit to Rachel's house would be more than just a casual meeting between friends.

Her intuition told her to get a couple of changes of clothes for Charlie and put them in his backpack. She also grabbed his mobile video game player.

*****

Fifteen minutes later, Sharon and Charlie stood on Rachel's front porch. Sharon knocked on the door and was greeted by Rachel's warm smile.

"Sharon! I'm so glad you could come." Rachel's eyes moved to Charlie. "And this must be Charlie." She stepped aside, gesturing them in. "Please, come in. Make yourselves at home."

Behind Rachel, David appeared, straining to see around her. His face lit up when he spotted Charlie.

"Hey David, you were right - we are seeing each other today!" Charlie exclaimed, his voice clear and confident. He turned to his mother. "Mom, this is my friend David."

David looked directly into Sharon's eyes with an intensity she had never before experienced in a boy so young. "It's nice to meet you, Mrs. Sullivan."

"Nice to meet you too, David," Sharon said, struck by something profound in the child's gaze.

David and Charlie immediately gravitated toward each other, finding a comfortable spot in the living room where they could talk. Sharon watched with amazement as her son settled in with such ease and familiarity beside this boy she'd never even heard of before today - still feeling that extraordinary moment of connection David had made with her through his eyes.

Rachel led Sharon toward the kitchen, where a woman was tidying up the breakfast dishes.

"Sharon, I'd like you to meet my momma, Nana," Rachel said. "Nana, I'd like you to meet my friend Sharon."

Nana turned with a welcoming smile, her eyes kind and attentive, and extended her hand. Sharon took it warmly. She noticed a young boy through the kitchen window, heading out with a backpack.

"That's my son, Sammy," Rachel said, noticing Sharon's gaze. "He already finished his breakfast and is going out to play with friends," Nana added.

"Would you like some coffee or tea, Sharon?" Nana offered.

"I'll have some coffee. I already had one cup, but if you have decaf, I'd love that."

"I do," Nana said. "And I have a selection of coffee pods, so I can make it quickly. I'll have it for you shortly. Do you take cream or sugar?"

"Yes to both, please."

As Nana busied herself with the coffee, Sharon turned to Rachel. "You know, Charlie knew David was going to be here because David told him in a dream. And Rachel, something else weird happened. Charlie stopped stuttering. He says he doesn't stutter when he's playing the Love Game that David taught him." She shook her head in bewilderment. "What is it about David? How is he affecting Charlie this way?"

Nana gave a knowing smile to that question.

"He is Love," Rachel said simply.

Sharon stared at her, confusion and wonder crossing her face. "What do you mean?"

"It's something you'll experience for yourself rather than being told. It's something that Charlie has already experienced," Rachel replied gently.

Sharon paused, remembering. "The way he looked at me when I came in made me feel like the deepest part of me was being seen."

"It was," Nana replied.

"Sharon, I can see you're carrying a heavy burden," Rachel said. "What brought you here today and how can I help?"

Sharon's voice broke. "Rachel, I'm drowning. I don't know how to protect my boys or myself. I'm afraid and uncertain about what's to come, but I know I need to separate my family from my husband's toxicity."

Nana sat Sharon's coffee in front of her and refilled Rachel's cup.

"Thanks, Nana," Sharon said gratefully.

"Thanks, Momma," Rachel added.

"I'll leave the two of you alone to talk," Nana said as she left the kitchen.

Rachel reached across the table and placed her hand gently over Sharon's. "You've already taken the hardest step - recognizing what needs to change. And look how you're already protecting Charlie, bringing him here shows your instincts are good."

Sharon took a shaky breath. "But I don't know where to start. Everything feels so overwhelming."

"Let's break this down," Rachel offered. "Sometimes it helps to think of this in phases - immediate safety, short-term stability, long-term independence. Which phase feels most important to focus on first?"

Sharon considered. "Safety, I think. I'm scared of what Les might do if he finds out I'm planning to leave."

"That's wise to think about. What feels like the most urgent need right now - physical safety, somewhere to stay, legal protection?"

"All of it," Sharon admitted, then caught herself. "But...maybe having a plan for where we could go if things got bad quickly."

Rachel nodded. "That makes sense. Have you had a chance to think about whether you'd want to stay in the area or start fresh somewhere else?"

"I don't know. Chris is in the hospital here, and Charlie's finally found something that helps him...but staying around here might mean Les could find us easier."

"There's no right or wrong answer," Rachel reassured her. "Some people find it helpful to have family or friends nearby for support. Others prefer the fresh start that comes with distance. What feels right for you?"

Sharon was quiet for a moment. "I think...I think I need to be somewhere where Chris can get the help he needs. He's finally getting care that seems to understand him."

"So, staying in the area, at least for now," Rachel reflected. "What resources do you already have that you might not be thinking of? Your AA network, savings, family?"

"I have some money saved that Les doesn't know about," Sharon said, a hint of strength in her voice. "And my sister is in the next town over...she's always said we could come there if we needed to."

"Those are real assets," Rachel affirmed. "Would it help to connect with some people who've been through similar situations? I know some women who might be able to share what worked for them - not to tell you what to do, but to give you options to consider."

Sharon nodded eagerly. "Yes, that would help. I feel so alone in all this."

"You're not alone," Rachel said firmly. "And Sharon, I know you've been working hard on your recovery. How are you feeling about maintaining your sobriety through all this stress?"

Sharon's face tightened. "It's been really hard. Especially with Chris...I keep thinking one drink would help with the anxiety."

"That's completely understandable," Rachel reassured her. "Crisis situations can make the urge to drink feel overwhelming. What's been helping you stay strong?"

"The meetings, mostly. And knowing that drinking would make everything worse, not better." Sharon paused. "But I'm scared about tonight, going home to that empty house."

"Do you have someone you can call if you feel triggered? Your sponsor?"

"Betty, yes. I should probably call her today anyway."

"That sounds like a good plan. Now, let's break down some of your needs and desires into priorities. Right now, Charlie's wellbeing is a priority. Then we'll start with what seems immediate. Next step is to gather information about possibilities - including legal advice and where you can go to feel safe temporarily. Then we can address long-term goals."

Sharon nodded with relief, looking more focused. "That makes sense. Charlie's safety does come first."

"Let's start with that then," Rachel said, then turned and called David and Charlie to the kitchen. They came in, both looking curious but comfortable.

Sharon turned to Charlie. "There's a lot going on at home and I don't think it will be helpful for you to be around your father at this time. We're considering some possible options."

Before she had a chance to talk about options, David interjected, "I would really like it if Charlie could stay with me. I'm sure my parents will agree, but I can give them a call. I told them how much we got to know each other when we were camping and dreaming."

"I would like that too," Charlie added.

Nana smiled from the doorway. "Sometimes Love allows things to unfold perfectly."

David pulled out his phone. "Mom, can Charlie stay at our house for a few days? Dad met him when he picked me up after the camping trip. He's my new friend and I would enjoy being with him." He paused, listening. "She wants to talk to Charlie's mom."

David handed the phone to Sharon.

"Hello, this is Sharon, Charlie's mom," she began, her voice slightly nervous.

"Hi Sharon, I'm Vicki. David has told us so much about Charlie. He said you might need some help?"

Sharon took a deep breath. "I'm in a difficult situation at home with my husband, and I don't think it's safe for Charlie to be around his father right now. David has had such a wonderful effect on Charlie - he's stopped stuttering and seems so much more confident. I was hoping...would it be possible for Charlie to stay with you for a few days while I figure things out?"

"Of course," Vicki responded warmly. "We'd be happy to have Charlie. Would you like to bring him by so we can meet properly, and you can see where he'll be staying?"

"I've packed some clothes and things for Charlie just in case. Would it be okay if David and Charlie walk to your house together? I have some urgent things I need to take care of right away."

"That's fine. David knows the way, obviously," Vicki chuckled. "Sharon, if you need anything else, please don't hesitate to call. David seems to think a lot of Charlie, and any friend of his is welcome here."

After Sharon hung up, David said, "I don't know all the details about what's happening, but Angela tells me that it would be really beneficial for you to call Mr. Lucas, our scoutmaster. Angela knows things, Mrs. Sullivan."

Rachel nodded. "If Angela suggested it, there's a gift you won't want to miss."

Sharon looked confused. "I thought Angela was your daughter who died."

"Yes," Rachel said gently, "but she's active in our hearts every moment, sharing wisdom at perfect times."

Rachel reached into her purse and pulled out a folded piece of paper. "I've been thinking about what you might need since I saw you Friday at the hospital, and I asked some friends for recommendations about divorce lawyers. Almost unanimously they mentioned Elin Young. She has a particular interest in helping women in abusive relationships. I thought you might want this information."

"I'll call for an appointment tomorrow, and I'll call Larry Lucas as well. I have his number," Sharon said, taking the paper. "Thanks so much, Rachel and Nana, for your support. I hope Les isn't home when I get back. I don't want to face him right now."

Rachel gave Sharon a hug, whispering in her ear, "I see the Love you are and I feel perfect. I know whatever happens will be for your highest good."

Sharon felt a warmth surge through her body, causing her to tremble slightly. "Thank you. Bye for now."

Charlie ran up to her for a goodbye hug. He whispered, "I know everything will be fine."

*****

Sharon entered the quiet, dark house alone with her thoughts. Charlie was safe now. It had been a stressful three days without much sleep, but as tired as she was, she couldn't stop worrying about the uncertainty ahead.

She flipped on a light and walked through the living room, her eyes falling on Les's bar setup. The bottles gleamed in the light - vodka, whiskey, gin. All the familiar escapes lined up like old friends.

Her hands shook as she reached for the vodka. It had been really rough the last few days, and she could really use a shot. One drink wouldn't hurt under these circumstances. It might help her sleep and ease the anxiety that Les might suddenly show up.

She poured herself a drink and stared at it, the clear liquid swirling in the light. The glass felt comforting and familiar in her hand. The smell hit her immediately - sharp, medicinal, promising relief from the constant knot in her chest. Six months sober, but at that moment it was nothing compared to the weight of everything falling apart.

She raised the glass halfway to her lips, then stopped.

"God, what the hell am I doing?" she called out to the empty house.

She threw the drink, the glass crashing into the bar sink.

The sound echoed through the quiet house, and suddenly she saw herself clearly, standing in her kitchen, about to throw away six months of hard work because she was scared and tired. She thought about Chris in the hospital, about Charlie finally finding confidence, about the lawyer's number in her purse.

She poured the rest of the bottle down the drain, watching the vodka swirl away. And she didn't stop there. One by one, she opened every bottle in Les's collection - the expensive whiskey and scotch he was so proud of, the gin, the rum, everything - and poured them all down the sink. The smell filled the room, but instead of tempting her, it made her feel stronger.

She threw the empty bottles in the trash with satisfying crashes, each one a declaration: I'm not going back. I'm not running away anymore. Exhausted but clear-headed, Sharon finally headed to bed, ready to face whatever came next.

Chapter 12: Guided by Love

Tuesday morning, August 26

Dr. Deera sat quietly in his office, Chris Sullivan's file open on his desk. The morning light filtered through his window as he took a moment to center himself before their second session together. He closed his eyes and breathed deeply, feeling the weight of responsibility for this young man's healing.

The silence in his office felt different today - expectant, almost alive. When he opened his eyes, Maggie was sitting in the chair across from his desk, her presence both familiar and comforting.

"I AM here," she said softly, her voice carrying the same gentle warmth he remembered from childhood.

"Maggie," he said, no longer surprised by her appearances. "I was just thinking about Chris, about how to help him."

"I know," she smiled. *"Mark, I've always watched over you, especially during your own dark times. Do you remember when you were Chris's age, feeling so alone after I died? When Dad poured himself into work and Mom withdrew into her grief?"*

Dr. Deera nodded, the memory still tender. "You were gone, and they were emotionally gone too. I felt invisible, like I didn't matter."

"That pain prepared you for this moment," Maggie said. *"You weren't ready to see me then, to accept my guidance in this form. Your heart was closed by hurt. But in the last few months, you've been opening to Love - through your own healing, through Rachel's influence, through the Peace Pond experience. Now you're ready."*

"Ready for what?"

"To be the healer you were meant to be. To approach Chris not just as a psychiatrist, but as someone who understands that Love is the greatest medicine." She leaned forward slightly. *"Chris doesn't need someone to analyze his trauma, Mark. He needs someone to see the Love he is beneath all that pain."*

Dr. Deera felt a warmth spreading through his chest. "Like you're doing with me right now."

"Exactly. You've spent years learning to diagnose and treat symptoms. I'm here to shine my light on you, inspiring you to open your heart and nurture the wellbeing of others with compassion, just like you did when you and Angela descended into the darkness to be with me. There is no better way to serve yourself or others. You don't have to give up your training and experience with conventional therapies, just offer it with compassion, checking in with the wisdom of your Loveself. You aren't alone. Angela and I are always with you. Love is here. Chris is ready to receive what you're ready to give - the kind of healing that comes from being truly seen and accepted."

He took another deep breath, feeling a shift in his energy. "So, when I'm with Chris today..."

"Trust what your heart tells you and trust the process," Maggie said. *"Let Love guide the conversation. Chris will feel the difference."*

"Will you be there with us?"

Maggie's smile brightened. *"I'm always there when Love is present. Chris will see me because his heart is open to healing. Trust that, Mark. Trust the process."*

Dr Deera stood, feeling more centered than he had in years. "Thank you, Maggie, for always watching over me, even when I couldn't see you."

"I never left you, brother. I just waited for you to be ready." Her image began to fade. *"Trust what your heart tells you, not just your training,"* Maggie said. *"Trust the Love you are, Mark."*

*****

Twenty minutes later, Dr. Deera entered the counseling room where Chris was waiting, sitting in the same chair as he did the day before. His posture seemed less rigid.

"Good morning, Chris," Dr. Deera said as he settled into his chair. "How are you feeling today?"

Chris looked up, surprised. "What?"

"How are you feeling?"

Chris stared at him for a moment. "I've never been asked that before. People usually tell me what I'm feeling or assume they know."

"Well today, I'm not going to assume anything."

Chris looked at him, locking eyes for the first time. "I feel good when Maggie is with me." He glanced at the third chair. "She listens without trying to fix me."

Dr. Deera followed his gaze and nodded. "Thanks, Maggie, for being here. I really appreciate how you've helped Chris express his emotions." He turned back to Chris. "I noticed that you've been talking to her at other times. Would you like to share what you've been talking about?"

Chris considered this, then spoke more openly than he had since his admission. "She told me that when she was alive, she felt despair and hopelessness and wanted to kill herself. She was on medications and in therapy but didn't feel like it was helping."

He paused, glancing at the chair where Maggie was sitting before continuing. "She told me she was sexually abused by a neighbor boy when she was twelve, and no one listened. She was so afraid, she waited a long time before she told her mother. Her mother called the boy's mother, but it was Maggie's word against the boy's, so nothing was done."

Dr. Deera looked toward Maggie, who nodded gently.

"She didn't bring it up again, even during counseling," Chris continued. "She couldn't focus and her schoolwork suffered. She thought if she tried to kill herself, then people would really listen. But she went too far and died."

Dr. Deera took a moment before responding. "Chris, you understand that the Maggie you're seeing is a spiritual presence, not a living person?"

"Of course, Dr. Deera."

Dr. Deera sat back, shaking his head slightly. "That's...that's remarkable, Chris." He paused, collecting his thoughts. "I'm sorry. That wasn't a very professional response. How do you feel about telling me this?"

Chris looked directly into Dr. Deera's eyes. "I'm okay with it, but I'm more interested in what you're feeling about what I told you."

The question surprised Dr. Deera. He glanced toward Maggie, who smiled encouragingly. "Chris, I see you - the real you, the Love that you are - and I feel perfect."

Chris's expression softened. "Really?"

"Chris, I've rarely had a patient ask me how I feel about something so personal. You and Maggie have been working together to find a way to help not just yourself, but me too." Dr. Deera's voice grew tender. "I'm having mixed feelings about what you told me. Some anger and sadness that Maggie had to suffer the way she did, but also appreciation that she's more a part of my life now, and gratitude to you for being part of my healing process as I am for yours."

For the first time in months, Chris smiled - a genuine smile that transformed his entire face. The session continued for another thirty minutes, with Chris becoming more animated and engaged than anyone at the hospital had seen. Before leaving, Dr. Deera said, "Chris, I want to ask your permission to discuss your care with Rachel. She's not a licensed professional, but she's an extremely intuitive healer whom I trust completely."

Chris looked at Maggie, who nodded. "Sure."

"I'll be meeting with your mother later this morning to give her an update on your progress."

Chris nodded, still wearing traces of that smile.

When Dr. Deera left the counseling room, his eyes were bright with hope. He walked to the ward secretary's desk and said, "Please call Mrs. Sullivan to set up a meeting this morning."

He then called his mother. "Mom, can we get together tonight with Crystal? I have something important I'd like to talk about."

"Of course," Amma responded. "What would you like to eat?"

"I don't want to put you out. Maybe I can bring some Thai food."

"Nonsense. I'll cook something. Let me check with Crystal, but I think around 6:30 would work."

Nearby, Rachel had been quietly working, and she watched Dr. Deera with knowing eyes. Something wonderful had happened - she could feel it. She hummed softly as she returned to her work.

*****

At 9:00 a.m., Sharon sat in her kitchen, staring at the lawyer's phone number Rachel had given her. Her hands trembled slightly as she dialed.

"My name is Sharon Sullivan," she said when the receptionist answered. "I need to speak with Ms. Young about a divorce. My situation is urgent - I have two sons and I'm in an abusive marriage."

"Let me check her schedule," the receptionist said. After a brief hold, she returned. "Ms. Young had a cancellation for this afternoon. Can you be here at 1:00 p.m. today?"

Sharon felt a wave of relief. "Yes, absolutely. Thank you so much."

After hanging up, she sat quietly, still unable to believe she was actually taking these steps. She hadn't heard from Les since Sunday when he picked Charlie up from camping, and she considers that a blessing.

Her phone rang, interrupting her thoughts.

"Sharon, it's Rachel. I wanted to give you an update on Chris. He had another session with Dr. Deera this morning, and something wonderful happened. Chris is really opening up and talking more. Dr. Deera will be calling you soon to set up a meeting."

"Thank you, Rachel. That's such good news."

Minutes after hanging up, her phone rang again. When Sharon saw the hospital number, her heart raced.

"Mrs. Sullivan, this is the Behavioral Health Unit. Dr. Deera would like to schedule a consultation with you this morning. Would 11:00 work?"

"Is Chris okay?" Sharon asked, her voice trembling.

"Dr. Deera seemed very positive when he made the request."

"Yes, that works perfectly." It would give her time to meet with Dr. Deera before her 1:00 appointment with the lawyer.

At 11:00 sharp, Sharon was sitting across from Dr. Deera in his office, her hands folded tightly in her lap.

"Mrs. Sullivan, thank you for coming in," Dr. Deera began. "I want to start by saying how much I've enjoyed working with Chris and how enlightening it's been for me professionally to get to know him."

He leaned forward slightly. "Chris has been on quite a journey in his first seventeen years, culminating with his suicide attempt, which was essentially a cry for help. Now he's getting the help he needs."

Sharon nodded, listening intently.

"Your son shows symptoms consistent with depression, anxiety, and PTSD. I attribute the PTSD to a history of lifelong verbal abuse from his father. When he was first admitted, he wasn't speaking to anyone. He's talking now, primarily to me, though he's still hesitant to open up to other staff and prefers to avoid social contact with other patients."

Dr. Deera's tone became more hopeful. "He's made remarkable progress in an unexpectedly short time. I believe if he continues on this path, you'll see him becoming the loving person he truly is. However, this progress will be threatened if he returns to an abusive environment."

"I've already taken steps to change that," Sharon said quietly.

"Good. We haven't started Chris on medications yet, and after today's session, I'm not sure that will be necessary. I do think he would benefit from continued counseling as he encounters situations that might trigger his PTSD responses. I'd be happy to continue with Chris's care after he leaves the hospital."

Sharon took a deep breath. "My friend Rachel works here and gave me a heads-up about Chris's progress. She mentioned that some staff are concerned about him talking to...spirits. Is that true?"

"Yes, but Chris understands he's communicating with spiritual energy. He's not hallucinating, and in my opinion, he's not psychotic. He has a spiritual guide who brings unconditional Love to him. I encourage that relationship because I've witnessed a change in him from complete self-absorption to beginning to care for others. That's a major shift." Dr. Deera paused. "Rachel mentioned that your other son, Charlie, is staying with David temporarily."

"You know David?" Sharon asked, surprised.

"I know David very well, and I want to assure you there's no better place for Charlie right now. David has a gift for bringing out the best in people."

"Charlie's been playing something called the Love Game with David, and he doesn't stutter when he's engaged with it. I know when he's anxious because the stuttering returns."

Dr. Deera smiled. "Mrs. Sullivan, I asked Chris this morning if I could discuss his care with Rachel, even though she's not a licensed professional. I told him I trust her completely and value her insights as an intuitive healer. He agreed. Do you also agree?"

"Yes, I know what you mean about Rachel. I've felt the Love she radiates."

"We'll keep you informed of Chris's progress," Dr. Deera said as their meeting concluded.

Sharon left the consultation room and found Chris waiting to see her. Initially, his face showed no expression and she hesitated, wanting desperately to hug him but uncertain if she should. Then Chris opened his arms to her.

She sobbed as they embraced. "I'm so sorry I let you down, my sweet son."

"Are you disappointed in me, Mom?"

"Absolutely not. Do you hear me? I am not disappointed in you." She pulled back to look at him directly. "Your cry for help was what I needed to inspire me to change how I care for you and Charlie, as well as myself."

She took a deep breath. "I want you to know, and I hope this won't upset you, but I'm going to divorce your father. I don't want his toxic behavior to hurt us anymore. We won't just survive, Chris - we'll thrive."

"It's okay, Mom. I don't want to be stuck in shame anymore. Maggie tells me I can continue to be a victim of Dad's behavior, or I can choose to move on. Let's move on. How's Charlie doing?"

"He's staying with a friend who's taught him something called the Love Game. It helped him stop stuttering when he's playing it. Maybe you could ask Maggie to teach you, too. But I have to leave now, I have an appointment with a lawyer. Have a wonderful day."

She gave him another hug and a kiss on the cheek. As she walked away, she noticed Chris standing a little taller, and for the first time in years, she felt genuine hope.

Chapter 13: Taking Action

Tuesday afternoon, August 26

Sharon pulled into the small parking lot at 12:40 p.m., giving herself a few minutes to gather her courage. The two-story brick building wasn't as imposing as the glass towers downtown where the big firms operated. A simple brass nameplate beside the entrance read 'Elin Young, PLLC - Family Law' in understated lettering.

She climbed the stairs to the second floor, her heart beating faster with each step. This was really happening. After years of making excuses and living in fear, she was finally taking action.

The reception area was modest but welcoming. Warm beige walls displayed a few tasteful prints of local landscapes, and two burgundy chairs sat across from a simple wooden desk where a woman in her fifties looked up with a genuine smile.

"You must be Sharon Sullivan," the receptionist said, rising from her chair. "I'm Janet. Ms. Young is just finishing up a call, then she'll be right with you."

"I'm a little early," Sharon admitted, glancing at her watch. 12:45.

"That's perfectly fine. Here, let me get you started with some paperwork." Janet handed her a clipboard with several forms attached. "Just the basic intake information - contact details, employment, children's information, that sort of thing. Can I get you some water or coffee?"

"Water would be great, thank you."

Sharon settled into one of the chairs, the clipboard feeling heavier than it should. The forms asked for facts - addresses, dates of marriage, children's names and ages, employment history. Simple questions that somehow felt monumental when she realized she was filling them out to end her marriage.

But thinking of Chris's transformation, of Charlie's healing, of Rachel's encouraging hug that still seemed to pulse with warmth through her body, Sharon pressed the pen firmly against the paper and began to write.

A few minutes later, the office door opened and a woman in her early forties stepped out. She had shoulder-length auburn hair, kind brown eyes behind wire-rimmed glasses, and wore a navy blazer over a cream-colored blouse. All professional but approachable.

"Sharon?" She extended her hand with a warm smile. "I'm Elin Young, but please call me Elin." Her handshake was firm and reassuring. "Come on in, let's sit over here where we'll be more comfortable."

Elin's office was as unpretentious as the reception area. She led Sharon to a small round table in the corner where two padded chairs sat facing each other, away from the imposing desk that dominated the other side of the room.

As they settled in, Sharon felt her shoulders relax for the first time in hours. There was something genuinely calming about Elin's presence - no rushing, no clock-watching, just patient attention.

Elin briefly reviewed the intake forms Sharon had completed, then set the papers aside and looked directly at Sharon.

"Janet mentioned you felt this meeting was urgent," she said gently. "How can I help you?"

"I want a divorce," Sharon replied, the words coming out clearer than she'd expected. "I don't know where to start."

She paused, gathering herself. "The turning point came when my seventeen-year-old son tried to commit suicide. He's in the hospital and doing better now, thank God. His psychiatrist believes he has PTSD from verbal abuse from his father - abuse that's been going on since he could walk. The doctor says Chris's recovery depends on getting out of that abusive situation."

Elin nodded, encouraging Sharon to continue.

"Chris's younger brother Charlie is thirteen, and he's received the same treatment. For years I knew it wasn't right, but I felt powerless and turned to alcohol." Sharon's voice caught. "I've been sober for six months now, and I can finally see clearly. My boys need to be safe." She looked directly at Elin. "I'm scared of what my husband might do when he finds out, but I can't let fear control me anymore. My friend Rachel gave me your name - she said you understand these situations."

With caring in her voice, Elin leaned forward slightly and said, "First, let me say how brave you are for taking this step. And congratulations on your sobriety - that takes tremendous strength." She reached for a legal pad. "You're absolutely right to prioritize the safety of your sons. Let's talk about protecting all of you."

"Les - my husband - and I both knew Chris was severely depressed," Sharon continued. "But Les refused to allow Chris to see a doctor or counselor. He said he didn't want to waste money on 'head doctors.'"

Elin made a note, her jaw tightening. "Has your husband physically abused you or your children?"

"No. It's all been verbal - constant criticism, name-calling, telling the boys they're worthless, stupid. He tears them down every single day." Sharon's voice grew steadier. "And he threatens them - he's always saying things like 'you'll be sorry' or 'you don't know what I'm capable of.'"

"Emotional abuse is just as serious as physical abuse," Elin said firmly. "The courts recognize that. Do you feel safe going home today?"

Sharon considered this carefully. "He's never hit us, but he throws things sometimes. Slams doors. His rages can be intense." She paused. "And he's very security conscious. He has cameras positioned around and inside the house that link to his phone. He says it's for our protection, but..."

"But it feels like surveillance," Elin finished gently.

"Yes. He checks everything - my phone call logs, where I go, who I talk to. He's told me repeatedly that I don't need anyone but him, and if I ever go behind his back, he'll find out and I'll be sorry."

Elin made several more notes. "That's textbook isolation and control. What about friends, family support?"

"He doesn't like my sister. He gets angry when I call her and says I call her too often. Over the years, he's made it very difficult for me to maintain friendships. He gets jealous, finds fault with anyone I try to get close to." Sharon's voice grew smaller. "He always says I have everything I need at home."

"Sharon, what you're describing is sophisticated psychological abuse designed to make you completely dependent on him. This isn't about you lacking judgment - this is about him systematically isolating you."

Elin sat back, her tone remaining professional but warm. "What kind of work does Les do?"

"He's in international business consulting. He travels constantly - sometimes he's gone for days or weeks at a time. He says he can't discuss his work because of confidentiality agreements with his clients."

Sharon's voice took on a bitter edge. "He left for another business trip right after dropping Charlie off from camp. Said he was heading to the airport. He does that a lot - appears and disappears without much explanation."

"And financially, how does that work for your family?"

"I haven't worked since the kids were born. I was a secretary before I met Les, but once Chris came along, I stayed home. Les said it made more sense financially, and honestly..." She looked embarrassed. "I was afraid to leave the boys alone with him. Even when they were babies, he had no patience."

Sharon paused, then continued. "But it wasn't just about finances. Les doesn't believe women should work outside the home after they're married. He says it reflects badly on him as a provider - that's his job as the head of the house." Her voice lowered. "My father believed the same thing. He had tight control over my mother too. I guess I didn't recognize the pattern until now."

"Your maternal instincts were protecting your children. Do you have any independent finances?"

"I have a few thousand dollars I've saved from household money over the years. I keep it hidden in the house. Les handles all our finances. He gave me a credit card with a credit limit for groceries, home supplies, and the kids' clothes, and he scrutinizes every purchase." Sharon looked down at her hands. "I feel so stupid admitting this. I don't even know what he earns or what assets we have."

"You're not stupid, Sharon. Financial control is one of the most effective tools abusers use. It's designed to make leaving seem impossible." Elin took more notes. "Once we file the divorce papers, I can legally demand full financial disclosure through the discovery process. He'll be required by court order to provide all financial records."

"I haven't seen Les since Chris was admitted to the ICU," Sharon said, her voice growing harder. "He picked Charlie up after his Boy

Scout weekend camping trip, dropped him off at the house, and said he was on his way to the airport for a business trip. He left Charlie alone while I was still at the hospital. He hasn't been back since and hasn't even called to check on Chris once."

Elin's eyebrows raised. "He abandoned a thirteen-year-old while his brother was hospitalized for a suicide attempt?"

"Yes. That's when I realized something I think I've known for a long time. Les doesn't really care about any of us. We're just things in his life that he manages when convenient."

"This abandonment is significant evidence of neglect," Elin said, adding to her notes. "For the emergency orders we need - temporary custody and exclusive use of the home - we have plenty with Chris's hospitalization, the psychiatrist's evaluation, and his abandonment of Charlie."

"I've already told the boys I'm getting a divorce. Chris seemed relieved when I told him at the hospital. And Charlie's been so much happier staying with David's family."

"Being honest with them shows you're taking their experiences seriously. Their positive responses will be helpful in court proceedings."

Elin glanced at her watch, then refocused on Sharon. "Before you go, we need to discuss your immediate safety. What happens if Les comes home before the emergency orders are granted?"

"I don't want to be home alone with him," Sharon said, anxiety creeping back into her voice. "But if I go somewhere else, he'll find me. He could track my phone."

"Do you have somewhere safe you could stay? Your sister's house?"

"My sister lives forty minutes away, but Les knows where she lives and she has her own family to think about. I can't put them at risk." Sharon paused. "I think Rachel might take me in for a couple of days until I can safely go back to the house. I have a feeling that Rachel and her mom wouldn't be intimidated by Les if he showed up."

"That sounds like a much stronger support system than a hotel room," Elin says approvingly. "Here's what we'll do. First, I will file the emergency papers today - within the next two hours. Second, I want you to pack a bag and keep it ready. Include important documents - birth certificates, social security cards, any medical records, your personal savings account information."

"What about Charlie? He's safe with David's family for now, but what if Les tries to take him?"

"I'll include language in the emergency order preventing him from removing Charlie from his current safe location. And I'll make sure David's parents understand the legal situation."

Elin wrote her cell phone number on her business card. "Third, if Les returns unexpectedly before we get the orders, leave immediately. Don't try to explain, don't pack, just go. Call me from wherever you end up safe."

Sharon felt more tension leave her shoulders. "So I might only have to avoid him for a day or two?"

"If everything goes smoothly, yes. But Sharon, promise me - if you feel unsafe for even a moment, you leave. Your instincts have kept you and your boys alive this long. Trust them."

Elin stood and extended her hand. "Sharon, what struck me today is how clearly you're thinking despite everything you've been through. You're not the victim Les tried to make you believe you were."

"Six months of sobriety changed everything," Sharon replied, shaking Elin's hand firmly. "I'm finally seeing things as they really are - including Les. Maybe he's not the powerful man he pretends to be. Maybe he's just as trapped as I was, but in his own fears."

"That's a remarkably compassionate perspective for someone who's been so hurt."

"I don't know where that comes from," Sharon said thoughtfully. "But holding onto anger and fear...it just keeps me in the same prison he's in."

"Remember - if anything feels wrong while you're at the house, abandon the mission and get out. Documents can be replaced, but you can't be." Elin walked her toward the door. "Call me the moment you're safely away."

"Thank you, Elin. For the first time in years, I feel like I'm not alone in this."

"You're absolutely not alone anymore. And Sharon? Trust those instincts that kept your children safe all these years. They'll guide you through this, too."

Chapter 14: Safe Harbor

Tuesday Evening, August 26

Sharon pulled into Rachel's driveway, her hands still trembling from the emotional intensity of the legal consultation. The two-story older home with its inviting front porch and gentle swing brought an unexpected wave of relief. She could practically feel the house embracing her as she walked up the steps.

Before she could even knock, the front door opened. Nana stood there with her warm, knowing smile, as if she had been watching for Sharon's arrival.

"Hi, Sharon, come right on in and tell me about your day," Nana said, stepping aside to usher her in.

They settled at the kitchen table, the same one where Sharon sat just days ago when Charlie and David were reunited. The normalcy of the setting felt surreal after everything that had happened since.

"Have you eaten today?" Nana asked, studying Sharon's face with concern.

"No, I haven't felt like it," Sharon admitted, suddenly realizing how depleted she felt. "I'm exhausted. Didn't sleep much last night."

Nana moved toward the refrigerator. "When did you last eat?"

Sharon had to think about it. "Yesterday morning, maybe? Everything's been such a blur..." She trailed off, not sure how to summarize the whirlwind of the past few days.

"Well, that won't do at all," Nana said, pulling ingredients from the refrigerator. "You need nourishment for the journey ahead, dear. Body and soul." She paused, looking directly at Sharon with her wise, compassionate eyes. "In this moment with me, Sharon, there's nothing to fight. Now is the opportunity to take a breath, get something to eat, and appreciate the gifts that you're discovering."

Sharon felt a peaceful sensation rising from her feet, softening and releasing each muscle as it traveled up her entire body.

Nana took some leftover stir-fried rice and vegetables in a bowl out of the refrigerator and put it in the microwave. As it heated, she poured Sharon a glass of iced tea, the ice cubes clinking softly against the glass.

Sharon watched in gratitude and amazement as the simple, caring gestures unfolded. "How did you know that's one of my favorite things to eat?"

Nana reached out and touched the side of Sharon's face. She didn't have to say anything.

Sharon ate with the enthusiasm of someone breaking a long fast. Nana watched in silence, her presence calm and patient. When Sharon finished, Nana took her empty dish to the sink and returned with a small plate holding three chocolate chip cookies.

Sharon raised her eyebrows and smiled.

"Now tell me all about your day," Nana said, settling back into her chair.

Sharon took a sip of her iced tea and let out a long sigh. "I don't even know where to start, Nana. This morning feels like a lifetime ago. It started with meeting Dr. Deera at the hospital - Chris's psychiatrist. He told me that Chris is really doing well, that something fundamental has shifted in him since Friday." She paused, her voice growing softer. "And then I saw Chris, and he was...different. Stronger somehow. He hugged me, Nana. Really hugged me, like he was choosing to move forward instead of staying stuck in the pain."

She took another sip, the weight of the day settling on her. "But Dr. Deera reinforced something I think I already knew deep down - that Chris's continued recovery from PTSD and depression will depend on getting away from Les's abusive behavior. Hearing a professional say it out loud made it impossible to ignore anymore."

She reached for a cookie, gathering her thoughts. "Then I went to see a lawyer - Elin Young - and for the first time in seventeen years, I told someone the whole truth about Les. I kept waiting for her to ask me why I stayed so long or tell me I should have left years ago, but she didn't. She just...listened. And believed me."

Sharon paused again, then continued. "You might be wondering why I stopped over today. Elin said it could take twenty-four to forty-eight hours to get a legal judgment that allows me to return home safely with a restraining order. You've been so helpful already and I hate to impose further, but could I sleep on your couch for the next day or two?"

Nana's expression grew serious. Shaking her head, she said, "I'm sorry, Sharon, but I can't let you do that." She paused, then with a gentle smile, continued, "I can't let you do that when there's a perfectly comfortable bed in Angela's old room. You're welcome to sleep there and I'm sure I speak for Rachel as well."

Sharon, holding her breath, let it out slowly and placed her hand over her heart, tears welling up in appreciation. Just then, her phone rang, breaking the moment. She glanced at the screen, then turned to Nana. "It's Vicki – I'm sorry, but I need to take this call."

"Hi, Vicki," Sharon said, wiping her eyes quickly.

"I've been thinking about you - how did everything go?" Vicki's warm voice came through the phone.

"It's all going better than expected. I got good news about Chris's progress today."

"That's wonderful. Charlie has been wondering. I think he'll be happy with the news."

"I also saw a lawyer today and she's getting the ball rolling so I can go back home with a court order restraining Les from contact. It will take one or two more days. I'm going to stay with Rachel and Nana until then." Sharon paused, gathering courage for her request. "I was hoping that Charlie could stay with you until I get the restraining order."

"Most certainly," Vicki replied without hesitation. "David is enjoying Charlie's company and they've been outside most of the day exploring nature. David hasn't had close friends other than Angela before. He's in heaven." Then she added, "I'd like to invite you to dinner at our house tonight. I'm baking lasagna and there will be more than enough. What do you say?"

"I would really like that," Sharon answered, her voice brightening. "I miss Charlie terribly, and it would be good to let him know what's happening - the positive news about Chris and the progress with the lawyer. I need to go home to pack a few things, then I can be at your house around 6:00. Will that work?"

"That sounds perfect. I'll see you then," Vicki replied. "Oh, and Sharon, I also invited Larry Lucas for dinner - David and Charlie's scoutmaster. The three of them had a real bonding experience on their recent campout, and David mentioned that Mr. Lucas, as a school counselor, might offer some additional support through these stressful times."

"That's great. David suggested that I call Larry, but I haven't had the chance yet."

"Perfect then. See you at six."

Sharon turned to Nana. "I'm going to stop by my house and pack some things. Vicki invited me to dinner tonight and I'm excited to see Charlie. If that's OK, I should be back here by eight."

"That's fine, Sharon," Nana replied. "Are you concerned about running into Les?"

"A little. I'm going to try not to think too far ahead. I'm trying to focus on one small moment at a time like I've been doing with my AA meetings. I've managed to survive Les's abuse for eighteen years, and I feel confident that I can hang in there for a couple more days."

*****

Sharon pulled into her own driveway, her heart beating faster as she approached the house that had been both home and prison for so many years. She noticed that Les's BMW wasn't there, which brought a wave of relief, but she knew the security cameras were tracking her every move.

She unlocked the front door and stepped inside. Everything looked exactly the same but somehow felt different - now filled with possibility, less like it owned her. She was the one changing.

Moving quickly, Sharon went to her bedroom and pulled a small suitcase from the closet. She packed enough clothes for a few days, some toiletries, and the few personal items that held special meaning for her. From Elin's list, she gathered her birth certificate, Social Security card, the boys' important documents, and their medical records from the file cabinet in the kitchen.

The most difficult part was retrieving her hidden money. Behind a loose baseboard in the back of her closet, she had carefully taped an envelope containing nearly three thousand dollars - money saved penny by penny over the years from grocery and household allowances. Her hands shook slightly as she peeled away the tape.

She was zipping up the suitcase when her phone rang. She jumped, her whole body tensing from the startling sound. Sharon looked at the screen - Les. Her breath caught and her heart pounded as she stared at his name on the display, her mind racing.

How did he know she was here? Then it hit her - the security cameras. He must have been alerted the moment she pulled into the driveway.

The ringing stopped, then started again immediately. Les wasn't giving up.

Sharon's hands were shaking as she grabbed her suitcase and headed for the front door. She could almost feel his eyes on her through those cameras, watching her every move. As she reached her car, the phone rang again. This time, she made a decision that would have been unthinkable just days ago.

She powered off her phone, removed the SIM card, and dropped it into her purse. He wouldn't be able to track her phone anymore.

Driving away from the house, Sharon felt a strange mix of terror and liberation. She was truly on her own now, cut off from Les's electronic leash for the first time in years.

*****

She headed for the Walden home and immediately felt a difference when she pulled into the driveway. Her spirits lifted as she saw warm lights glowing from the windows of the modest two-story home. She opened the car door and heard genuine laughter drifting from the backyard - a sound foreign to her own home, where tension usually stifled any joy, the kind of easy, joyful sound that happened when people felt safe with each other.

Vicki answered the door with a welcoming smile that reached her eyes. "Sharon! Perfect timing. Come on in. The boys are out back with my husband Jesse and our son Tommy. Larry texted that he's on his way."

As they walked through the house toward the back door, Sharon immediately caught the rich aroma of lasagna and garlic bread. But more than that, she noticed how the house felt - lived in but not chaotic, comfortable without being sloppy. Family photos lined the hallway, capturing moments of genuine happiness. There was no tension in the air, no sense that anyone had to walk on eggshells.

She stepped onto the back deck and took in the scene before her. Charlie was animated in a way she hadn't seen in months, gesturing excitedly as he told a story. David stood beside him, grinning and occasionally adding details. They were both facing a man in shorts and a polo shirt sitting at the patio table with a glass of iced tea in his hands. He was nodding with genuine interest, not the polite tolerance she'd seen adults show children, but real engagement.

"Mom!" Charlie's face lit up when he saw her. He bounded over and wrapped her in a fierce hug that nearly knocked her off balance.

"Hey, sweetheart," Sharon whispered, holding him tight. "You look...happy."

"I am happy," Charlie said simply. "And I'm even more happy seeing you."

Jesse stood and extended his hand. "Hi, I'm Jesse. We're so glad you could join us." As they shook hands, Sharon was struck by the genuine warmth in his eyes - no judgment, no hidden agenda, just honest welcome. Jesse then gestured to the other boy present. "This is Tommy, David's younger brother."

"Nice to meet you both," said Sharon, observing how Tommy, despite being the youngest one present, was included naturally in the conversation rather than being ignored or dismissed. "Thank you for everything you've done for Charlie. He seems like a different boy."

A few minutes later, Vicki opened the screen door and Larry stepped through. His warm smile transformed his entire face. Charlie immediately rushed over to him and gave him a hug that spoke of complete trust and affection. Sharon watched in amazement - she had never seen her son embrace a man with such openness.

Charlie grabbed Larry's hand and led him to Sharon. "Mr. Lucas, this is my mom."

"Hi. I'm Larry," he said simply, extending his hand.

As they shook hands, Sharon found herself looking into Larry's kind eyes longer than she intended. There was something about his presence - a gentleness mixed with strength - that felt unfamiliar but safe. She quickly looked away, suddenly self-conscious.

"Dinner's ready!" Vicki called from inside.

Around the dinner table, Sharon found herself in a foreign world. The first bites taken brought appreciative murmurs around the table.

"Wow," Larry said, taking another forkful.

"Vicki, this is incredible," Sharon added, genuinely surprised by how delicious the lasagna was.

"I'm loving this," Jesse smiled as he licked his lips.

Conversation flowed naturally from person to person. Jesse asked the boys about their day without interrogating them. Everyone listened to each other with genuine interest.

Sharon noticed an extra chair at the table and asked, "Who is the extra chair for?"

"That's for Angela," David answered matter-of-factly. "It's a reminder that she's always here with us and always welcome."

Larry nodded. "I had the privilege of meeting Angela at Peace Pond with Charlie and David. She made my heart sing."

"I saw her, too," Charlie said. "She stayed with me after Mr. Lucas and David left."

"When did this happen, Charlie?" Sharon asked, confused.

"Monday night."

"That can't be, Charlie. I was with you Monday night."

"Mom, we were dreaming."

"All three of you had the same dream?"

"Yes," David and Larry answered in unison.

Vicki, seeing the confused look on Sharon's face, said gently, "Unexplained things have been happening in our lives ever since we started playing the Love Game."

"Rachel mentioned the Love Game once but didn't explain how to play."

Charlie's eyes lit up. "Oh Mom, it's amazing! The Love Game starts with appreciation and dropping judgments of right or wrong, to open your heart. Then you look for how many places you can see Love or what some people call God."

As Charlie began to explain more, Sharon watched his animated face, the joy radiating from him. She glanced around the table - at David and Tommy listening intently despite their young ages, at Larry's rapt attention to every word Charlie spoke, at Jesse's warm smile as he listened. This is what family dinner looked like when fear wasn't at the table.

Sharon shook her head in wonder. "Five days ago, Charlie couldn't say three words without stuttering. What happened?"

"Love," David responded.

The realization hit her like a wave. Her sons could have had this their entire lives. Every single day, they could have come home to this warmth, this safety, this unconditional acceptance. Instead, they'd spent their whole lives in fear, tiptoeing around Les's moods, measuring their words, dimming their natural light to avoid triggering his rage.

But as Sharon watched the easy love flowing around the table, the contrast between this warmth and her own family's reality felt crushing. Another realization cut even deeper. She hadn't just stayed because of Les's control - she had accepted it because somewhere deep inside, she believed that's all she was worth. All those years...all those lost years...

Her chest tightened as the weight of understanding settled over her. The room started to feel too warm. Charlie continued explaining the Love Game, his voice full of wonder, but Sharon could barely focus on his words.

"I'm sorry," she said abruptly, standing up so quickly her chair scraped against the floor. "I need to step away for a moment."

Vicki immediately stood. "Of course. Down the hall, second door on the right."

Charlie stopped mid-sentence, watching as his mother headed towards the bathroom. "Did I say something wrong?"

"Oh no, sweetheart," Vicki answered gently, reaching over to touch Charlie's arm. "You didn't do anything wrong at all. Sometimes when people hear beautiful truths, it can bring up a lot of feelings. Your mom just needs a moment to process everything."

In the bathroom, Sharon splashed cool water on her face and stared into the mirror, trying to steady her breathing. *Who is this woman in front of me?* She wondered. *How could I possibly play the Love Game? I can't seem to find anything to appreciate about myself. I know I can't go back to the way things were, but how do I go forward and create the kind of loving interactions that I've just witnessed?*

Suddenly, an image of a young black girl appeared beside her reflection in the mirror.

"Angela?" Sharon whispered.

"*I AM here,*" she heard, the same words she heard when with Rachel. "I feel so much guilt and shame about my life. I thought I wouldn't see Love unless I let go of my judgments, yet I'm seeing you."

"*The beauty of the Love Game is that when you're surrounded by people who are playing, it opens your heart to see, too,*" Angela told her. "*This is the perfect time for you - this is the moment to appreciate. You don't have to direct your appreciation toward yourself if that feels too hard right now. Anything or anyone you appreciate will start opening your heart."*

"I can appreciate Charlie's transformation," Sharon said softly. "And the warmth I feel here tonight."

"Absolutely. The contrasts you're witnessing are exactly what you need to create desire. How your desire gets fulfilled isn't by focusing on what you lack, but by experiencing the feelings of fulfillment that you can manifest moment by moment. Are you ready to go back and soak up more of that divine Love?"

Sharon took a deep breath, feeling something shift inside her. By the time she returned to the table, she felt far calmer.

"I feel much better," she said as she sat back down. "Sorry for interrupting you, Charlie."

Charlie resumed talking about his experience playing the Love Game, his words flowing.

When he finished, Sharon reached over to squeeze his hand. "That was beautiful, sweetheart." Jesse nodded in agreement. "You've learned something really special." Sharon looked around the table. "Jesse and Vicki, thank you so much for caring for Charlie, and Vicki, your dinner tonight was outstanding. This has been such a roller coaster week for me, exhaustion is catching up, so I need to excuse myself. I appreciate everyone seeing me with open hearts, and someday I hope to see myself and feel the way I do when you look at me."

A round of hugs followed, each embrace leaving a small crack in her armor of unworthiness. Jesse's hug was fatherly and protective, Tommy's was sweet and genuine, Vicki's was warm and understanding, while David's hug caused full-body goosebumps - there was something otherworldly about this boy, a presence that spoke directly to her soul. Larry's hug felt different - safe in a way she'd never experienced with a man, like coming home to something she didn't know she'd been missing. And Charlie's final hug was pure love and gratitude.

"Good night, everyone. I'll see you tomorrow," Sharon said, feeling lighter and more loved than she had in years.

Chapter 15: Reunion

Tuesday Evening, August 26

Mark and Crystal arrived together at Amma's house - the same house where Mark grew up, the house where Maggie was found dead all those years ago. Mark knocked briefly, then immediately walked in, a familiar routine.

"Mom, we're here!" Mark called out.

They walked toward the kitchen where Amma stood at the stove, just putting down her spoon after stirring the boiling pasta. She turned with a warm smile and came over to hug each of them.

"I've been eager all day to find out what this mysterious information is that you'd like to share," she said, her eyes bright with curiosity.

Mark exchanged a glance with Crystal. "Let's wait until after dinner. It's nothing to worry about."

"Well, now you've got me even more intrigued," Amma laughed. "Crystal, how are you doing, dear? You look radiant."

"Thank you, Amma. I feel...different lately. More at peace somehow."

"That's wonderful to hear. Mark, there's something different about you too – you're lighter, if that makes sense." She studied her son's face. "There's something in your eyes that I haven't seen before."

Mark nodded, feeling the truth of her words. "A lot has been happening, Mom. Good things. Healing things."

"Well then, let's eat and you can tell me all about it. I made your favorite - spaghetti and meatballs." She paused, then added gently, "I'd like to set a place for Maggie tonight, to remind us that she's still present in our hearts."

Mark's eyes filled with tears at his mother's suggestion. "Mom, that would mean everything to me."

Amma looked at her son with surprise and tenderness. "Oh, sweetheart. I haven't seen you respond to Maggie's name like that in...well, ever. You're not pulling away or changing the subject as you usually do at the mention of her."

Crystal watched Mark's reaction with growing curiosity. She'd never seen him this emotionally open about his sister.

"No," Mark agreed. "I'm not running from her memory anymore. But time to eat. I'm starved," he added, trying to lighten the moment. "I've been looking forward to this dinner all day."

They served themselves from the bowls on the counter and sat down around the table, with Maggie's place setting creating a gentle presence among them.

Crystal asked, "Amma, what have you been up to lately?"

"I've been spending more time at Peace Pond, especially since learning about the Love Game from Angela and David. Sometimes I meet Roy there - he likes to sit with his feet in the water." Amma paused, twirling her spaghetti thoughtfully. "He's been teaching me more about seeing Love in everything."

Crystal's eyes widened with recognition. "The Love Game? I remember the day Angela taught me to play. Amma, weren't you dream-sharing with Angela and David in the beginning when David first started playing the game?"

"Yes. I didn't even know it was a dream until Mark told me. We kept going back and forth between dreams and what we think of as physical reality until it became really confusing. Eventually I discovered reality is reality for the person who is creating it, whether it's in the physical world or the spiritual realm."

As they finished their dinner, the conversation quieted, each lost in their own thoughts about dreams, reality, and spiritual encounters. Mark helped clear the dishes while Amma prepared coffee.

"Let's take our coffee to the living room," Amma suggested. "I think it's time you told me about this mysterious information you wanted to share."

They settled into the comfortable chairs, steam rising from their coffee cups. Mark took a deep breath, knowing the moment had finally arrived.

"I had a dream last Thursday where Maggie came to me and said she was there for me. I thought about the dream over the weekend, trying to figure out what she meant. On Monday, I was sitting with a seventeen-year-old boy who tried to commit suicide last Friday. He hadn't spoken since waking up from his coma."

Mark paused, gathering his courage. "We were sitting in the counseling room and he pointed to the empty chair. I asked what he saw and he said he saw a teenage girl. I encouraged him to introduce himself and ask her name. He said, "I'm Chris, what's your name?" Then he told me she said her name was Maggie. I looked at the chair again, focusing with my heart open, and then I saw her, too."

Crystal leaned forward, her eyes wide with amazement.

"I saw Chris a second time this morning. Again, Maggie was there, but the two of them had been having conversations since I left on Monday. The boy has miraculously improved between sessions."

Mark hesitated, uncertainty flickering across his face. He wasn't sure about Amma's reaction to what he's about to reveal. After all, he had no way to verify whether Maggie's story was true. Then again, he thought, was Maggie's spirit even capable of lying? Since Maggie shared her story, he had faith that it was meant to be revealed to Amma.

"Maggie told us something, Mom. About what happened to her." He took another deep breath. "She said she needs you to know the truth."

Amma's face went very still, her coffee cup frozen halfway to her lips. "The truth? What truth, Mark?"

Crystal reached over and gently placed her hand on Amma's arm, her own face showing concern. "Are you okay with hearing this?" she asked softly.

Amma set her cup down with shaking hands. "I've wondered for thirty-seven years what really happened that day. If Maggie...if my daughter wants me to know something, then yes, I need to hear it."

"Mom," Mark began, "what I'm about to tell you might be difficult. But Maggie wanted you to understand that what happened wasn't your fault."

Mark looked directly into his mother's eyes. "Maggie says her death wasn't intended - it was an accident. She wanted you and Dad to take her cry for help seriously." He chose his words carefully. "Maggie told me she had been sexually abused and was so afraid she kept it hidden for a long time. When she did reveal it, she didn't think anyone really believed her or that anything would be done about it. She couldn't talk about it, even with her counselors."

Amma's hand flew to her mouth, tears immediately filling her eyes. Then the color drained from her face as a memory surfaced. "Oh my God. Oh, Maggie." Her voice became a whisper. "She did tell me. She did tell me, and I...I couldn't...I didn't want to believe it."

Crystal moved closer to Amma, wrapping an arm around her shoulders as she began to shake.

The room fell silent, except for Amma's increasingly labored breathing. Mark reached over and took his mother's trembling hand.

"I remember now," Amma said, her voice breaking. "She came to me one day, so scared, trying to tell me what that neighbor boy had done to her. And I...God forgive me, I told her she must have misunderstood what happened. I said she shouldn't make up stories that could hurt people." She covered her face with her hands. "I was so overwhelmed by the possibility that I chose not to believe her. I was a coward."

"Mom..." Mark started, but Amma continued.

"She never brought it up again after that. She just...withdrew. Got angrier, more distant. And I told myself it was just teenage behavior. I convinced myself I had handled it right, that she had just been confused." Amma's tears were flowing freely now. "But deep down, I knew. I knew and I failed her completely."

Crystal squeezed Amma's shoulder, her own eyes filled with tears. "You were scared too. You didn't know how to handle something so terrible."

"That's not an excuse," Amma groaned. "She was my baby, she came to me for help, and I turned my back on her because I was too frightened and overwhelmed to face the truth."

Mark's voice was gentle but firm. "Mom, Maggie specifically said it wasn't your fault. She understands why you reacted the way you did. She knows you were human, fallible, trying to protect yourself from unbearable knowledge."

Amma looked up at him through her tears. "How can she forgive me when I can't forgive myself? I was supposed to protect her, and instead I sent her the message that she was alone with this terrible secret."

"She's not angry, Mom. She's full of love and understanding. She sees things differently now - she sees how fear can make people do things they never thought they would do."

Amma sat quietly for several long minutes, her body still shaking as years of suppressed guilt came flooding back. "All this time, I told myself we didn't know, that there were no signs. But the truth is, I knew and I chose to look away."

"She doesn't want you to carry that guilt anymore," Mark said softly. "She's here to heal, not to punish."

Amma took a shuddering breath. "I need to tell her how sorry I am. I need her to know that not believing her was the worst mistake of my life. That I've lived with that cowardice every day since she died."

Mark nodded. "She knows, Mom. But yes, I think it's time you had some conversations with her. She can share her experiences and address regrets and guilt. Mom, I know you've experienced Divine Love - well, Maggie is Divine Love. She's not in some hell because she tried to take her life, and you're not condemned for your very human mistake."

Mark paused, looking at his mother with infinite tenderness. "Are you ready to face her? To receive her forgiveness?"

Amma nodded, still crying but sitting up straighter. "I've been running from this moment. Yes, I'm ready."

Mark called softly, "Maggie?"

The room filled with a gentle presence, and Amma's tears began to slow as she felt something she hadn't felt in twenty-three years - her daughter's love surrounding her.

The three of them sat in reverent silence, their coffee forgotten and growing cold on the table in front of them. Mark and Crystal watched as Amma's face transformed, moving from anguish to wonder as she began to sense Maggie's presence. No words were needed in those sacred moments - they simply held space for a mother and daughter to reconnect across the veil between worlds.

*****

Sharon got back to Rachel's just after 8:00 p.m., her headlights sweeping across the now-familiar front porch. The long day felt like a week had passed already – the meeting with Dr. Deera about Chris, the legal consultation with Elin, the tense trip to her house, and then the transformative dinner at Vicki's with her family. She sat in the car for a moment, processing everything that had happened.

The front door opened before she even turned off the engine. Rachel appeared, backlit by the warm house lights, waiting with the loving, patient smile Sharon had come to treasure.

"How was your evening?" Rachel asked as Sharon approached, carrying her small suitcase.

"Life-changing," Sharon responded. "I saw what real family love looks like. I watched Charlie laugh - really laugh - in a way I haven't seen in years."

Rachel studied Sharon's face in the porch light. "You look different than when I saw you earlier today at the hospital. Lighter somehow, but also..." she paused, searching for the word.

"Sad?" Sharon suggested. "Because I am. I'm happy and heartbroken at the same time."

"I've already started brewing some chamomile tea," Rachel said with a knowing smile. "Why don't you sit on the porch swing? It's pleasantly warm tonight, and the stars are clearer than usual. I'll bring the tea out in a moment."

Sharon settled into the gentle swing, feeling it rock as she pushed off with her feet. The night air carried the scent of jasmine from Nana's garden, and above her, the stars seemed brighter somehow, as if the universe was celebrating her day of awakening.

Rachel appeared with two steaming cups and settled beside Sharon on the swing, their shoulders naturally touching. She handed Sharon the mug of tea without a word, simply being present and listening.

Sharon began sharing the events of her day - the lawyer's kindness, the terror and liberation at her house, Charlie's joy at dinner, the way Larry embraced him with genuine affection, the overwhelming realization of what her sons had missed over the years. Rachel listened without trying to fix or analyze, simply witnessing Sharon's journey with complete acceptance.

"I spent so many years thinking I was completely alone," Sharon said quietly, watching the steam rise from her cup. "But tonight, I realized I'm surrounded by love - Charlie, David's family, Larry, you and Nana, even your wonderful Angela who appeared to me. All these people and spirits are rooting for me, seeing me as Love itself."

Rachel's hand found Sharon's, their fingers intertwining naturally. "You've never been alone, sweetheart. Love has been here the whole time. You're now discovering how to see Love, and when you do, you will not only know God, you will know yourself."

The swing rocked gently as they sat in comfortable silence, shoulders and hands touching. In the stillness, both Rachel and Sharon heard those now-familiar words, *"I AM here."*

They looked into each other's eyes, simultaneously saying, "In this moment, I feel perfect."

Sharon closed her eyes and breathed deeply, carrying this perfect moment of Love into her dreams.

Chapter 16: Mothers Healing Circle

Wednesday, 3 a.m., August 27

Five mothers who struggled with guilt and regret about how they raised their children found themselves dream-sharing at 3:00 a.m. In that surrealistic realm, they were walking in the park, heading toward Peace Pond. Their feet seemed to know the way without their minds needing to understand.

David walked beside his mom, Vicki. Neither questioned how they came to be there together; it simply was.

Sharon sensed familiar hands reaching for hers and looked to find Chris and Charlie on either side of her, their fingers intertwining as naturally as breathing.

Rachel met up with Nana and Angela along the path, three generations drawn by the same invisible current toward the water's edge.

Amma walked alone, watching the others as they converged ahead of her. As she neared the pond, an indescribable feeling of peace washed over her. She turned to see Maggie. An overwhelming sense of love surged through her body. She stopped to look into Maggie's eyes - experiencing the deep peace of Love's presence. "I'm so glad you came to be with me," Amma said with tears welling up. "I have really missed you."

"Mom, I never left your heart. Your beliefs and suffering simply drowned out my voice. The walls of grief and pain surrounding your heart have been crumbling lately. Now is the time for you to know me."

Amma reached for Maggie's hand and together they strolled leisurely toward the Peace Pond, appreciating every step. Tears burst forth when she felt Maggie's touch. It had been thirty-seven years since she experienced Maggie's presence. A moment later, she felt another familiar presence and turned to see Mark approaching, his face soft with wonder at seeing his sister again. The three of them stood together - mother, daughter, and son - a family reunited in the space where Love makes all things possible.

Eleven souls with open hearts formed a sacred circle, creating a compassionate space for healing - seeing each other not as broken, but as souls learning to create new experiences aligned with Divine Love.

A voice spoke, not from any one person but from the Love that connected them all, *"I AM here. You are here because you have opened your hearts enough to hear my voice. Today you will witness and experience deep healing."*

The words settled into their hearts like gentle rain on thirsty earth. In this sacred space, there was no need for explanation or doubt - only the profound knowing that they were being held in perfect Love.

"Each mother will share the guilt she carries," the voice continued, *"and each child will respond from Love, not victimhood. This is how wounds become wisdom and suffering transforms into compassion."*

A gentle hush fell over the circle. Nana spoke first, her weathered hands trembling slightly as she looked at Rachel.

"I was a good mother to you for the first years of your life," Nana's voice carried the weight of decades of sorrow. "William and I loved you so completely. But when that truck driver fell asleep at the wheel and killed your daddy in that accident...his death shut me down completely.

She paused, took a deep breath, and continued. "My grief over losing the love of my life, my rage at that driver - it consumed everything. You lost both your parents that day, Rachel, even though I was still breathing. I watched you acting out, crying for help, needing your mother desperately, and I couldn't find the strength to reach for you. I withdrew from you when you needed me most, right when you'd already lost your father. I bear the weight of knowing my emotional death stole your childhood and sent you searching for love in dangerous places."

Rachel stepped slightly forward in the circle, her eyes shining with understanding rather than pain. "Mom, I didn't know it at that time, but I do now. You gave me exactly what my soul was requesting - an opportunity to learn about resilience and finding my own way to Love.

Your struggles taught me that mothers are human, that we all do the best we can with what we have. Every hard moment led me to search for something deeper, something that couldn't be taken away. You didn't fail me - you gave me the gift of knowing I could survive anything and still find my way back to Love."

Rachel then looked around the circle. "It is easier to forgive Nana than myself. When I try to say those same words to myself, they stick in my throat."

She paused, gathering courage. "My addiction consumed me so completely that I chose drugs and alcohol over my babies. Angela and Sammy needed their mother, and I left them when they were small and innocent. For a short time, I was doing better, but when Angela was diagnosed with cancer, my life came crashing down. The thought of losing her the way I lost my daddy terrified me - I couldn't let myself be that close only to have it snatched away. I had to protect my heart. The alcohol took away the 'why me?' questions, but the more I stayed away, the harder it became to face my beautiful daughter. I convinced myself they were better off without me, but the truth is I was a coward, running from everything because of my own pain. I'm haunted by stealing their childhood security, making them feel unwanted and unloved."

Rachel's voice trembled with gratitude as she continued. "I may not even have entered Angela's hospital room if it weren't for Mark and David. They supported me as I faced Angela, and I never expected in a million years she would receive me with unconditional love. I have never experienced that kind of energy surging through my body. When she passed, she entered my heart and has never left. She absorbed the guilt and gave me purpose to serve others with the Love I AM."

Angela's spirit moved closer to her mother, radiance emanating from her young face. "Mom, your leaving taught me the most important lesson of my life - that Love never abandons us, even when people do. Because you left, I learned to find the Divine mother within, to trust the Love that is always present. Your addiction was your way of trying to survive unbearable pain. Witnessing your journey provided the contrast I needed in order to find my way to the Love I Am. I see your courage now in being here. Look at you, momma, you are compassion, kindness, and pure love that brings your perfection to this moment. All is perfect."

The circle held the power of those words, each soul feeling the transformation that occurs when guilt meets understanding.

Vicki stepped forward next. Her face was etched with years of protective vigilance and hidden pain. She held her head down as she spoke, avoiding eye contact with anyone in the circle. "I failed Michael and David in different ways. I kept running from abusive situations, trying to protect my boys. I sent Michael away to protect him from David's biological father, but in his mind, I abandoned him. He felt unworthy to be loved. I abandoned David when I sent him to live with another family so I could work two jobs. I managed my fears by trying to control everything. I learned to parent through fear. I didn't often spank the boys with a wooden board - I didn't have to. It hung on the wall in the kitchen, and if they were misbehaving, I just pointed to it. I wanted to protect them so desperately that I became the very thing I was trying to protect them from. I taught them that love comes with threats. Throwing the paddle away was easy compared to throwing away my guilt."

At the end of her confession, David looked at her with infinite tenderness. "Hold your head up, Mom," he said gently.

She lifted her eyes to meet his and immediately started sobbing.

"Mom, you don't need my forgiveness. Look how everything worked out - I'm here, Michael's here, we're all okay. You were doing the best you could." He paused, his young wisdom shining through. "What was, was. Now is now and now is what matters. You have been, you are now and will forever be the perfect mom for me. My soul wouldn't have wanted it any other way."

Vicki wiped her tears away before holding David's face in her hands. She kissed his cheek and said, "Words aren't enough to express how much you mean to me. I used to think of myself as unworthy of love, but you have shown me a way to honor the Love I AM."

The circle held the power of this healing, and then Sharon stepped forward, her voice trembling as she looked at Chris and Charlie.

"I failed to protect you both from your father's control and abuse. I grew up watching my mother take my father's verbal abuse in silence, never showing anger, never fighting back. I was taught that women should be subservient, that a good wife supported her husband no matter what. My parents told me I wasn't smart enough for college, that my dreams of being an artist were impractical. They said my place was to find a good husband, be a good housewife, and have children.

"When they met Les, they thought he was perfect - a powerful, successful man who would take care of me. They loved that he believed the man should be the boss. I turned to alcohol the same way my mother did - to numb the pain of feeling powerless, to escape the reality that I had trapped my children in the same cycle I grew up in. But my deepest guilt isn't that I didn't stand up for myself - it's that I didn't have the guts to fight for my boys. I watched Les control and diminish you, and I said nothing. I let him make you feel small and afraid because I was too afraid to fight for you. I was so emotionally absent because of my drinking that even when I was physically present, I wasn't really there when you needed me most. I'm tormented by choosing my own survival over protecting my children, of teaching you that your voices didn't matter, that you should accept being treated as less than you are. I am so, so sorry I let you boys down. Can you forgive me?"

Chris stepped closer to his mother, his voice gentle but clear. "Mom, I was really angry at Dad, but it wasn't safe for me to express anger toward him. I redirected my feelings toward you, making you at fault for them. I said some mean things. Dad made it clear that women are second-class citizens and should take the blame. I'm just starting to learn that no one but myself is responsible for my feelings. You always took the blame for my feelings, and I let you because it meant I didn't have to change my behavior. I'm sorry, Mom. I feel bad for the way I treated you."

Sharon looked at her son with tender understanding. "Chris, I know you're trying to help me feel better, but you are in no way responsible for my guilt. That burden is mine to release."

Charlie nodded, reaching for Sharon's hand. "I see who you really are underneath all the guilty feelings. You don't need us to forgive you, Mom. You need to forgive yourself."

The voice of Love spoke softly through the circle: "*I don't need to forgive any of you because I never judged or condemned you in the first place. Forgiveness implies that something was wrong, but I see souls learning, growing, doing their best with what they have in each moment. The forgiveness - letting go of your guilt - will come when you accept the Love you are at the core of your being, even when you can't feel it or express it.*"

Sharon's tears flowed freely as she struggled with hearing those words. "I don't know how to see myself as Love. I've only just learned what Love looks like through Rachel. It's so new to me...I don't know if I have it in my own heart."

A chorus of support rose from the circle: "You don't have to do it alone. We are here."

The circle held Sharon in tender vulnerability for a few minutes of silence as she turned to look deeply into the eyes of each person around the circle.

Then all turned toward Amma, the final mother to share her feelings. She looked at Maggie and Mark, reunited with her in this sacred space, and her voice trembled with twenty-three years of unspoken anguish.

"Maggie, I bear the deepest guilt a mother can know - I couldn't save your life, and then I withdrew from Mark when he needed me most." Amma's voice broke but she continued, speaking directly to her daughter. "You tried to tell me about the sexual assault, and I shut down completely. I convinced myself it probably wasn't true because I couldn't bear to think about my beautiful daughter suffering something so terrible. When you died by suicide, I realized I had failed you in the most fundamental way - I didn't believe you when you told me your truth.

"After losing you, I became so consumed with grief that I emotionally abandoned Mark. He had just lost his sister, and instead of being the mother he needed, I withdrew into my own pain. Mark, I was so lost in my guilt and anger at myself that I couldn't see you were drowning too. I lost both my children - Maggie to death, and you to my own grief."

Maggie moved closer to her mother, her spirit radiating the same love that had touched Chris in the hospital. "Mom, I see how much you've been hurting. I see how much you loved me then and how much you love me now." She paused, her presence pure compassion. "I'm here with you. I've always been here with you. The love between us never ended - it just changed form. I am whole now, and I am Love. And so are you.

Mark stepped forward, his voice gentle but strong. "Mom, after Maggie died, I knew how overwhelmed you were with your own grief. You couldn't be there for me in the way I hoped for at the time, but look what happened - your withdrawal forced me to find my own strength, to discover my own path to healing. It led me to become someone who could help others the way I wished I could have helped Maggie. Your pain became my purpose." He paused, his eyes soft with compassion and understanding. "Thank you for acknowledging what I experienced. It means everything to have you see me in this moment."

Maggie reached for both her mother's and brother's hands. "We were never broken, Mom. We were always whole, always loved, always exactly where we needed to be for our souls to learn what they came here to learn." She then turned to address the entire circle, her angelic presence encompassing everyone. "Your guilt may have served some need you had to be unkind to yourselves in the past, but I question the need at this time to maintain it. Guilt imprisons regret, keeping you stuck in yesterday's pain. You aren't the same people now. You are all now able to see life and possibilities in new ways – creating new realities.

"You are all functioning more from a present-moment Love focus. If you want to bring the memory of regrets and mistakes forward from the past, and re-experience them now in this moment, observing them from a Love perspective, you might notice that they won't have the same power and will slip away. We're telling you a new feel-good story for you to consider. Try it on and see if it fits. Or you could simply offer it to the Peace Pond."

As Maggie's words settled into their hearts like seeds of healing taking root, the circle began to dissolve. One by one, the mothers and children faded from the dreamscape, their souls carrying profound peace back to their sleeping bodies. Only Angela and Maggie remained, sitting in reverence at the Peace Pond's edge, watching their reflections shimmer in the water - two angels witnessing the power of Love to transform even the deepest wounds into wisdom.

Chapter 17: Anger

Wednesday Morning, August 27

Sharon woke to the smell of coffee drifting up from the kitchen. She stretched, feeling unexpectedly rested despite the vivid dream that still lingered in her mind like morning mist. The healing circle at Peace Pond felt both distant and immediate, as if it happened in another lifetime yet was still happening now.

She made her way downstairs to find Nana and Rachel sitting at the kitchen table, their voices soft in the early morning quiet.

"...and when Maggie told me I could offer my guilt to the pond, I felt this incredible sense of relief," Nana was saying. "Like I'd been carrying a heavy suitcase for decades and finally got to set it down."

Sharon paused in the doorway, confusion crossing her face. "That was my dream!"

Rachel looked up with a knowing smile. "It was a dream for all of us. We were there too."

"How is that possible?" Sharon asked, settling into a chair beside them.

"We are all connected, Sharon," Nana explained. "And when we are aware of the presence of divine Love, we can dream-share."

Rachel poured Sharon a cup of coffee. "What did you do with your guilt after we left?"

"I remember throwing it in the pond," Sharon said slowly, the memory becoming clearer as she spoke. "When I woke up this morning, I felt lighter, with an insight that came from the pond: Sharon, you don't have to forget the past, your regrets, or the guilt you felt. You can practice focusing on this moment and the power you've given to past experiences will fade. It's like the way you are abstaining from alcohol by focusing on one day at a time. This day."

"That's a really helpful invitation," Rachel said, standing up. "I'm sorry but I have to run. My fun in the psych unit is awaiting."

Sharon and Rachel hugged good-bye - one of those hugs that penetrated your whole being.

Sharon sat down and took a sip of her coffee. "What did you do with your guilt after I left, Nana?"

"Much of my guilt dissipated, seeing how my family has come together in a beautiful and loving way. The guilt is still there, but it feels powerless, and I can more and more quickly move out of that energy by appreciating what is now.

"I have a secret strategy. It's Angela. She is always in my heart, and when I need to show kindness to myself for feelings that bring me down, I call to her. By the way Sharon, Angela is not exclusively in my heart. You witnessed her presence last night and she will be forever in your heart as well. Don't forget Maggie, too. What are your plans for the day, Sharon?"

"I'm going to get a temporary burner phone so I can stay in touch with my lawyer as well as with others that were in our healing circle. Les is probably going crazy that he can't find me. It wouldn't surprise me if he showed up at the hospital - not to check in on Chris, heaven forbid. It would be to express his anger about losing control of me."

*****

Meanwhile, at the hospital, Rachel was making her way through the psych unit, greeting patients with her characteristic warmth. She stopped by Chris's room and smiled at him.

"How are you feeling this morning about the dream? About helping your mother with her guilt?"

Chris looked up, surprised. "I know you were in the dream, but I thought it was mine."

"Your mother said that very same thing to me this morning," Rachel said, smiling.

Karen, the head nurse, was passing by but stopped abruptly. "What do you know about his dream this morning? He hasn't shared that with anyone."

"I was in the dream too," Rachel responded.

"How can that be?" Chris asked, still puzzled.

"What are you talking about?" Karen interrupted, her voice strained with confusion.

"We had a shared dream," Rachel explained calmly.

"I've never heard of such a thing. Get back to work," Karen directed tersely, walking away with visible frustration.

A little later, when Karen saw Rachel talking kindly to another patient, she pulled her aside. "We have to talk. I thought I told you to stay clear of patients," she snarled, her voice tense with irritation. "You're not trained in how to communicate with mentally unstable individuals. I don't want you to upset them and trigger a crisis."

Rachel looked at her steadily. "I hear your concern about patient safety, Karen. With respect, I won't stop being civil to them and I will not ignore their presence. They need to have someone around who can see them as whole and not broken. I'm not doing therapy. I am one human interacting in a kind way with another. If that is not appropriate or good enough, then take it up with Dr. Deera."

"You can't tell me what the patients need or don't need. You know I can have you transferred to another part of the hospital."

"Yes, you can, but you can't stop me from speaking to the patients with compassion and kindness."

Karen turned away, muttering to herself, "We'll see."

Dr. Deera arrived for his early rounds. Karen immediately approached him with her jaw clenched and hands gripping her clipboard as if it might try to escape. "We need to talk about Rachel. I don't want her interacting with patients. Today she was talking to Chris about a dream he had in the night. He hadn't shared it with anyone, yet Rachel knew about it. She shouldn't be talking to patients about personal things such as dreams. She is a housekeeper, not a licensed therapist. She has no business interacting with our patients regardless of her good intentions. I don't think this is the right place for her. I feel compelled to let HR know about my concerns in case there are any legal issues that need to be addressed."

"Do what you think you need to do, but I will support Rachel. By the way, I know all about Chris's dream. Both Rachel and I were in his dream. It was our dream too."

Karen responded, "This is utterly ridiculous. You are just taking her side because she's your girlfriend."

"Be careful what you are accusing me of, Karen. I have observed that Rachel isn't going out of her way to interact with patients. Patients gravitate to her. You know why, Karen? She radiates the energy of unconditional Love. Something I am learning to allow for myself.

Unconditional Love is the most powerful tool we have to positively impact a person's life. If you're curious about shared dreams, you're welcome to observe my counseling session with Chris today and see how we process this dream."

*****

Across town, Vicki was sitting at the breakfast table with David and Charlie. The morning light filtered through the kitchen window as they processed what they had experienced together.

Vicki turned to Charlie, "How are you feeling about your dream and what your mom shared?"

Charlie answered, his young voice earnest, "I could feel that she was suffering, but she never talked about it openly like that before. I didn't know the background story of how she was raised. I haven't had much contact with my grandparents after they moved away. I remember my grandma being very quiet and Grandpa doing most of the talking. I feel closer than ever to mom now. I see how she has been changing over the last 6 months starting with her decision to stop drinking."

"You're very perceptive to notice those changes, Charlie. Recovery takes tremendous courage."

"I also was touched hearing all the stories of moms suffering with guilt. All I could do is see them as Love. What about you Mrs. Walden, how did you experience sharing in the group?"

Vicki looked at Charlie with surprise and tenderness. "Thanks for asking. And you seeing us as Love is the best thing we could ask for. David and I have talked about my past before, but I'd never opened up to a group of people like that. It wasn't just my healing," she reflected. "Watching Sharon and Amma and all the mothers, seeing how guilt was affecting their self-worth, it gave me perspective on my own journey. I wasn't alone in carrying that weight. It was freeing. I felt lighter afterward.

"My experiences have led me to be suspicious of people. I didn't trust that they wouldn't use my vulnerabilities against me. I put on a mask of strength. I also didn't want to burden others with my negative energy. I have spent my life playing the survival game and I suspect your mother has done the same. It's only been a couple of months since David taught me the Love Game and your mom just started. I think you will notice big changes coming."

"I hope so," Charlie responded. "I wish my dad could learn to play the Game. Maybe he would be nicer to us."

"Some things we just can't control. There is a perfect time for everything," David said. "We can't make things happen if it isn't the perfect time. What you can control is how you choose to see your dad. You can choose to see the Love that your dad is beyond his unkind actions instead of judging him. Maybe when the time is right for his journey, he will awaken to what you see in his heart."

Vicki nodded, "I agree. He is more apt to be inspired by Love than he would be by anger or hate."

*****

Les sipped the beer in his first-class seat and turned to face Janet, his attractive 34-year-old executive assistant with long blond hair and blue eyes, sitting beside him. He was glad he could mix business and have a little vacation with Janet at the same time.

"Sharon's disappeared," he told her, keeping his voice low. "I suspect she might be seeking a divorce. I might need to move some money to protect my assets before she can freeze them."

Janet's eyes lit up. "Finally, we can be open about our relationship."

"I don't want to reveal anything about us that she could use against me in a divorce settlement."

The plane landed on time at 9:00 a.m. As they collected their bags, Les asked Janet if she would mind getting an Uber. "I feel I should go straight to my house."

Les collected his car from the long-term parking lot. On the way home, his frustration grew. It wasn't because Sharon probably wanted a divorce, but that she got a jump on him before he could protect his assets. It was unlike her to take such a bold move. *I should have known, damn it.* The uncertainty about losing control terrified him. If he could just talk to her, he thought, he could slow down the process. By the time he pulled into his driveway, he was ready to explode.

Inside, an unsettling silence greeted him - no sounds of Sharon moving about, no television murmur, no signs of life.

"Sharon!" he called out, his voice echoing through the empty rooms. "Charlie!"

He moved through the house with growing agitation. In their bedroom, Sharon's dresser drawers had been pulled open, some clothes missing but most still there. Her small suitcase was gone from the closet. In Charlie's room, his backpack was missing along with his handheld video game, but the rest of his belongings appeared untouched.

This isn't permanent, Les realized. *They're planning to come back.*

He strode into his private office and pulled up the security recordings on his computer. The screens showed Sharon and Charlie leaving on Tuesday. Charlie was carrying his backpack. Les's jaw clenched as he watched them walk out the front door.

"Damn it," he muttered, scrolling through his contacts. He found Sharon's sister's number and hit dial.

"What do you want, Les?" her cold voice answered after two rings.

"Where's Sharon? She's not here and her phone's been disconnected."

"Good for her."

Les's voice hardened. "Don't play games with me. Where is she?"

"I'm not telling you anything. She finally got smart and left your sorry ass."

"You tell me where she is right now or..."

"Or what? You'll threaten me too? Leave me alone, Les. She's done with you and so am I." The line went dead.

Les stared at the phone, his control slipping. Two days. She'd been gone for two days and no one bothered to tell him. His hands shook as rage boiled in his chest.

The hospital. Maybe Sharon was there visiting Chris, or maybe Chris knew where they were staying. Les grabbed his keys and stormed out of the house.

*****

When Dr. Deera entered the counseling room, he found Chris talking to Maggie.

"I'm sorry for interrupting you two," Mark said. "Let's talk about your dream. Would you like to share your experience with dream-sharing and what insights you came away with?"

Chris looked at Maggie, smiling. He felt his shoulder muscles soften and his heartbeat slow. "I didn't realize it was dream-sharing until Rachel told me that the others in the dream were also dreaming the same thing at the same time. Is that true?"

"Yes, it is," Dr. Deera replied. "You know that I was there also."

"Yes. You were with your mother and Maggie. Rachel and her mother and Rachel's daughter Angela were there. And David and his mother were there. I never met any of them before. How did they end up in my dream?"

Dr. Deera explained, "Because we are all connected on a spiritual level as one with Love. You may have not realized it in your dream, but like Maggie here, Angela is an angel. They have both passed from this physical existence and are here in our hearts to remind us of our true nature as Love."

"I thought there was a radiance about her," Chris noted.

Dr. Deera continued, "To review your dream, there were eleven people gathered in a healing circle at Peace Pond. There were five mothers including yours and mine, and six children including you, me, Maggie, Angela, David, and Charlie. The focus was healing mothers' guilt. Is that a pretty good overview of the setting?"

Chris nodded enthusiastically. "Yes. Perfect. I felt honored to be included in the circle, hearing the mother's experiences with guilt and how that feeling has limited them and how they are now freeing themselves. It was like being surrounded by pure love and acceptance."

"What was your reaction to your mother's story?" Dr. Deera asked.

"I have never seen her open up like that. She said things about the way she was raised, the attitudes of her parents about the role of women that I didn't know. Now her behavior makes sense to me. I feel she is becoming more supportive of me than ever as she is learning how to better support herself. The whole experience felt perfect - like this is what healing is supposed to feel like."

In the observation room next door, Karen stood with Dr. Taft and Dr. Lewis, the intern who was following Chris's progress. They watched through the one-way mirror as Chris continued his animated conversation with what appeared to be empty space.

Dr. Taft frowned, making notes on his clipboard. "First, we're supposed to accept the empty chair technique with an invisible 'angel,' and now they're claiming multiple people shared the same dream simultaneously?"

Dr. Lewis shifted uncomfortably. "The patient seems calmer when he's...talking to her. His vitals have improved significantly since these sessions began."

"That's not the point," Dr. Taft replied. "We can't validate delusions, even if they appear therapeutic. Dream-sharing? Multiple people having identical dreams? It's impossible. Chris was suicidal less than a week ago, and we still haven't started him on antidepressants or antipsychotic meds for his delusions."

Standing behind him, Karen whispered, "Are we actually witnessing the impossible? How did Dr. Deera know that?"

*****

Les was banging on the locked double doors leading to the Behavioral Health Unit, yelling for someone to let him in.

The nurse opened the door slightly but blocked his entry. "How can I help you?"

"I'm Les Sullivan, Chris Sullivan's father and I demand to see him. Is my wife in there?"

"No, your wife isn't here. I'm sorry, but Chris has restricted visitors. You're not on the approved list."

Les tried to push past her. "That's my son! You can't keep me from seeing him!"

"Stop, or I'll call security," the nurse said firmly, stepping back and beginning to close the door.

Fuming, Les shouted, "I demand to speak with someone in charge!"

"I'll get someone. Step back," she said, closing and locking the door.

The nurse hurried to find Karen, who was observing Dr. Deera's counseling session. She quietly opened the observation room door and whispered urgently about Chris's father being at the Unit's door, demanding to see his son, and wanting to know where his wife was. She mentioned she'd called security.

Karen knocked on the counseling room door and opened it slightly. "Dr. Deera, I'm sorry to interrupt, but may I have a word with you before you proceed?"

Dr. Deera excused himself to Chris and came out with a concerned look - something really important must be happening for him to be interrupted during a session. He closed the door behind him. Karen quickly explained that Chris's father was at the door, demanding to see Chris, and asking about his wife's whereabouts.

"Thanks, Karen. Let's go have a chat with him," Dr. Deera responded, his voice calm but his expression serious as they walked toward the unit entrance.

A couple of chairs sat outside the entrance. Dr. Deera and Karen went to meet Les outside, and Dr. Deera said, "I'm Dr. Deera and this is our head nurse, Karen. And you are?"

"Les Sullivan, Chris's father."

"Let's sit down and talk."

Les remained standing. "I want to know why I can't see Chris and I want to know where my wife is."

"First of all, Mr. Sullivan, your wife is not here," Dr. Deera stated calmly. "As for visiting Chris, your presence is not permitted because Chris does not want to see you, and his mother supports that decision. In my professional opinion, it is too soon after Chris's suicide attempt for him to deal with your antagonistic relationship."

Les shifted his approach, his voice becoming more controlled. "I'm sorry for yelling at your nurse before. This is so stressful for me. In the last few days, first Chris trying to kill himself and then my wife and son disappearing. I just lost it. I think there must be some misunderstanding about our relationship. The boy has had problems all his life and he doesn't understand how I've been trying to toughen him up to face the world. I want the best for him."

"I hear what you are saying, Dr. Deera responded. "Then I hope you can respect that at this time the best thing for Chris is for him not to see you until the 'misunderstanding' is worked out."

Les's controlled facade cracked, his voice rising with fury. "I don't accept this. I have rights as a father. I'll take him out of here and if you refuse, I'll sue your ass and the whole hospital."

"Well, Mr. Sullivan, you can try that. But for now, you must leave." Security staff had arrived in case he needed to be escorted. Les stormed off red-faced, pushing the security guard's outstretched hand away. "I don't need your help."

Karen turned to Dr. Deera as they watched Les leave. "I don't know how you kept so calm with that man."

Dr. Deera shrugged his shoulders. "I wasn't going to give him the power to upset me. Let's go back and resume the counseling session."

When Dr. Deera returned to the counseling room, Chris looked up expectantly, still glowing from their conversation about the healing circle.

"I just talked to your father who was demanding to see you," Dr. Deera told him.

Chris could feel the hair on the back of his neck stand up. His shoulders hunched and fists clenched at the thought of his father. The feeling of peace, joy, acceptance, and love from the healing circle seemed to vanish instantly. His head dropped and his hands began to shake.

Dr. Deera noticed the dramatic change in Chris's demeanor. "Chris, I can see that hearing about your father's visit has affected you. The high you were feeling from the healing circle - it's natural for that to feel threatened when faced with the harsh reality of your father's behavior."

Chris nodded, looking down. "Yeah, it's like...for a moment I felt so hopeful, and now I'm wondering if any of it was real."

Dr. Deera leaned forward. "Can I share something personal with you? Something that might help you understand what you're experiencing?"

Chris looked up, curious.

"A few months ago, I had my own profound experience of love consciousness. I was with David, Angela, and Rachel - you met them in the dream circle. We were playing what David calls the Love Game, and suddenly my heart opened in a way I'd never experienced before. I felt connected to divine Love, completely peaceful, seeing everyone around me as expressions of that same Love."

Dr. Deera paused, his voice becoming softer. "It was transformative. But then I went back to my regular life, my work here at the hospital, dealing with administrative pressures and difficult cases. Within a week, I noticed my heart closing again. The walls I'd built up over years of protecting myself were rebuilding."

"What did you do?" Chris asked.

"I was discouraged at first, thinking I'd lost it. But then I returned to spending time with David and Rachel, and my heart opened again - even more easily the second time. I began to understand something important."

Dr. Deera gestured with his hands. "Think of the space around your heart like a spring that's been compressed for years forming a protective shield. When you experience Divine Love, it's like stretching that spring open for the first time, letting the light of Love pass through. When you return to a survival mindset, the spring contracts and close again."

Chris nodded, following the metaphor.

"Each time the spring gets stretched open, it becomes easier to open and takes longer to close. It never contracts all the way back to where it was before." Dr. Deera looked directly at Chris. "Once you've experienced the light radiating from your open heart, you'll never be thrown into complete darkness again."

"So even though hearing about my dad upset me…"

"You're not back where you started," Dr. Deera confirmed. "The light you experienced in the healing circle and even the light you experienced when you first talked to Maggie is now part of you. You've experienced something most people go their entire lives without seeing. Your father's anger can't take that away, though it might temporarily make it harder to access. The work now is learning to return to that open-hearted state more easily each time."

At the end of the session, after Chris and Dr. Deera left the counseling room, Dr. Lewis rushed to catch up with Dr. Deera.

"Is dream-sharing really a thing?" Dr. Lewis asked urgently.

Dr. Deera smiled. "Research it and get back to me with your findings. I'm writing a case study journal article that presents incidences of dream-sharing. Just because something is beyond your experience or your beliefs about what is possible, doesn't mean that it isn't within the realm of another person's reality."

Chapter 18: A Step Forward

Wednesday Midday, August 27

Sharon sat in her car outside the electronics store, her new burner phone in hand. She dialed Elin Young's office with trembling fingers, hoping for good news but bracing for complications.

"Elin Young's office, this is Patricia."

"Hi, this is Sharon Sullivan. I need to speak with Ms. Young about my case."

"Hold on, she's been waiting for your call."

Within moments, Elin's confident voice came through the phone. "Sharon, I have excellent news. The emergency restraining order was granted, and the court also issued a temporary order giving you exclusive use of the marital home. Both documents will be served to Les today."

Sharon caught her breath. "Really? That fast?"

"Judge Angelo reviewed your documentation yesterday evening. Les will have twenty-four hours from the time of service to vacate the premises. If he's still there after that, he'll be arrested for violating a court order." Elin's voice carried a note of satisfaction. "He cannot contact you, cannot come within 500 feet of you or the children, and cannot enter the family home."

"What if he doesn't comply?"

"Then he'll be arrested. The police take these orders seriously, especially when there are children involved. However, Sharon, I need you to do a few things. First, do not go to the house until tomorrow afternoon at the earliest. Let's give him the full twenty-four hours to clear out. Second, when you do return, I recommend having a police escort."

"How do I arrange for police to be present?"

"Call the non-emergency number and explain you have a restraining order and need police present when you return to your home. They do this regularly."

"Where will Les go?"

"That's not your problem, Sharon. He's an adult who made choices that led to these consequences."

"What else do I need to do?"

"Document everything. If he tries to contact you through intermediaries, if he shows up anywhere you are, if he violates the order in any way - document it. Take photos, save messages, get witness names. The more evidence we have of violations, the stronger our case becomes for a permanent order."

"This is such a huge, meaningful step," Sharon said softly.

"It absolutely is. You've taken back your power, Sharon. How does that feel?"

"Terrifying and liberating at the same time. I'm having a hard time not thinking something really bad is going to happen."

"That's a normal response after years of walking on eggshells. But you're protected now, legally and practically. Trust the process."

After hanging up, Sharon sat in the parking lot for a moment, processing the magnitude of what just happened. She started the car and headed toward David's house to see Charlie, then planned to go visit Chris at the hospital.

*****

At the Walden's, Sharon found Charlie and David up in the treehouse Jesse built while David was in the hospital two months ago. When Charlie saw his mom pulling into the driveway, he quickly climbed down the wooden ladder, David following behind.

"Mom!" Charlie ran over and hugged her tightly. "I missed you. How are you doing?"

Sharon held him close. "I missed you too, sweetheart. I'm feeling hopeful for the first time in a long time. What have you two been up to?"

Charlie's face brightened. "David and I were talking about the Love Game and how hard it can be trying to see love in someone who has hurt you."

David nodded. "I was explaining to Charlie that sometimes when people are mean, it's because they have built walls around their hearts to protect themselves."

Sharon listened intently, realizing she'd never heard anyone explain Les's behavior this way before.

Charlie looked thoughtful. "Dad's mean actions are like a wall? To protect his heart from getting hurt?"

"That's right," David replied. "Those walls come from suffering that he doesn't talk about. It's a way that he learned to take care of himself - to survive."

Charlie paused, his expression serious. "It's really hard to think that he's suffering too."

David nodded encouragingly. "When you can see the Love he is behind those walls, your own upset feelings will start to fade. That doesn't mean his behavior should be okay or that he shouldn't have consequences. Sometimes consequences help people realize they need to tear down those walls so they can be happier."

"David, you're helping Charlie understand something I've struggled to explain for years," Sharon said softly.

Charlie suddenly perked up. "I almost forgot. We haven't talked about the dream we shared last night. How do you feel about what happened, Mom?"

"The healing circle was amazing. It gave me support and insights that I've never had in my entire life. I feel different after the dream. I'm much calmer."

Charlie looked into her eyes. "Are you still scared?"

"A little, but much less when I remember to keep my thoughts on this moment rather than thinking too far ahead." She stroked his hair. "How about you, Charlie? How do you feel about my story?"

"I feel closer to you than ever. I want to be there for you."

Sharon looked at both of them thoughtfully. "We had some good news from the lawyer today. It looks like we can go back home tomorrow afternoon. Your dad is not allowed to come near us or go into the house until things can be sorted out in the courts."

Charlie's eyes widened. "Really? We can go home?"

"Maybe as soon as tomorrow afternoon."

Charlie's expression grew serious. "Dad is going to be really mad." He looked down at his feet, then back up at his mother. "I feel sad about Dad being unhappy. I don't like it when he is mean to us, but who will take care of him?"

Sharon nodded. "Yes, he will be sad and angry. He may feel like we betrayed him. It was his choice to act the way he did. There are consequences for the way he behaved toward us all these years. Now is the time for us to heal and claim our worth."

"Mrs. Sullivan, you aren't alone," David said quietly.

"I know. The healing circle...it's like I have this whole network of support now that I didn't have before." Sharon looked at Charlie. "Are you okay staying here a little longer? I want to go see Chris at the hospital."

"Can I come with you?"

Sharon considered this. "Not today, sweetheart. Chris is still processing a lot, and the hospital has restrictions. But soon, I hope we'll all be together again."

Charlie hugged her again. "Tell Chris I love him. And that I'm proud of how brave he's being."

"I will." Sharon felt tears prick her eyes. "I love you so much, Charlie."

"I love you too, Mom. And I'm proud of how brave you're being too."

*****

Les was standing in his kitchen when he heard a sharp knock at the front door. He opened it to find a policewoman in uniform standing on his porch, clipboard in hand.

"Leslie Sullivan?"

"Yeah, what do you want?"

"I'm Officer Martinez. I have a restraining order to serve you." She extended the official documents toward him.

Les stared at the papers without taking them. "A what?"

"A temporary restraining order filed by Sharon Sullivan. You are ordered to stay away from her and your minor children, Chris and Charlie Sullivan. You cannot contact them directly or indirectly, and you cannot come within 500 feet of their location. In addition, you have twenty-four hours from the time of service to vacate this house so your wife and children can return. It is 3:10 p.m. now. If you are still here after 3:10 p.m. tomorrow, you will be arrested for violating a court order."

"This is bullshit!" Les exploded, then slammed the door in Officer Martinez's face without taking the documents.

Officer Martinez placed the papers in a manila envelope and tied them in a plastic bag to the front doorknob, then documented the attempted service on her clipboard before leaving. Her body cam recorded the whole interaction.

Inside, Les's rage erupted. He grabbed a glass vase from the hallway table and hurled it at a framed picture on the wall. Glass shards flew everywhere.

After several minutes of pacing and cursing, he retrieved the manila envelope from his front door. Hands shaking, he tore it open and read through the restraining order, his eyes focusing on the lawyer's name at the bottom: Elin Young, Attorney at Law.

"I could really use a drink right now," Les muttered to himself. He walked to his liquor cabinet and yanked it open, finding it completely empty.

Another surge of anger hit him. "That bitch. She'll be sorry."

He grabbed his phone, his mind racing through his options. Who can help him fix this? Who will listen to his side? His business contacts, his lawyer, someone has to see this is all a misunderstanding.

He dialed the number listed on the letterhead.

"Elin Young's office, this is Patricia."

"This is Les Sullivan. I need to speak to Elin Young immediately about my wife's case."

"I'm sorry, Mr. Sullivan, but Ms. Young cannot speak with you. You'll need to contact your own attorney if you wish to respond to this matter."

"There's been a misunderstanding. I need to explain—"

"Sir, I cannot put you through. You'll need to contact your own attorney."

"You don't understand. That lawyer boss of yours has turned my wife against me. I need to know where Sharon is. She's not thinking clearly and..."

The line went dead.

Les stared at the phone, his control slipping further with each failed attempt to regain power. The walls felt like they were closing in. No one would listen. No one understands.

He dialed another number - his business lawyer, Richard Walsh.

"Richard, this is Les Sullivan. My wife just had me served with a restraining order and she's trying to kick me out of my own house!"

"Slow down, Les. What exactly does the order say?"

Les read through the papers with shaking hands, his voice getting more agitated with each detail. "She wants me to stay away from her and the kids, and I have to be out of the house in twenty-four hours or I'll be arrested!"

"I need to refer you to a family law attorney - this isn't my area. But Les, you need to comply with the court order. This is just a temporary order until things can be worked out in court. I would call a friend, rent a U-Haul, take what's really essential, and stay in a hotel or with a friend. Don't leave anything that would be difficult to replace in case Sharon's anger turns destructive."

"This is insane! She can't just—"

"Les, listen to me carefully. If you violate that order, you'll be arrested and it will only make things worse for you in court. Comply for now."

Les ended the call, his mind racing. Twenty-four hours. Her lawyer wouldn't talk to him. Sharon's phone was disconnected. His sister-in-law hung up on him. The hospital won't let him see Chris. His liquor is gone.

And now he has twenty-four hours to pack up his life and leave his own house.

The silence in the house was oppressive. For the first time in years, there was no one to control, no one to direct his anger toward, no one who had to listen to him.

"Fuck it, I need a drink." He grabbed his keys and headed for the liquor store, the weight of his isolation pressing down on him with each step he took.

Chapter 19: Unwanted

Wednesday evening, August 27

Les returned from the liquor store with a bottle of bourbon, the amber liquid sloshing as he set it down hard on the kitchen counter. He filled a glass half full and took a long drink, feeling the burn settle into his chest. The alcohol helped quiet the panic, but his mind still raced.

He sat down at the kitchen table, staring at the restraining order paperwork scattered in front of him. Twenty-four hours to clear out. But maybe that's not long enough. Maybe he needs to move faster, get ahead of whatever Sharon and that lawyer were planning.

The bourbon worked its way through his system, and something shifted. His rage crystallized into cold calculation. He couldn't just pack some clothes and leave. There were things in this house that could destroy him if they fell into the wrong hands.

Les drained his glass and poured another, then headed into his home office. The room looked ordinary enough - desk, computer, filing cabinets, a few framed certificates on the wall. But Les knew what secrets it contained.

He started with the security system, methodically disconnecting the cameras and recording device, unaware of the backup recordings hidden elsewhere in the system.

Next, he opened his safe. Thirty thousand dollars in cash sat in neat stacks - money from deals that never saw a tax form, payments for services that existed only in handshake agreements. The cash went into a leather briefcase along with files documenting his shell corporations. Those papers were more valuable than anything else in the house because they represented his real assets - the properties Sharon didn't know about, the accounts that don't appear on any joint tax returns.

He emptied his filing cabinets systematically, pulling every document that could reveal the scope of his side businesses. The

Worcester property deal, the partnership agreements with investors who preferred anonymity, the records of artwork accepted as payment for his services - all of it went into boxes.

The artwork presented a problem. Three pieces hung on his office walls, each worth more than Sharon would guess. A small Marc Chagall sketch that was a signed limited edition lithograph worth about $35,000, and two small paintings he'd accepted instead of cash from a client who couldn't afford his usual fees. The paintings were valued at more than $50,000 each. They were far too valuable to leave behind.

Les made his decision quickly. They all came down. The Chagall and the two paintings were wrapped carefully in blankets and loaded into his BMW SUV along with the boxes and cash.

He had clothes at the condo already - part of maintaining his double life with Janet meant keeping a second wardrobe in the city. The secret condo was owned by one of his shell corporations, completely off Sharon's radar. If he could just get there tonight, he would have space to think, to plan his next moves.

The bourbon steadied his nerves and also sharpened his focus. This wasn't just about complying with a temporary restraining order. This was about protecting everything he'd built outside of the marriage, everything Sharon never even knew existed.

He loaded the last box into his car and took one final look at the house. Sharon didn't want him here anymore. Fine. She had no idea what she was losing or what he was truly worth. If he could just get Sharon to slow down the legal process, he could return and handle this more carefully. But for now, he needed to disappear into his other life, the one where he wasn't just Sharon's husband but a man with real power and hidden wealth.

Les drove away from the house that no longer felt like his, heading toward the city and the condo where Janet occasionally stayed. The restraining order said he had to leave the house, but it didn't say he couldn't fight back.

****

Sharon parked and walked Charlie to the entrance of the church's activity center. "David's dad will pick you guys up after the meeting," she reminded him.

"Thanks, Mom," Charlie said.

Sharon spotted Larry near the entrance as Charlie headed inside to join his troop.

"How are you holding up?" Larry asked, stepping forward to greet her.

"Better than I expected. The legal protection helps, and I feel like we're finally moving forward. I will be able to move back home tomorrow afternoon."

"When is Chris coming home?"

"I'm not sure. Dr. Deera says he is improving rapidly and maybe on Friday."

"Let me know if there is anything I can do to help," Larry offered. "School is starting soon so my days will be filled, but evenings and weekends are open."

"Well, there might be something you can do. I go to AA meetings on Friday nights. So, this Friday, I will be gone from 6:30 until about 8:00. I really don't want to leave Chris and Charlie alone."

"I would love to watch them when you go. I may be overstepping, but I volunteer at the Humane Society. I'll be there this Saturday and could use some help caring for the animals - feeding the dogs, cleaning kennels, that sort of thing. Do you think they'd be interested if I asked them on Friday if they'd like to come with me?"

"Oh, my gosh, Larry. I think they would love that. They have always wanted a pet, but Les wouldn't allow it. This would be great."

"I'll stop by on my way over Friday and pick up a pizza. What kind do they like?"

"They both like pepperoni. I really appreciate this, Larry."

"That's wonderful. I should go in and get the meeting started. See you on Friday."

"Bye, Larry."

After Larry headed inside, Sharon drove away, leaving Charlie in what she hoped would be a supportive environment.

Inside the meeting, the scouts who hadn't been on the camping trip were hearing David's story for the first time - how he claimed to see and hear God, how it affected the whole group. The whispers and sideways glances start almost immediately. The boys focused entirely on David's "craziness," completely overlooking the remarkable story of the rescued fox.

"So, you really think you talked to God?" one of the older scouts asked David during a break, his tone skeptical and mocking.

"It's not like talking on the phone," David tried to explain. "It's more like knowing something in your heart."

"That's crazy," another boy chimed in. "People who hear voices or see things that aren't there are psycho."

Charlie stepped closer to David, his loyalty clear. "It's not crazy. God taught David to play the Love Game."

"The what game?" The mockery in the older boy's voice spread to others nearby. "What happened to your stuttering? Did God take that away too?"

Charlie felt heat rise in his cheeks. These boys didn't understand. They were making fun of something beautiful and turning it into something ugly.

"But it's true..." Charlie started to protest.

"Alright, scouts, let's gather around," Mr. Lucas's voice cut through the chatter. The talking continued until he held up the scout sign of three fingers. Silence followed as the boys held their fingers up in response. "Let's focus on tonight's lesson. We're working on knots. Later in the evening, David will get his Tenderfoot badge."

David's face lit up at the mention of his badge, the excitement temporarily overriding the sting of his peer's reactions.

Mr. Lucas recognized the dynamics at play - David's spiritual experience made him a target for ridicule, and Charlie was trying to defend his friend. As the evening progressed, he kept a careful eye on both boys to make sure the teasing didn't escalate into something more harmful.

During the knot-tying lesson, Mr. Lucas paired David with one of the quieter, kinder scouts, and did the same for Charlie. When it came time for David's badge ceremony, he spoke directly to the troop about the importance of respecting each other's beliefs and experiences, even when they were different from their own.

"David showed courage, kindness, and leadership on our camping trip," Mr. Lucas told the group. "These are the qualities that matter in scouting, not whether we all believe the same things."

As the meeting ended and Jesse arrived to pick up the boys, both David and Charlie seemed subdued. The joy of David's new badge was tempered by the realization that sharing something sacred could sometimes make you feel unwanted, even among friends.

Chapter 20: Desires

Thursday morning, August 28

Sharon sat at Nana's kitchen table with her coffee and new burner phone as she began making the calls that would secure her new life. First on the list was the locksmith, who would be able to come by her house between 3 and 4:00 p.m. to change all the locks.

She called a different security company than the one Les had been using to install a monitoring system that she would control, not Les. The security company secretary told her a representative would be there at 3:00 p.m. to assess her needs. "Then if you decide, we can have a technician come Friday morning to install the system. You'll have complete control through an app on your phone." It felt surreal, planning security measures for her own home, but it gave her some relief. She felt good - things seemed to be falling into place.

Her phone rang. She saw it was Elin's office calling and answered the call.

"Sharon, the divorce papers have been filed and served to Les at his office. He wasn't too pleased. His lawyer contacted me within an hour - they want to negotiate. Can we talk?"

"Of course."

"Les has hired Marcus Webb, a family law attorney. He's asking what you want in terms of settlement. I told him we'd get back to them, but I need to know what you're thinking. What are your priorities?"

"I honestly don't know, Elin. I've never planned for this moment. I know I want some protection from any further abuse. What do you suggest?"

"I'll give you a possible starting point. Of course, this is hypothetical until we know Les's financial situation. What I would ideally like is if we can settle the divorce uncontested instead of a stressful long-drawn-out process. From what you told me about Les's ego, he will think he needs to fight. It would be nice if you can get what you want while Les thinks he has control. I'll let you sit with the question of what you really want to see happen. Give me a call back when you know. In the meantime, I will call Les's lawyer back for what Les might propose as a fair settlement for a non-contested divorce."

"Okay, Elin. I'll let you know later today. Bye."

"Bye."

After the call ended, Sharon found Nana in the garden, tending to her roses in the morning sun.

"Nana, I need your wisdom. The lawyers asked what I want from Les in the divorce. I don't know how to approach this."

Nana put her pruning shears down and looked at Sharon thoughtfully. "Are you asking from a place of love or a place of fear and revenge?"

The question stopped Sharon short. "I...I'm not sure. I want to protect the boys and myself, but I also don't want to be vindictive."

"Let's sit quietly and ask your heart what you truly want." Nana guided Sharon to the garden bench. "Close your eyes and take a few deep breaths. Imagine yourself at the Peace Pond."

Sharon settled into the meditation, following Nana's gentle guidance. She visualized herself at the pond's edge, feeling the cool water around her feet. With each breath, a profound sense of calm spread through her body, releasing tension she didn't even realize she was carrying. The peace rose through her legs, into her torso, filling her heart with light, relaxing her shoulders and arms, softening her face, until finally reaching the crown of her head where all her stress dissolved and flowed away like ripples on the pond's surface.

In that state of perfect stillness, Sharon asked her deepest questions about what she truly wanted for herself and her sons.

Nana gave Sharon about five minutes of silence. "When you are ready to come back, wiggle your toes in the water. Squeeze the grass you're sitting on. Notice the sensations coming back into your body. When you are ready, open your eyes to a new reality of clarity."

Sharon opened her eyes, her face bright with a smile. "Wow, I haven't been that relaxed in forever."

Nana nodded approvingly. "The Peace Pond has that effect. What did you learn from your experience?"

"I learned that I am the creator of my experiences. I want to start my life fresh from this moment. I want to align with the Love that I AM. I want to see Love everywhere and create new realities from that perspective. I want the freedom to experience life in new ways, to move beyond limiting beliefs. I want to create joy as I eagerly move forward into the infinite opportunities awaiting me. I want to see myself as worthy and valuable, appreciating my blessings and gifts. I want to attract people into my life who are kind. I want to radiate the energy of wellbeing. I want the same for my sons, but I realize each of them are on their own path. I can choose to see the Love they are."

"What amazing clarity," Nana said, her face lighting up with a smile. "What do you want from Les?"

"When I asked the Peace Pond that question, I got the message: *What you came here for today is to feel better. You don't need anything from Les to feel better or to experience all the things you want.* Nana, I don't need Les to create my happiness or wellbeing. In the practical day-to-day living, it would be nice to have a house, a car, food, and some money for basic expenses, but I'm not going to fight him for it - that won't make me feel better. I prefer that Les not live with us anymore and not interact with the boys until they have more time to heal."

"Sounds like you had an amazing experience. You know that you also don't need me. You can go right to the Source. You can go to the Peace Pond anytime you want to feel better."

"Yes, but it also brings me joy to do it with others who see the Love I am."

Sharon called Elin right away. "Elin, I have given it some thought. I don't want revenge or to make demands out of fear. What I want is an uncontested divorce. I want to live with my sons without the presence of Les. I'll wait until we hear back from Les's lawyer with his proposal. In the meantime, may I continue to live in the house with the boys until some settlement is made?"

Elin was surprised that Sharon wasn't making more demands other than for Les to stay away from her and her sons. "Aren't you concerned that Les will take advantage of your approach and take more than his fair share?"

"No, and I'm not being passive. I am 'actively' creating what I really want by focusing my attention in alignment with Love, to feel better, to experience joy. I'm 'actively' practicing focusing on one moment at a time. I know everything will work out perfectly."

Elin was stunned by Sharon's response. "This is quite a turnaround from the fearful woman I saw in my office earlier this week. What happened?"

"A lot," Sharon took a deep breath and let out a sigh. "I have been surrounded by kind support that helped me see the Love I am. My heart has opened up to see others the same way, including Les, if you can imagine. I want the best for Les even though I am not interested in having him present in my life any longer."

"Okay, we'll wait for Les's lawyer to get back to me with his proposal."

"Thanks, Elin. Bye."

"Bye, I'll call as soon as I know anything." Elin hung up confused about Sharon's requests. She'd never had a client approach divorce with the calmness she felt with Sharon today.

*****

At his secret condo, Les paced while Marcus Webb told him what Sharon's lawyer relayed to him. "Sharon wants an uncontested divorce and does not want you to live with her and the boys any longer. She wants to know what you will offer as a fair settlement."

"Nothing," replied Les with disdain.

"Come on Les, there must be something that is acceptable between nothing and more than half of all your assets if it goes to court."

"I suppose so."

"It would be in both your best interests if we can avoid court. I am inviting you to consider what you really want the outcome of this divorce to be. How do you want to feel when it's all over?"

"I want to feel respected. I don't want anyone to think they can walk all over me. I want to feel like a winner. I actually want to feel free from the daily drama that Sharon and the two loser kids lay on me. And I want to be free to be with my girlfriend without hiding."

"Okay, so what will it take to make this happen so that you get what you want?"

"I'll give her the house and the Kia Soul."

"How about any money to support the boys?"

"Yeah, I'll give them $500 per month."

"For each of them or total for both?"

"Total for both."

"Will you assume all current debts, credit card balances, and loans that are present at this time?"

"I guess so. After all, I am a fair man."

"Is there any more that you can offer and still feel like a winner?"

"I'm not sure."

"What about keeping your boys on your company's health insurance plan?"

"Yes, I'll do that. But she has to pay all the copays for health services. I'm not paying for every little doctor visit."

"Anything else?"

"No, that's all. I think I'm being more than generous. Most men wouldn't give their ex-wife a house."

"I will call Elin back and let her know what you are offering. I'll get back to you with Sharon's decision."

*****

At the hospital, Dr. Deera sat across from Chris in the now-familiar counseling room.

"Chris, you've made remarkable progress. I'm meeting with my colleagues this afternoon to discuss discharge planning. But first, I want to ask you something important. What do you want? Not what you think others want for you, but what do you truly desire for your life?"

Chris considered the question carefully. "I want to go home and be with my family. I want to help my mom and Charlie feel safe. I want to keep talking to Maggie when I need guidance. And I want to go back to school without feeling like I have to hide who I am."

"Those are beautiful desires. They show how much you've grown. What about your relationship with your father?"

"I hope someday he can learn the Love Game too. But I'm not responsible for his happiness or his anger anymore. That was a big lesson for me."

Dr. Deera smiled. "You're ready to go home, Chris. Let's make that happen."

Later that morning, Dr. Deera met with Dr. Lewis and Dr. Taft to discuss discharge plans.

"His progress has been remarkable," Dr. Lewis admitted. "The unconventional approach seems to have worked."

Dr. Taft shook his head. "I still don't understand how you can dismiss his claims about talking to a dead person. That's textbook psychosis."

"Is it?" Dr. Deera asked. "Tell me, what are the outcomes of his 'delusion'? Has it made him more functional or less?"

"Well, more functional, but..."

"Has it increased his capacity for love and connection with his family?"

"Yes, but that doesn't mean..."

"Has it given him hope, reduced his suicidal ideation, helped him make better decisions?"

Dr. Taft paused. "I see your point, but we can't just ignore diagnostic criteria because the results are positive."

Dr. Deera leaned forward. "What if we're asking the wrong question? Instead of 'Is this experience real according to our consensus reality?' what if we asked, 'Does this experience create healing and wellbeing?' Or perhaps more fundamentally, 'Are delusions without dysfunction or distress something we should be concerned about?'"

"You're suggesting we validate delusions?"

"I'm questioning whether we should call them delusions at all. Think about what we already accept as therapeutic practice. We use affirmations - that's imagination. We use hypnosis to help people stop smoking - that's guided imagination. We encourage patients to pray or meditate - both involve visualizing or imagining divine presence or healing outcomes."

Dr. Taft looked uncomfortable. "But those are conscious techniques..."

"Are they intentional? Does it matter whether they are intentional or not? We know placebo effects can create real healing through the power of belief and imagination. People aren't intentionally taking medicine they know is a placebo."

Dr. Deera continued, "What if Chris's experience with Maggie is simply his psyche using imagination in the most therapeutic way possible by creating exactly the guidance he needed to heal? Whether we call it divine communication or therapeutic imagination, the healing is real."

Dr. Taft shifted in his chair. "But we can't just ignore when someone's perception doesn't match reality..."

"Can't we? When someone sees a rope and jumps thinking it's a snake, are they delusional? Fear creates false perceptions, but we don't hospitalize people for being afraid of things that aren't actually threatening them."

Dr. Taft considered this. "But pathology is about persistence and dysfunction. If that person then avoids parks because of possible snakes, that's a problem."

"Exactly my point. Chris's experience with Maggie made him more functional, not less. Same type of perception, completely different outcome."

Dr. Taft furrowed his brow. "But you actually encouraged it. You confirmed your sister was there."

"I did. When he asked who the presence was, I spoke from my heart and said it was Maggie."

"Why?"

"Because I'd recently dreamed about my own sister Maggie, who died by suicide. She said she came back to help me. Something beyond my rational mind guided my response."

Dr. Taft looked stunned. "You responded intuitively rather than clinically?"

"If you were counseling a child with an imaginary friend that kept her from being lonely, and she wanted to introduce her friend to you, would you say no because the friend wasn't real? Probably not. You'd engage with the child and her friend to see how that relationship was helping her feel better. If the imaginary friend was scaring her, then you'd change your approach. That is how I was with Chris."

Dr. Taft nodded slowly. "It's beginning to make sense. I'm really interested to see whether Chris can maintain this progress."

"I'm comfortable discharging him tomorrow," Dr. Deera said. "I will personally follow him after discharge. Chris has found what he was looking for – he knows who he is and what he wants. I'll let you know how he's doing. By the way, Dr. Lewis, what did you discover about dream-sharing?"

"There's not much written about it, but dream-sharing has been documented, mostly between two people who are intimately close. Nothing about dream-sharing between strangers or groups of people."

"Do you accept that it might be unlikely but not impossible?"

"There have been a lot of strange things happening in the last week that are shaking up my beliefs. I'm starting to open to unconventional possibilities."

Dr. Deera smiled, saying, "Open your heart, let go of expectations, and you will witness miracles all around you. For example, you saw the drawing that Carlos did the other day. Carlos gifted the drawing to Chris, and Chris loaned it to me." He placed the drawing on the table. "Chris said the name of the girl is Maggie."

Dr. Deera then placed a photo of his sister Maggie, taken before she died 37 years ago, next to the drawing done by Carlos. Dr. Taft and Dr. Lewis were stunned by the incredible likeness.

"How is this possible?" Dr. Taft asked.

Dr. Lewis murmured, "That is incredible."

"Carlos said he saw the girl talking to Chris. Sit with that for a while and ask yourself, *Is Carlos really hallucinating, or is there something going on we just don't understand?*"

He then left to find Rachel and tell her the plan for discharging Chris. "Would you let Sharon know? And I'll talk with both her and Chris tomorrow morning."

"That is wonderful. I would love to tell Sharon. I'm sure she will be ecstatic."

Chapter 21: Opportunities

Thursday Afternoon, August 28

At 1:00 p.m., as she was organizing files in Dr. Deera's private office, Darla received a call from Patricia in HR.

"Is Dr. Deera available to meet with me, the hospital medical director, and the director of maintenance this afternoon at 4:00?"

"May I ask what this meeting is about?"

"We need to discuss Rachel and whether the Behavioral Health Unit is the best placement for her. We've received some concerns about her interactions with patients."

Darla immediately called Dr. Deera's private cell phone number. "Dr. Deera? Patricia from HR wants to meet with you, Dr. West, and Jim from maintenance at 4:00 today. It's about Rachel and concerns her patient interactions."

Dr. Deera's voice came through the phone, concerned but calm. "I see. Yes, 4:00 works. Administrative conference room?"

"I'll confirm with Patricia."

At exactly 4:00, Dr. Deera entered the administrative conference room. Patricia was sitting at the head of the table with a manila folder, flanked by Dr. West and Jim Peterson.

"Thank you for coming, Dr. Deera," Patricia began. "We need to discuss Rachel's role here and some concerns that have been expressed about her interactions with patients."

Dr. West leaned forward. "Let me be clear, there are no complaints about Rachel's work quality. Jim conducts periodic inspections and her cleaning work is consistently excellent."

Jim nodded. "Rachel's one of our best housekeepers. Always thorough, professional work. That's not the issue."

Patricia opened her folder. "The concern is whether the psychiatric unit is the best placement for her, given how she interacts with patients. She's been described as unusually friendly, talking to patients beyond what's expected of housekeeping staff."

"Can you be more specific?" Dr. Deera asked.

"Karen Williams documented an incident where Rachel approached a patient who was acting violently while security was on their way. Another time, she was overheard discussing a patient's dream with the patient."

Dr. West added, "There haven't been any specific incidents where patients complained or had adverse reactions to Rachel. But Karen is concerned that Rachel might give advice to patients when nursing staff isn't present."

Patricia looked directly at Dr. Deera. "Karen has also indicated that your personal relationship with Rachel may be affecting your judgment. Dr. Deera, can you address these concerns? We take all staff concerns seriously and want to find the best solution for everyone."

"Yes, I can. I believe Rachel's presence in the Behavioral Health Unit has uplifted the spirits of many patients. Her interactions have been friendly and compassionate. I have not heard that she ever gave any patient advice. Regarding the violent patient she approached, witnesses told me she didn't say one word to him. She just looked into his eyes. He then turned, apologized to the staff for his behavior, and walked back to his room. And the patient who wanted to talk to her about his dream spent less than a minute with her. I have observed patients spontaneously coming up to her more often than they tend to with the professional staff. She has a loving energy.

"About my relationship with Rachel, yes, we are friends. She was a patient here in the unit in June and I counseled her until recently. We have some mutual friends as well, and I had a connection to her daughter who passed away. My friendship with her in no way affects my observation of her being a valuable asset to this hospital and a compassionate presence for anyone she interacts with. I am not attached to Rachel staying in the Behavioral Health Unit, although I would miss the positive energy she brings. I think it would be a major mistake for the hospital to let her go or to put her in an area where she wouldn't have contact with people. If you feel it's best to move her to another part of the hospital, I highly recommend moving her to the pediatric oncology ward. To give you a heads up, Dr. Welling also has a connection with Rachel, having treated her daughter."

"Thanks for your time to address these issues," Patricia said. "We'll talk to Dr. Welling and let you know what we decide. We have no intention of letting her go," she added. "We simply want to ensure she's in the position where she can best serve both the hospital and our patients."

*****

After her transformative morning with Nana, Sharon drove to the grocery store to stock up on essentials before the locksmith and security company arrived. She felt oddly peaceful pushing the cart through familiar aisles, selecting foods she actually enjoyed rather than what Les preferred.

When she pulled into her driveway at 2:45 p.m., a police car was parked in front of the house. Officer Martinez rolled down her window. "Mrs. Sullivan? Your lawyer arranged for us to do a welfare check. I'll stay until you're safely inside and everything looks okay."

Sharon nodded gratefully. The house felt different as she unlocked the door – peaceful, and somehow lighter. She did a quick walk-through while the officer waited, then waved to let her know all was well.

A few minutes after the patrol car left, a white van pulled up. "Secure Home Systems," the technician announced. "I'm here to assess your security needs."

As he examined windows and entry points, Sharon asked, "When your installation team comes tomorrow, will they be able to remove the existing security cameras?"

"Absolutely. We'll disconnect the old system completely and install your new one. You'll have total control through your phone app."

At 3:30, the locksmith arrived. The sound of lock mechanisms being replaced felt symbolic - each old lock removed was another tie to Les being severed. The locksmith also helped her reprogram the garage door remote.

"Make sure you dispose of any old remotes," he advised. "You don't want anyone else having access."

Alone in the house for the first time in years without fear of Les returning, Sharon looked around at the furniture, the decorations, the remnants of their life together. She headed to the garage and retrieved several empty boxes.

It was time to start clearing his energy from this space entirely. Sharon moved methodically through the house, collecting items he left behind. His clothes from the bedroom closet and dresser went into one box. His toiletries, electric razor, and cologne from the bathroom went into another. She found his reading glasses on the nightstand, a coffee mug with his company logo in the kitchen sink, and the remote control he always hogged tucked between the cushions of his favorite chair.

Each item she removed felt like a weight being lifted from her shoulders. His favorite throw pillow, the one that always smelled faintly of his aftershave. The stack of car magazines by his chair. Even his protein powder from the kitchen counter - everything went into the boxes.

She carried the boxes one by one to the garage, stacking them against the back wall. Standing there among the cardboard containers, she realized she didn't know what she would ultimately do with his belongings. The clothes could go to Goodwill. But the rest? She wasn't sure she cared enough to sort through what might have value. The trash might be the simplest solution.

For now, though, it was enough that his presence was contained in the boxes, removed from the living spaces where she and the boys could heal and start fresh.

The house already felt different - like it was exhaling after holding its breath for years. With it feeling lighter and more like her own, Sharon prepared to leave. She wanted to show her gratitude to the women who'd carried her through this transformation. Just then, her phone rang. It was Elin.

"Sharon, I received Les's proposal from his lawyer Marcus. Marcus apologized for Les's offer but is compelled to pass it on." Elin paused. "Sharon, it's really disrespectful."

Sharon listened as Elin read through the terms: the house and car, $500 monthly child support total, health insurance with Sharon paying copays.

"I think I could make it work if there are minimal unexpected costs," Sharon said calmly.

There was silence on the other end of the line. "Sharon, this is far below what you're entitled to. We might be able to negotiate him into offering more as we fine-tune a settlement contract. Even his own lawyer is uncomfortable with these terms."

"Elin, I appreciate your expertise, but I'm not interested in a long, drawn-out fight. This gives me what I need to start fresh."

"What if we could get more without a fight?" Elin asked.

Sharon paused. "Sure, any help is welcome in making the transformation easier."

"I think it's prudent to get additional information before agreeing. For example, it would be nice to know what liabilities you'll be faced with. For example, the mortgage payments and balance owed and taxes. What are your utility expenses? Are there any outstanding credit card debts, real estate taxes, etc.? We're collecting information, not engaging in a threatening audit of all his assets. We want to know if Les might be setting you up for a windfall of unexpected expenses. Would that be a reasonable approach?"

"Yes, okay, go for it," Sharon agreed.

"I'll have Marcus provide these details as part of finalizing any settlement. It's standard due diligence - we need to know what you're actually agreeing to take on."

Sharon felt the wisdom in this approach. Getting practical information wasn't the same as fighting or being vindictive, it was just being informed about her financial reality.

"How long will this take?"

"Probably a few days. Marcus will have most of this information readily available. Then you can make a truly informed decision."

*****

Sharon drove to a local gift boutique downtown, taking her time to select each item thoughtfully.

For Nana, she found a leather-bound journal with "Miracles Happen Daily" embossed on the cover, and a delicate silver wind chime that would sing softly in her garden's breezes. For Rachel, she chose a silver necklace with rose quartz beads and an angel pendant. The beads represented unconditional love and healing, perfect for a mother who'd lost her child but continues to help others heal.

Sharon's next stop was Flora's Flowers. She wandered inside, immediately struck by the heady floral scents and creative beauty of the arrangements. A woman in her early sixties with shoulder-length white hair pulled into a ponytail hummed softly while arranging an elaborate display of white lilies and eucalyptus fronds. Her hands moved with practiced grace, each stem finding its perfect place.

Sharon watched, mesmerized. Something stirred deep within her as she observed the creative process - the way colors blended, how different textures complemented each other, the complementary scents, the artistry in something so natural yet carefully crafted.

"That's beautiful," Sharon said softly.

The woman looked up with a warm smile. "Thank you! I'm putting this together for a wedding this weekend. I'm Flora, by the way. Are you looking for something special?"

"Hi, I'm Sharon. Yes, I'd like an orchid plant, something in full bloom with care instructions." Sharon paused, still drawn to watch Flora's skilled hands. "I've always loved flowers and enjoy cutting the ones in my garden. My arrangements are fairly simple, but I love seeing combinations that aren't ordinary. I've never seen the professional arranging process up close. It's fascinating."

Flora beamed. "It's my passion. Been doing this for twenty-two years and I still get excited about each arrangement. I was about 40 when I first started. I had gone to school to be a lawyer, but after nine years in that cutthroat business, I found the courage to follow my passion and opened up this shop."

"Then it's not too late for me to find my passion."

"Never!"

Sharon took a deep breath, feeling something urging her forward. "Any chance you're looking for help in your store?"

Flora paused, studying Sharon's face with interest. "You know, it's funny you should ask. I was just thinking this morning about how busy things are getting with wedding season coming up." She reached behind the counter and pulled out a help-wanted sign. "I was planning to put this in the window tomorrow. Are you interested?"

"I haven't worked in a florist shop before, but I'm really eager to learn. I'm a hard worker, and something about this just feels right."

Flora put her pruning shears down and gave Sharon her full attention. "Tell me, what draws you to this work?"

"There's something about creating beauty, about taking individual elements and bringing them together into something that makes people feel joy. I've been going through a major life change, and I'm discovering parts of myself I never knew existed."

Flora nodded thoughtfully. "I can see the passion in your eyes. You know what? Sometimes the best employees are the ones who bring genuine enthusiasm rather than just experience." She smiled. "When can you start?"

"My son will be coming home tomorrow, so I could start Saturday or Monday."

"Saturday would be perfect! You can help me deliver flowers for a wedding. It's a great way to start learning the business and see how our arrangements look in their final settings."

"Thank you so much. I won't let you down." Sharon's heart leapt. It felt like another piece of her new life was falling perfectly into place.

Back at home, she wrote heartfelt notes to accompany each gift, her pen flowing easily as gratitude filled her heart. She carefully wrapped the journal and chime in beautiful gift paper.

She stopped at Nana and Rachel's house first. Ringing the doorbell, her hands trembled slightly as she held the carefully wrapped packages. Rachel opened the door with a warm smile.

"Sharon! What a wonderful surprise. Come in, come in."

"I can't stay long, but I wanted to give you each something in appreciation." Sharon's voice caught with emotion. "Rachel, you changed my life with that first hug at the AA meeting. I could never have imagined how much support the two of you have been to me since then with your compassionate kindness. These gifts don't even begin to adequately reflect my level of appreciation."

Nana appeared from the kitchen, wiping her hands on a dish towel. "Child, you didn't need to bring us anything."

"Yes, I did," Sharon said firmly, handing Nana the first package. "You both gave me hope when I had none left."

Nana unwrapped the journal slowly, running her weathered fingers over the embossed words. "Miracles Happen Daily," she read aloud, then looked up with tears in her eyes. "Oh honey, this is perfect. I've been wanting to start writing down all the beautiful things I see each day." She opened the second package and lifted out the delicate silver wind chime. "And this beautiful chime will sing to me in my garden every day, reminding me of your sweet heart."

Rachel opened her gift next, gasping softly at the rose quartz necklace. "Sharon, this is absolutely beautiful."

"The lady at the store said rose quartz represents unconditional love and healing," Sharon explained. "It reminded me of you - how you help people heal even after losing Angela."

Rachel fastened it around her neck, her fingers touching the angel pendant. "I'll treasure this always. But Sharon, seeing you find your strength again - that's the greatest gift you could ever give us."

Rachel hugged Sharon warmly, then Nana pulled her into a gentle hug. "You're going to be just fine, sweetheart. You've got Love on your side."

"I feel I have a new family," Sharon said, tears in her eyes.

She left Rachel and Nana, then headed to Vicki's to deliver the orchid. Once there, she rang the doorbell with the gift in hand. When Vicki opened the door, her face lit up with surprise and warmth.

"Sharon! What a lovely surprise. What's all this?"

"Just a small thank you for everything you've done for me and the boys. It has given me peace of mind to be able to have Charlie stay here surrounded by so much loving energy," Sharon said, handing over the flower. "The orchid comes with care instructions."

Vicki's eyes welled up as she read the heartfelt note attached. "Oh, Sharon, you didn't need to do this. But thank you - it's beautiful." She admired the orchid's delicate white blooms. "While Charlie's getting ready to come home with you, would you like to have some tea? I just put the kettle on."

"I'd love that," Sharon replied, following Vicki into her cozy kitchen.

As they settled in with steaming cups of chamomile tea, Vicki studied Sharon's face. "You look different, more peaceful. How are you feeling about everything that's happened?"

Sharon took a sip and smiled. "Like I'm finally waking up from a long, bad dream. I actually got a job today, at a florist shop. I start Saturday."

"Sharon, that's wonderful! You're really building a new life."

"It feels like everything is falling into place. For the first time in years, I'm excited about the future."

They chatted for another few minutes before Charlie appeared in the doorway with his backpack, David right behind him.

"Ready to go home, Mom?" Charlie asked, though his voice carried a hint of sadness about leaving.

Sharon set her teacup down and stood. "Ready when you are, sweetheart."

David put both hands over his heart, then opened and spread his arms, silently requesting a hug. Sharon, surprised, accepted the invitation, feeling a vibration similar to what she felt hugging Rachel.

"I didn't expect that," she said softly.

David looked directly into her eyes, saying, "I really enjoyed having Charlie here. We've had so much fun. He's my best friend. Maybe we can play again tomorrow? I can ride my bike over to your house."

Charlie's face brightened. "Can he, Mom?"

Sharon smiled, touched by David's sincere affection for her son. "Of course. We'd love to have you visit."

As they walked toward the car, Sharon told Charlie, "By the way, Chris is coming home tomorrow."

"Great! He can meet David," Charlie said excitedly.

David looked at Charlie with a puzzled expression. "Don't you remember? We already met at the Peace Pond."

Charlie stopped walking and hit his forehead with his palm. "Oh yes, I forgot!"

"See you later," David said with a grin.

Charlie gave him one more quick hug. "See you tomorrow!"

Sharon and Vicki exchanged amazed glances as they watched the boys' easy friendship, both mothers recognizing the special connection their sons shared.

Vicki wrapped Sharon in a hug. "Call me if you need anything at all. And I want to hear all about your first day at the flower shop."

Charlie gave Vicki a tight hug. "Thanks for everything."

"Our door is always open," Vicki said.

Back at home, Charlie threw his backpack on his bed and stretched out with a big smile. "It's good to be back," he commented, looking around his room.

Sharon watched from the doorway, her heart full. "How do you feel?"

Charlie took a deep breath. "Different. Something about being here feels more peaceful than I ever remember."

Sharon nodded, understanding exactly what he meant. "It does, doesn't it? But I don't think it is just the house. We are not the same people that were here a few days ago."

"I think we're all going to sleep better tonight."

Charlie bounced on his bed a few times, testing the familiar comfort. "Mom. Thank you for taking care of me."

Sharon's eyes welled up with tears of gratitude. "We're going to be okay, sweetheart. Better than okay."

Chapter 22: Crystal Love

Thursday Evening, August 28

Crystal got off work a little early and decided to cook dinner for Mark. They'd been going out to eat a lot lately, and Mark would be really happy to have a homecooked meal in a more private place.

He arrived at Crystal's house a little early and watched as she finished preparing dinner. It was a warm day, so she made summer pasta primavera with fresh broccoli, peppers, peas, and cherry tomatoes, with a light lemon vinaigrette. She'd also prepared iced tea with fresh lemon.

"Is there anything I can do? Set the table?" Mark asked.

"You could do that or you could sit down for a while and let the day settle before it's time to eat," Crystal suggested.

"Good idea," Mark sat down, feeling himself sink into the comfort of the padded chair.

The next thing he knew, Crystal was gently shaking his shoulder. "Hey, it's time to eat."

He stood up, stretched his arms and shoulders and took a deep breath. "I can't believe I actually fell asleep."

"I guess you needed it."

They sat down, Mark commenting on how good everything tasted while hardly taking the time to breathe. It wasn't long before he was going for seconds.

"Are you okay if I tell you something that's been bothering me at work?" Crystal asked.

"I am ready. My heart is open," Mark replied.

Crystal told him about a 7-year-old boy named Nathan at the hospital who has leukemia. "He cries all the time, doesn't want to engage with the other kids, or even talk. His parents are just as depressed and grieving, expecting him to die at any moment. From the lab tests, it appears his organs are beginning to shut down. The medical treatments aren't working anymore, and we're running out of options. I don't know how to help him. Do you have any suggestions?"

Mark closed his eyes, sitting in silence for a few moments. Then he opened his eyes wide. "Yes! I do."

"I need to first tell you about a meeting I had today. I'm not trying to change the subject," he said. He told her about Rachel and how they were considering moving her out of the psych unit because Karen doesn't like her. "I think she's jealous that patients gravitate to Rachel and doesn't like it when patients talk to her. In any case, they are considering moving her to another part of the hospital, just to keep everyone happy. I highly recommended that Rachel be placed on the pediatric oncology floor. I expect Patricia in HR will call you in the morning for your approval."

Mark paused, choosing his words carefully. "This might sound unconventional, but I have a strong feeling about this. What if we invited Rachel to come and sit with Nathan and his family for a few minutes? I'm sure Angela would show up."

Crystal looked thoughtful. "Rachel certainly understands what these families are going through."

"Exactly. And Crystal..." Mark hesitated. "I keep thinking about your father's crystal, that beautiful piece he gave you to represent unconditional love. What if we asked Nathan's parents to let him hold it for a while? Sometimes children find comfort in holding something from nature, something beautiful and smooth."

Crystal's hand instinctively went to her necklace, where she kept the crystal close to her heart. "You want me to let Nathan hold my father's crystal?"

"Only if his parents are comfortable with it. We could explain that it's something meaningful to you that represents love and see if they think Nathan might enjoy holding it. Some children find comfort in crystals - the way it feels warm in their hands."

Crystal sat quietly for a long moment, her fingers still touching the crystal through her shirt. She thought about Nathan's constant tears, his parents' devastation, the feeling of helplessness that's been weighing on her.

"Mark, that crystal is the most sacred thing I own. It's my connection to my father." She paused, her voice becoming thoughtful.

"When my father gave it to me, he said it represented love that never dies, love that keeps flowing from person to person."

She looked up at Mark. "I've been holding onto it like...like love is something you possess, something you keep safe by not sharing it. But that's not what love is, is it?"

Mark shook his head gently.

"Love is something you give away. The more you share it, the more it grows." Crystal took a deep breath. "If my father's love, channeled through that stone, could bring even a moment of comfort to Nathan..." Her voice became stronger. "Yes. Let's do it. I'll ask his parents first, of course. And I'll call Rachel tonight and see if she would be willing to stop by and see him."

"You're not concerned about how unconventional this is?"

"After what I saw today, with Nathan sobbing, his parents' devastation, and our medical team running out of options, I know that conventional methods aren't working. If there's even a chance this could help..." She shook her head. "I'd rather try something that sounds unusual than do nothing and watch that family suffer."

Mark nodded. "No one needs to know the details. If the nurses or staff wonder why Rachel is there, you can tell them that what Rachel experienced being with Angela in her final days might bring some peace to Nathan and his family."

Crystal nodded slowly. "That's perfect. It's completely true, Rachel does understand what it's like to lose a child. And it gives a clear reason for her presence that everyone can accept."

"Exactly. We're not asking anyone to believe in anything mystical. We're just arranging for a grieving mother who works at the hospital to spend time with another family facing loss. And offering a child a beautiful stone to hold if his parents think he might like it. The rest...well, the rest will speak for itself."

Crystal picked up her phone. "I'm going to call Rachel now, before I lose my nerve."

As she dialed, Mark reached across and squeezed her free hand. "Thank you for trusting this."

"Thank you for helping me understand that love isn't something you hoard," Crystal replied. She tapped Rachel's number into her phone, her heart beating a little faster as it rang.

"Hello?"

"Rachel, it's Crystal. I hope I'm not calling too late."

"Not at all, Crystal. How are you?"

"I'm well, thank you. Rachel, I have an unusual request, and I want you to know you can absolutely say no if this doesn't feel right to you."

"What is it?"

"There's a seven-year-old boy in my unit named Nathan. He has leukemia and he's...he's not doing well. He cries constantly, won't engage with anyone, and his parents are devastated. The medical treatments aren't helping anymore. I was wondering if you might be willing to come sit with him and his family tomorrow morning around 11:00. After what you experienced with Angela in her final days, your understanding and presence might bring them some much-needed peace."

There was a pause on the other end of the line.

"Of course, I'll come," Rachel said softly. "11:00 works perfectly."

"Thank you, Rachel. He is in room 314. One other thing I want to mention. HR might be transferring you out of the psych unit and Dr. Deera, with my support, has recommended that you come and work in the pediatric oncology unit. Would that be too emotionally difficult for you, being around children who are sick and possibly dying?"

Rachel paused again, then responded, "It might be if Angela wasn't with me. But she is."

Crystal felt a familiar warmth at Rachel's words. "I understand. I'll let you know what HR decides."

"Crystal? Thank you for thinking of me. Sometimes the hardest part of losing Angela is feeling like her death was meaningless. If being with Nathan's family can honor her memory in some way..."

"I think it will, Rachel. I really do. We'll see how tomorrow goes. See you at eleven."

Crystal ended the call and turned to see Mark standing close behind her, smiling.

She whispered, "Thank you."

He reached for her hand. "Thank you for understanding that the most sacred things become even more sacred when we share them."

*****

Rachel set her phone down after the call from Crystal. Nana looked up from her book. "Who was that?"

"Dr. Welling from the hospital. She wants me to come in tomorrow and sit with a patient of hers - a seven-year-old boy, Sammy's age, who is dying."

Nana put her book down, giving Rachel her full attention. "How do you feel about that?"

Rachel sat down across from her. "Part of me is excited, and another part of me is curious about whether the energy in that ward will be overwhelming and bring me down."

"What does your heart tell you?"

"My heart says this is why I'm still here - to help other families going through what we went through. But my mind worries about being around all that sadness and fear."

Nana nodded thoughtfully. "When you were with Angela in her final days, did being around her illness and pain overwhelm you, or did love carry you through?"

Rachel considered this. "Love carried me through. Even in the darkest moments, there was so much love."

"Then trust that same love to carry you tomorrow. You won't be going alone."

Chapter 23: Healing Energy

Friday morning, August 29

Crystal stood at the nurses' station reviewing charts before making her rounds, her father's crystal carefully wrapped in her pocket. Her phone rang, showing a hospital number.

"Dr. Welling, this is Patricia from HR. Do you have a moment to talk?"

"Yes, I've been expecting your call."

"Good. We're considering transferring Rachel from housekeeping duties in the Behavioral Health Unit to pediatric oncology. Normally we wouldn't involve you in staffing details, but Karen, the head nurse in that unit, has concerns about Rachel and thinks she might be better suited somewhere else. Dr. Deera spoke highly of Rachel yesterday, and even though he doesn't entirely agree with Karen, he suggested a move to your unit might benefit everyone. Would this placement work in your department?"

"Yes, I think she would be a wonderful addition to our team," Crystal responded. "I want to let you know that I invited Rachel to come in and sit with one of my patients today. I want to see how Rachel responds emotionally to being around sick and dying children. Even though it is her day off, she will be here at 11:00. I'll call you this afternoon with an update."

Patricia responded, "That's a nice idea, Dr. Yes, please let me know if you want Rachel to work in your oncology unit."

At 11:00 sharp, Rachel arrived to find Crystal waiting outside the door to Nathan's room.

"Good morning, Rachel. How are you feeling?"

"Eager and curious with my heart open."

"I talked to Nathan's parents about you visiting and they agreed. They said they trust me and they are willing to try anything to ease Nathan's suffering."

Rachel and Crystal entered the room. Nathan was lying listless in bed, his parents sitting nearby looking exhausted and heartbroken. His mother's eyes were red and swollen from both lack of sleep and tears.

"Mr. and Mrs. Johnson, this is Rachel. She works here at the hospital. Sometimes patients feel better when she visits. And I brought something that my father gave me, a crystal that represents unconditional love. Would it be okay if Nathan holds it for a while?"

The parents nodded wearily.

Rachel sat beside Nathan's bed and gently took his small hand. "Hi, Nathan. I'm Rachel."

Crystal placed the crystal in Nathan's palm and asked him to hold it against his heart.

"What's this?" Nathan asked weakly.

"It's a very special crystal that is full of love."

"It's warm." Nathan turned and looked into Rachel's eyes, his breathing becoming easy and relaxed.

"I can see right into your heart, Nathan, and I see the love you are."

"You can?"

"Yes. May I put my hand on top of yours as you hold the crystal?" Rachel asked.

"Okay."

Rachel gently placed her hand over his. Nathan surprised everyone when he burst out laughing. "That tickles all over my body."

His mother and father, watching the exchange intensely, opened their eyes wide in surprise. His mother covered her mouth, and his father whispered, "What?" Crystal was equally surprised. None of them had seen a smile from Nathan in weeks, and now he was laughing.

"Nathan," Rachel said softly, "I want you to know that you are very loved. I had a daughter named Angela who died, and she's now an angel who is with me all the time, even right now."

Nathan asked, pointing to the space next to Rachel, "Is that her?"

Rachel's eyes filled with tears of recognition and joy. "Yes, it is."

Nathan smiled at Angela.

His mother gasped and reached for his father's hand.

"She's beautiful," Nathan whispered, still holding the crystal close to his heart. "She is telling me not to be scared. Everything will be fine."

The transformation in the room was palpable as Nathan continued to interact with Angela, his spirits lifting visibly with each moment. He began talking with animated hands and glowing eyes. His mouth moved in soft whispers heard only by Angela.

The door opened and Carolyn, the head nurse, stepped in, immediately noticing the almost joyful energy in the room. She asked, "What's happening here?"

Crystal turned to her. "Nathan is talking to Angela. Remember? She was a patient here in June."

The nurse leaned toward Crystal and whispered, "Didn't she die?"

"Yes, she did. She came with her mother Rachel to be with Nathan today."

The nurse looked confused. "I'm not following..."

"Have you seen Nathan acting so alive recently?" Crystal asked quietly. The nurse looked at Nathan, who was still smiling and holding the crystal, then back at Crystal. She shook her head slowly.

"That is what Divine Love can do," Crystal said softly.

The nurse stood there for a moment, watching Nathan's animated interaction with the space beside Rachel, his parents holding hands and crying tears of relief rather than despair for the first time in weeks.

"I...I'll be at the nurses' station if you need anything," she said quietly, stepping back out and closing the door gently behind her.

Back at the nursing station, the head nurse was still shaking her head in disbelief. The ward secretary looked up from her computer and asked, "Is something wrong?"

The nurse sat down heavily in her chair. "I thought I had seen everything in my twenty years working pediatric oncology, but what I witnessed in Nathan's room today is mind-boggling. I can't even put it into words."

"What happened?"

"Nathan Johnson, you know, the little boy with leukemia who hasn't smiled or spoken much in weeks? He was laughing. Actually laughing and talking animatedly to...well, to someone I couldn't see. His parents looked like they'd witnessed a miracle."

The secretary's eyebrows rose. "That's wonderful news, isn't it?"

"It is, but..." Carolyn trailed off, staring down the hallway toward Nathan's room. "There was a woman in there with Crystal. Rachel, I think her name is. She lost her daughter Angela here in June. Nathan was talking to Angela like she was right there in the room with them."

Another nurse said, "I remember Angela. She and another patient, David, really connected. They radiated Love. I always felt good when I saw them together."

The ward secretary said, "Kids have vivid imaginations when they're scared..."

"Maybe. But I've never seen or felt anything like the energy in that room. It felt..." Carolyn paused, searching for words, "it felt sacred."

*****

Rachel turned back to Nathan's parents: "There is nothing more beautiful than seeing a child laugh." She turned to Nathan. "I have to leave, Nathan, but now that Angela has entered your heart, she will be with you as long as you want."

Nathan sat up, his eyes bright, still holding the crystal to his heart. "Thanks for coming and bringing Angela. Will you come back and see me?"

Rachel touched his cheek, "You sweet child, of course I will."

"What about the crystal?" Nathan asked. Rachel looked at Dr. Welling.

"Why don't you keep it for now," Dr. Welling offered.

As Rachel prepared to leave, Nathan's mom and dad stood up. His mother's voice broke slightly as she asked, "May I give you a hug?"

Rachel opened her arms to both parents. She could feel the tension in their bodies melt as their shallow, irregular breaths slowed into a smooth rhythm. For the first time in weeks, they were breathing like people who had hope.

Crystal followed Rachel out into the hallway where they hugged.

"Mark wasn't wrong. You carry a powerful healing energy and I want you on my team."

Rachel responded, "My heart tells me this is just what I need."

Crystal immediately called Patricia. "Rachel is perfect. Please assign her to our unit."

"Thanks Crystal, I'll talk to the Housekeeping supervisor and we will make it happen."

She then called Mark, who was standing at the nursing station in the Behavioral Health Unit preparing the discharge orders for Chris. "Mark, you are absolutely right about Rachel. Her healing presence is Godsent. I'm excited to have her on my team."

"Thanks for letting me know, Crystal."

Mark turned to Karen. "I have to thank you for bringing your concerns about Rachel to HR. It worked out well. Rachel will be in pediatric oncology where families often appreciate compassionate support during difficult times. She's going to a place where her gifts can shine."

Karen looked at him for a moment, then said defensively, "I did what I needed to do."

"I understand. Sometimes what seems like a problem in one setting turns out to be exactly what's needed somewhere else." Mark then turned back to completing Chris's discharge paperwork.

Chapter 24: Home Again

Friday Afternoon, August 29

Chris walked down the hallway of the Behavioral Health Unit, no longer the fragile, withdrawn young man who was admitted a week ago. Other patients looked up as he passed, and instead of avoiding their eyes, he offered genuine smiles and words of encouragement.

"Morning, Mrs. Patterson," he said to an elderly woman sitting alone in the common area. "How are you feeling today?"

She looked surprised but pleased. "Better, thank you for asking, dear. You seem different today."

"I am different," Chris replied, settling into the chair beside her. "I've learned that we're all more than our struggles."

Nurse Karen watched from the nurses' station, shaking her head in amazement. "I've never seen anything like it," she whispered to Dr. Taft. "Four days ago, he wouldn't speak to anyone except that empty chair. Now look at him."

Dr. Taft, who had been the first to evaluate Chris in the ICU, nodded thoughtfully. "It's remarkable. I expected we'd be discharging him on antipsychotics and antidepressants."

Chris moved on to Carlos, the middle-aged schizophrenic artist who had drawn Maggie's portrait. "How's the drawing coming along, Carlos?"

Carlos held up his sketchpad, showing a new piece - a serene landscape with a young girl sitting peacefully by a pond. "I keep drawing her," he said quietly. "She keeps appearing in my mind. The visions of her don't make me angry or afraid like the visions I've had in the past. I guess the medications are working."

Chris studied the artwork, his eyes widening with recognition. "That's the Peace Pond. I've been there. Maybe it's not only the medications that are helping you feel better, but Maggie, the girl you are drawing, is calling you to the Love you are."

"I don't understand, Chris."

"I don't know how to explain it exactly, but...maybe you could ask Maggie how Love can help with the scary stuff. She really helped me figure things out."

Dr. Deera approached from behind, observing quietly. In over twenty years of practice, he'd never witnessed such a complete shift in a patient's energy and connection to others. Dr. Lewis joined him, equally amazed.

"Chris," Dr. Deera said. "Your mother will be here in an hour for our discharge meeting. Are you ready to break out of here?"

Chris turned, his eyes clear and confident. "I'm ready, Dr. Deera. More ready than I've ever been for anything. I have to tell you that I am glad I won't be seeing my father. I think I need more time to ground myself."

*****

An hour later, Sharon was sitting across from Dr. Deera in his office, Chris beside her in the chair he'd occupied during several sessions this week. But unlike those earlier meetings, there were no observers today - no residents taking notes, no case study atmosphere. Just the three of them and Maggie's presence.

"I have to admit, Dr. Deera, I'm terrified," Sharon began, her voice barely steady. "A week ago, my son was unconscious in the ICU. Now you're telling me he doesn't need any medication at all? What if I take him home and...what if he tries again?"

Chris responded, "I'm not the same frightened person I was a week ago. I didn't really want to die. I just didn't want to feel anything bad about myself for a while. I won't do that again. I know things about myself now that I didn't know then. Mom, I have seen what Love is. Maggie taught me."

Dr. Deera nodded. "Chris has always been an extraordinarily sensitive young man. He feels the emotions and energies of everyone around him - their anger, their pain, their fear. For years, especially with the abuse from his father, he internalized all of that negative energy and believed it was his fault, taking him into the depths of unworthiness."

Sharon's eyes filled with tears. "He always blamed himself for everything."

"What I'm discovering, Mom, is that my sensitivity - which felt like a curse to me - might actually be a gift. With Maggie's guidance, I'm learning to...I don't know, transform how I handle all those overwhelming feelings."

Sharon leaned forward, her tears momentarily forgotten as she listened intently.

"Instead of absorbing others' pain and drowning in it, I'm finding ways to be present with it, to accept that it is a part of their journey. Their experience doesn't have to be mine; their opinion of me doesn't have to be how I see myself."

Dr. Deera nodded, recognizing the profound shift in Chris's understanding.

"When someone, like Dad, wants to put me down or hurt me, I can change how I see it. I can see their actions as coming from their fear, their need to control me to feel better about themselves. It has nothing to do with my value as a person." Chris took a deep breath, glancing at both adults before continuing. "I want to help people feel better, but I can't fix everyone's problems. Maggie says to first understand that people's suffering is part of their learning, then focus on creating a better feeling moment for myself. When I feel better, it helps others see what that looks like, but they don't have to choose it."

Dr. Deera added thoughtfully, "I have to admit, Sharon, much of the way I've been caring for Chris has come from my own conversations with Maggie. I know how that sounds, but I've witnessed something profound happening here."

Sharon stared at him. "You've...talked to her too?"

"I have. And she's helped me see both your son as well as myself in ways that all my training and experience as a psychiatrist couldn't. That's why I am confident that Chris has the perspective and tools to create a joyful and fulfilling life, even though he, like us all, will continue to face challenging situations."

"Listening to you two talk has been enlightening for me," Sharon said. "I feel myself relaxing just being in the room with you."

Dr. Deera smiled. "I would like to see Chris in my office once a week for the next three weeks, then we can decrease the frequency to once a month. Will that work for you?"

Sharon nodded. "I have a job and will be working now, and Chris starts his senior year at school next week. Can our appointments be late afternoon or early evening?"

"I think we can make that happen," Dr. Deera replied. "My secretary will give you a call to set up the appointments."

Chris stood, looking at both adults. "Thank you, Dr. Deera. For everything. And for believing in what you couldn't see."

Sharon rose as well, gathering her purse. As they walked through the unit toward the exit, Chris stopped to say goodbye to the people who had become part of his journey. He hugged Mrs. Patterson gently. "Take care of yourself. Remember, you're more than your struggles."

He found Carlos still sketching. "Keep drawing, Carlos. And remember what we talked about. Ask Maggie for help when you need it."

Carlos looked up with a small smile. "I will. Good luck out there, Chris."

At the nurses' station, Chris shook hands with Dr. Taft. "Thank you for taking care of me when I couldn't take care of myself."

Even Nurse Karen managed a grudging smile. "Take care, Chris. I have to admit, I'm amazed by how far you've come."

"Are you ready to go home, Chris?" Sharon asked as they reached the exit.

"More than ready," he replied, his voice full of quiet confidence.

Later that afternoon, Dr. Deera sat at a conference table with Nurse Karen, Dr. Taft, Dr. Lewis, and Janet, the evening shift head nurse. The fluorescent lights hummed overhead as coffee cups and patient charts created a familiar backdrop to their discussion.

"I know you all have things to do, but I wanted to take a short time to discuss what we've experienced with Chris in the last week," Dr. Deera began, his voice thoughtful. "I'm also interested in how much you value your intuition in caring for the patients here, beyond what is the usual or ordinary way to treat them."

He paused, looking at each colleague in turn. "And lastly, I'm curious what value you place on the healing capacity of unconditional love in service to our roles here in the behavioral health unit."

Dr. Taft shifted in his chair, clearly uncomfortable with the direction of the conversation. "Mark, Chris's recovery has been remarkable, but we can't ignore standard protocols. He was talking to empty chairs, claiming to see deceased people. In any textbook case, that would warrant..."

"Antipsychotics and mood stabilizers," Dr. Lewis interjected, but his voice carried uncertainty. "I mean, that's what the guidelines say, but..."

Dr. Deera cut in, "The key word there is 'guidelines' not laws or absolute rules."

Nurse Karen crossed her arms. "I've been concerned about this approach from the beginning. Patients need structure, medication compliance, evidence-based treatment. Not...whatever this was."

"Karen, I might be mistaken, but I sense you are afraid that if you don't follow the rules, mistakes will be made and some adverse outcome will occur. Am I wrong?"

"No, you're not wrong. I am more comfortable following established protocols."

"But what if protocols themselves could limit healing?" Dr. Lewis asked hesitantly. "I mean, Chris is functional, connecting with people, showing empathy. Isn't that what we want?"

Dr. Taft looked at the young resident. "Dr. Lewis, we can't just abandon evidence-based medicine because one patient had an unusual outcome."

"I'm not suggesting we abandon anything," Dr. Deera responded. "I'm asking whether we should expand our therapeutic options, rather than limiting them, to enhance the possibility of favorable outcomes."

Karen frowned. "But Chris was having delusions. That required..."

"Did it?" Dr. Lewis interrupted, surprising himself with his boldness. "I keep thinking about what you said, Dr. Deera, about children having imaginary friends. We don't medicate them for that."

"That's different," Karen said quickly.

"But why?" Dr. Lewis pressed. "Because we've decided children are allowed to have spiritual experiences, but adults aren't?"

Janet, who had been quiet up to this point, spoke. "I've been working evenings this week, and I have to say, Chris's presence on the ward changed things. Other patients seemed calmer when he was around."

Dr. Deera nodded. "I think it matters when a person's experience is lifting them up, allowing them to function more effectively, as opposed to pushing them down into despair and disfunction. Chris found healing through his connection with Maggie. He is functional, purposeful, and connecting with others in meaningful ways."

Dr. Lewis leaned forward. "That's what I keep coming back to. The outcome. He's better by every measure we typically use."

Dr. Taft shifted uncomfortably. "But how do we know it will last? How do we measure spiritual healing?"

"How do we know any treatment will last?" Dr. Lewis asked. "We follow up, we stay connected, we adjust as needed. Same as always."

"Spiritual healing shows up in thoughts, feelings, and actions," Dr. Deera added. "Thinking unity over separation, feeling joy and peace, acting with compassionate kindness. We can observe those things."

Karen looked uncertain. "But what about liability? What if other patients start claiming to see dead relatives?"

"Then we evaluate each case individually, looking at function and outcomes rather than just symptoms," Dr. Lewis suggested, gaining confidence. "We use our clinical judgment."

Dr. Deera smiled at the young doctor's growing understanding. "Professional judgment turns diagnostic criteria from rigid rules into suggestions. It allows us to treat the whole person, not just the diagnosis."

The room grew quiet as his colleagues considered this.

"I appreciate all of your individual perspectives and strengths," Dr. Deera concluded. "I believe as a team we can bring them together to be most effective serving our patients."

Dr. Lewis nodded thoughtfully. "Maybe we need to be more open to unconventional healing when conventional methods aren't working."

Janet added quietly, "I've seen a lot of patients over the years. Sometimes the ones who get better fastest are the ones who find something to believe in, something bigger than their diagnosis."

Even Karen seemed to soften slightly. "I still think we need protocols, but...maybe there's room for more flexibility when the outcomes are positive."

*****

The ride home from the hospital was quiet. Sharon gripped the steering wheel, her mind racing ahead to what awaited them. Chris stared out the window, unable to focus on the present moment, caught between what just happened and what would come next. He was aware of how tired his body felt - an actual physical weariness that came from extended, long-term stress even though much of the stress had eased.

Sharon pulled into the driveway just as David and Charlie rode up on their bikes. Charlie dropped his bike and ran quickly toward his brother. "Hey, Chris. I'm really glad you're home." Chris nodded, his hands in his pockets, not quite meeting Charlie's eyes. "Yeah. Thanks."

Charlie hesitated, then added quietly, "I was scared."

"I know," Chris said, his voice rough, looking deep into Charlie's eyes. "I'm sorry."

Charlie rushed forward again and wrapped his arms around his brother in a tight hug. Chris hugged him back, feeling deep love and relief. Sharon watched, her heart opening as she took a deep breath, her shoulders relaxing.

As they broke from the hug, Charlie said, "I have to say again, Chris, how glad I am you're home. I have so many things I want to talk to you about."

Chris replied, "I'm looking forward to talking to you, too. A lot of crazy sounding things have been happening."

"Great." Charlie paused, then gestured toward David. "I want you to meet my best friend, David."

Chris looked at David, his eyes squinting, trying to remember where he had seen him before. "I feel like I've met you before."

"In our dream," David said simply.

"Oh yeah, now I remember. Nice to see you again."

Chris entered the house and paused just inside the door. He noticed that his mom had moved some furniture around and covered his father's bar with a cloth and flowers. He appreciated the effort, but the house still felt heavy with everything that had happened here. The walls remembered, even if the couch was in a different spot.

"It looks...different," he said carefully.

"I was trying to change the feeling of the place, one step at a time," Sharon said. "I think it's going to take many more steps. I want everything to be all right. I made some cookies and lemonade to celebrate your homecoming." She paused, her voice uncertain. "Am I trying too hard to make things right?"

He heard Maggie's voice say, *"I AM here. Let's create some new feelings."* He noticed himself smiling and thinking, *this is perfect.* "This is perfect, Mom. It's fine. You know how much I love chocolate chip cookies." David chimed in enthusiastically, "Me too!" as they headed toward the kitchen.

Chapter 25: Connections

Friday Evening, August 29

Mr. Lucas rang the bell at Sharon's house. When she opened the door, he announced with a grin, "Pizza delivery!"

Sharon smiled, "Come on in Larry." She glanced at her watch. 6:15. The AA meeting started at seven, and she still needed to drive across town. "The kitchen is this way."

"Charlie! Chris! Mr. Lucas is here!"

The sound of footsteps on the stairs - one set quick and light, the other slower, more hesitant - then Charlie appeared in the kitchen doorway. He immediately opened his arms to Larry. They embraced warmly, their connection evident to everyone in the room.

Chris followed more slowly, his body still recovering from the extended stress. He was quieter and more reserved as he entered the kitchen.

"You must be Chris," Larry said, extending his hand. "I look forward to getting to know you."

Chris stepped forward and took Larry's hand, his grip firm despite the wariness in his eyes. "Nice to meet you."

"Thanks for coming over this evening," Sharon said, grabbing her keys from the hook by the door. "I should be back by eight fifteen."

She caught Chris's eye, and he gave her a small nod. They had talked about this - about her going to meetings, about Larry being here, about the careful rebuilding they were all doing.

As Sharon headed toward the door, Charlie called after her, "Have fun!"

She paused and looked back at him. "Are you kidding?"

Charlie grinned. "Why not?"

"We'll be fine," Mr. Lucas said, his voice carrying the steady reassurance Sharon needed to hear. He nodded thoughtfully. "I know you boys don't need me here, but since this is your first day back home, it would really help your mother feel better." He smiled. "You guys ready for some pizza?"

"What kind is it?" Charlie asked.

"Your mom told me you like anchovies."

"Oh," Charlie and Chris responded in unison, trying not to turn their noses up.

Mr. Lucas chuckled, "I'm kidding, it's pepperoni with extra cheese."

"Alright!" Charlie said with a big smile. "I'll get some plates."

Chris took two root beers out of the refrigerator for Charlie and himself, then turned to Mr. Lucas. "What would you like to drink?"

"Do you have an extra root beer?"

"Sure do."

Once they were all seated around the kitchen table, Mr. Lucas looked at Chris. "Has your brother told you about our camping trip last weekend? Some amazing things happened."

Chris glanced at Charlie, then back at Mr. Lucas. "I just got home from the hospital today and we haven't had that much time to talk."

"Welcome home, Chris. I'm glad you're here." Mr. Lucas turned to Charlie. "Why don't you tell Chris about the unusual things that happened while camping out this past weekend?"

Charlie's eyes lit up immediately. He launched into the story with dramatic gestures and exaggerated voices. "...and then Mr. Lucas came out of the woods holding a fox wrapped up in his shirt!" Charlie threw his arms wide to demonstrate.

Chris looked skeptical. "A fox? Just let you hold it?"

"I'm telling you, it happened!" Charlie insisted, grinning at Mr. Lucas for confirmation. Even Chris found himself smiling at his brother's enthusiasm.

When Charlie finally caught his breath, Mr. Lucas turned to Chris with genuine curiosity. "How about you, Chris? Is there anything you'd like to share about your hospital experience?"

Chris paused, a slice of pizza halfway to his mouth. He put it down and looked at Mr. Lucas carefully. There was something about the older man's quiet attention that felt different from what he was used to.

"I met someone there," Chris said slowly. "Dr. Deera's sister Maggie. She died when she was fifteen." He glanced at their faces. Charlie nodded knowingly, Mr. Lucas listened with interest. "I know how it sounds, but I could see her and talk to her. She helped me understand things about myself."

"The other doctors and nurses just saw me talking to an empty chair," Chris continued. "They thought I was losing it. But Dr. Deera could see her too - his own sister. And then this artist, another patient, drew a picture of her. Perfect likeness. Dr. Deera saw it and said, 'That's my sister Maggie.'"

Chris picked up his root beer. "The staff kept waiting for Dr. Deera to put me on medication, but he didn't. He listened to me. There was this woman Rachel who worked there too..."

"Rachel's great," Charlie said with a grin. "She had us over for dinner."

Chris looked at his brother with a small smile, then turned to Mr. Lucas. "She didn't see me as broken either." He looked between Charlie and Mr. Lucas. "It was the most real thing that's ever happened to me."

Charlie reached over and gave his brother's arm a quick squeeze. "It doesn't sound crazy to me. When I couldn't talk right, everyone treated me like something was wrong with me. But David and Mr. Lucas just...saw me differently."

Chris turned back to Mr. Lucas with genuine curiosity. "Charlie mentioned something else amazing happened on your camping trip?"

Mr. Lucas set down his pizza, his expression shifting to something between wonder and disbelief. "Well, Charlie told you about the fox. But something else happened that I still can't quite wrap my head around." He glanced at Charlie, who nodded encouragingly.

"A chickadee landed in Charlie's hands. Just flew down and perched there, looking at both of us. And then..." Mr. Lucas paused, as if testing whether he should continue. "It spoke to me. Not out loud, but I heard it clearly in my mind, *'I am glad you are open to learning more about the joy of playing the Love Game. David is a true way-shower.'*" He looked at Chris directly. "I value science, what I can see and measure. This was completely outside that realm. But it happened. Charlie was right there."

"It did happen," Charlie confirmed. "The chickadee looked right at Mr. Lucas when it said that."

Chris nodded slowly, something in his posture relaxing. "Like Maggie appearing to help me. Or that artist drawing her without ever seeing her."

"Exactly," Mr. Lucas said.

The sound of the garage door opening broke into their conversation. All three of them looked up, startled.

"Is it eight-fifteen already?" Mr. Lucas checked his watch, surprised.

Sharon walked in, setting down her keys. "Hi guys, how was your time together?"

"I had a great time. I really enjoyed talking to the boys," Mr. Lucas responded. "They shared some remarkable experiences."

"It was awesome! Chris talked about how Maggie helped him and Mr. Lucas told us about his reaction to meeting Chickadee," Charlie exclaimed.

"I've longed for interacting the way we did," Chris said. "It was a breath of fresh air."

Sharon smiled. "The meeting went well too. For the first time, I felt like I could actually help someone else instead of just taking. Rachel was there. She's always such an inspiration."

"That's wonderful, Sharon," Mr. Lucas said. "Actually, that reminds me - I was thinking the boys might enjoy helping out at the humane society with me tomorrow. We could use some extra hands."

Charlie bounced in his seat. "Really? Mom, please can we go?"

"I'd like that," Chris said quietly.

Sharon looked at her sons - Charlie's enthusiasm, Chris's cautious interest - and felt something shift. "That sounds great. I'm starting at the florist shop tomorrow, so the timing works out perfectly."

"I'll pick them up at nine," Mr. Lucas said. "Should be a good day."

Chapter 26: Transformation

Saturday Morning, August 30

Crystal was making her rounds at the hospital, but when she entered Nathan's room, she stopped short. Nathan was sitting up in a chair - not lying in bed for the first time in a week - coloring and talking quietly to himself. The crystal sat beside his coloring book.

"Nathan?" Crystal stepped closer, hardly believing what she was seeing. "You're out of bed."

He looked up with a brightness in his eyes she hadn't seen since his admission. "I'm feeling better. Can I get something to eat?"

Crystal blinked, her throat tightening. "Of course. What would you like?"

"Chocolate pudding."

She nodded, not trusting her voice for a moment. "I think we can arrange that."

Nathan returned to his coloring, adding careful strokes of blue to what looked like a sky. "Dr. Welling, did you know Angela was an artist?"

"Yes, I did."

"She drew a picture of me with Dr. Deera." He didn't look up from his coloring. "Angela told me that I'm a creator. That I can use my imagination to create feelings." He paused, considering his next color choice. "She taught me about the Love Game. Do you know how to play?"

Crystal knelt beside his chair so she could see his face. "Tell me more."

"I can create peace, love, and joy right now, in this moment. I don't have to wait for something to happen." He looked at her directly. "I don't even have to wait until the cancer goes away."

Crystal felt tears prick her eyes. This withdrawn child who hadn't spoken more than a few words in days was suddenly explaining a profound truth about living in the present.

"Nathan, would you like to take a walk with me?"

He nodded and reached for her hand. As they passed the nursing station, Crystal asked a nurse to bring chocolate pudding to the playroom - two cups.

They walked slowly down the hall, Nathan's steps careful but determined. When they passed a room with an open door, he leaned in. "Hi!"

The patient inside looked up, startled, then smiled.

A nurse coming out of another room froze when she saw Nathan walking. "Nathan? Oh, my goodness, look at you!"

"It's nice to get out of my room for a change," he said simply.

Crystal squeezed his hand, watching him greet the world again.

They were halfway down the hall when Nathan's parents emerged through the unit's double door entrance. His mother stopped in her tracks, her hand going to her mouth. His father's eyes widened in surprise.

"Nathan?" His mother rushed forward, dropping to her knees to pull him into her arms. "You're walking. You're...oh my God, you're walking."

She looked up at Crystal, tears streaming down her face. "What does this mean? Is he...is he getting better?"

Crystal chose her words carefully. "Nathan has had a surge of energy. I can't make predictions about his condition, but something has shifted for him."

"What happened?" his father asked, one hand on Nathan's shoulder as if to confirm he was really there.

Nathan looked up at them. "I've been talking to Angela. She taught me a game."

"A game?" his mother asked, confused.

"It's called the Love Game," Nathan explained. "You try to find love in everything, even when things are hard. You don't have to wait to feel better."

His parents looked at Crystal for help understanding.

"From what I understand," Crystal said, "Nathan has found a way to be present with joy despite his circumstances. To create peace for himself in this moment, rather than waiting for his situation to change."

"But the cancer..." his father started.

Nathan tugged on his father's hand. "I know I'm still sick, Dad. But I don't have to be sad every second. Angela showed me that."

His mother pressed her fingers to her lips, fresh tears coming. "Oh, sweetheart."

His father laughed through his own tears and pulled Nathan into a hug.

Nathan said, "Let's go back to my room. I want to show you what I've been coloring."

As Nathan and his father headed down the hall, his mother caught Crystal's arm, her voice dropping to a whisper. "Dr. Welling, what does this mean? This surge of energy. Is he getting better?"

"I honestly don't know, and I wish I could give you a clearer answer. It may be a temporary surge before his organs shut down. I'll run some blood tests - a complete blood count to check his leukemia markers and kidney and liver functions - to see if we can get a better understanding of what's happening. I'll meet you back in the room."

She watched them disappear into Nathan's room, then stopped at the nursing station to order the blood tests.

Later that afternoon, Crystal's phone rang as she was reviewing patient charts.

"Dr. Welling? This is Linda from the lab. I have Nathan Johnson's blood work results and...well, they're not what I expected."

Crystal sat forward. "Go ahead."

"His white blood cell count has stabilized for the first time in weeks. Liver enzymes have actually improved slightly, and his eGFR shows marginal improvement in kidney function. I ran everything twice because I thought there might be an error."

Crystal sat back slowly. "The deterioration has stopped."

"For now, yes. The improvements are modest, but the decline we've been tracking for weeks has halted."

After ending the call, Crystal stared at Nathan's chart for a long moment before calling Mark.

"Mark, Nathan's labs came back."

"The boy Rachel visited?"

"His counts have stabilized. Not dramatically improved but declining has stopped." She paused. "Kids with his level of organ involvement don't do this, Mark. They don't just...pause."

"But he has."

"He's walking the halls, talking to everyone, asking for chocolate pudding. It's like he's a different child." Crystal's voice carried both wonder and uncertainty. "I'm trying to stay grounded in medical reality, but something beyond our usual understanding is happening here."

Mark was quiet for a moment. "Are you going to tell his parents?"

"I'll share the results. But I need to be careful - this could still be temporary. I don't want to promise a miracle." She glanced toward Nathan's room. "Even if that's what it feels like."

*****

Sharon arrived at Flora's shop fifteen minutes early, her hands trembling slightly as she reached for the door. The bell chimed as she entered and the scent of fresh flowers immediately surrounded her - roses, lilies, something sweet she couldn't quite name.

Flora looked up from a workbench covered in pink roses and white hydrangeas, her silver hair pulled back in a practical bun. "Sharon! Right on time." She wiped her hands on her apron and came around the counter. "How are you feeling? First day jitters?"

"A little," Sharon admitted. "I haven't worked in seventeen years."

"Well, you're in the right place." Flora gestured to the flowers spread across multiple tables. "We have a wedding delivery today — you'll jump right into the deep end. But don't worry, I'll show you everything you need to know. Let's start with how we load the van so nothing gets damaged."

Sharon nodded, grateful for Flora's matter-of-fact kindness. No questions about why she's been out of work so long, no judgment, just forward motion.

"Come on," Flora said, already heading toward the back. "Let me show you how we keep these beauties safe during transport."

Sharon followed her through the workroom, taking in the organized chaos of ribbons, wire, foam blocks, and buckets of flowers in various stages of arrangement. Flora moved with the efficiency of someone who'd done this for decades.

"The key is proper spacing and stability," Flora explained as they reached the back door where the van was parked. "Flowers are tougher than they look, but one sharp turn can send everything sliding."

Sharon secured the last corsage box in the van, the scent of roses and lilies filling the enclosed space. Table arrangements, bridal party flowers, and two large displays for the ceremony arch - everything Flora had been working on for days was finally ready.

"That's the last of the small pieces," Flora said. "Now for the bride's bouquet. Sharon, can you grab that special holder from the workbench?"

Sharon retrieved the water-filled container, handling it carefully. This was her first day, and she was determined not to make a mistake. It had been seventeen years since she had a job, seventeen years since she made her own money or had somewhere to be that was just hers.

Flora lifted the bridal bouquet of pink roses nested among white lilies, wrapped in ivory silk ribbon and positioned it in the holder. "There. That'll keep the stems hydrated during the drive."

"It's beautiful," Sharon said, meaning it.

"The bride chose well. Classic, elegant." Flora glanced at Sharon. "First day, first wedding delivery. You picked a good one to start with."

Sharon nodded, feeling nervous but also something else; something unfamiliar. For the first time in years, she'd chosen something for herself. Not what Les demanded, not what she had to do to survive, just a simple choice to work with flowers and be part of someone's celebration.

"Let's go make someone's day," Flora said, closing the van doors.

The drive to the resort took them through winding country roads, past fields of late summer wildflowers and tall grasses turning golden. Sharon watched the landscape slip by, still getting used to the idea that she was actually doing this - working, contributing, choosing her own path.

"You're quiet," Flora observed.

"Just taking it all in." Sharon glanced at the flowers secured in the back. "I keep thinking I'm going to wake up and find out this is a dream."

Flora smiled. "It's real. And you're doing fine."

The day was a comfortable seventy-five degrees with cloudless blue skies, perfect late summer wedding weather. Flora talked Sharon through what to expect - an outdoor ceremony on the lawn overlooking the lake, reception under a pavilion, resort staff handling setup while they placed the flowers.

When they arrived, Sharon stepped out of the van and stopped. White chairs were arranged in precise rows facing an archway draped with sheer fabric that moved gently in the breeze. Beyond it, the lake stretched out like glass. Round tables covered with white linens waited under the pavilion, empty spaces at their centers ready for Flora's arrangements.

"Beautiful, isn't it?" Flora said, already gathering the bridal bouquet and personal flowers. "Never gets old, seeing people celebrate love."

Sharon nodded, something catching in her throat. She spent years in a marriage where love felt like survival. Seeing all this hope and joy laid out so carefully - it meant something different now.

"Come on," Flora said gently. "Let's find the wedding planner and get these to the bridal party."

They located her near the bridal suite, a woman in her forties with a headset and tablet, radiating controlled efficiency. "Perfect timing," she said, accepting the boutonnieres and corsages. "The bridesmaids are almost ready."

"Now we can focus on the displays," Flora said as they walked back toward the ceremony site. "Let's start with the altar arrangements."

Sharon carefully positioned the larger arrangements on either side of the archway. As she adjusted them to sit level, she noticed how the pink and white flowers stood out against the lake and trees beyond. There was something satisfying about getting it just right, seeing how the pieces came together.

"Perfect," Flora commented. "Now the reception tables. Each centerpiece goes in the exact center. See those small marks on the tablecloths?"

They worked their way through the tables, and Sharon found herself falling into a rhythm. Her hands were steadier than expected. Each placement mattered - she could see how the flowers changed the space, making it ready for celebration.

They were nearly finished when a caterer rushed past with a tray of glasses, bumping a table. The centerpiece tipped, spilling water and flowers across the white linen.

"Oh no! I'm so sorry!" The woman looked mortified.

Sharon was already kneeling before she consciously decided to move. Her hands gathered the scattered blooms, checking stems for damage. In her old life, she would have frozen, waiting for someone to tell her what to do, worried about doing it wrong. But right now, she just knew what needed to happen. Within minutes, she had the arrangement reassembled and the tablecloth cleared.

"There," she said, adjusting the final spray of greenery.

Flora had been watching. "You've done this before."

"No, I really haven't." Sharon stood, surprised at herself.

"Could have fooled me. When my assistant was in the car accident last week, I thought I'd have to cancel this wedding. Then you walked in." Flora smiled. "Perfect timing."

Sharon again felt something unfamiliar: trust without criticism, competence without someone second-guessing her every move.

They finished the last few tables in comfortable silence. When Sharon stepped back to look at the completed space, she felt a quiet pride. She had helped create this.

"How does it feel?" Flora asked.

Sharon considered. "Like I'm actually good at something and could keep doing this."

"You could. You should." Flora started packing the empty containers. "We've got the afternoon free. Want to help me prep for Tuesday's orders? Monday is Labor Day. We'll be open, but it'll be quieter."

On the drive back, Sharon watched the fields pass, already thinking about what other arrangements she might learn. Tomorrow the shop would be closed, but Tuesday she'd be back. The thought made her smile.

When they returned to the shop, Flora unlocked the door. She had posted a sign saying they'd return at 1:00. She took it down and said, "Let's get these containers cleaned and prepped for Tuesday's orders."

As Sharon rinsed buckets and reorganized supplies, with the cool water running over her hands, something shifted inside her. This wasn't simply a job she liked. Working with flowers, creating beauty for people's most important moments - it already felt like she'd found something she was always meant to do. She wasn't just looking forward to Tuesday. She was already thinking about what she might learn next, what arrangements she would create and master, how many celebrations she would help make beautiful.

For the first time in longer than she could remember, Sharon felt like she was exactly where she belonged.

*****

On the drive to the Humane Society, Charlie bounced in his seat with excitement while Chris sat quietly, looking out the window. Mr. Lucas glanced at him in the rearview mirror, remembering what Sharon told him about Chris's love of animals - all those books he read, the nature shows he watched. Today might be the first time he got to actually work with some.

As they pulled into the parking lot, several volunteers were walking dogs along a nearby path, the animals eager for exercise and attention.

"Ready for your first day as volunteers?" Mr. Lucas asked as they got out of the car.

Charlie nodded enthusiastically, but Chris hung back, quieter and more observant.

As they entered the main building, sounds hit them immediately – dogs barking, whining, the rustle of movement. Chris stopped, taking it all in. Where most people might have found the noise overwhelming, he seemed drawn to it. Mr. Lucas noticed his attention fix on an open doorway down the hall. Through it, they could see a veterinarian struggling with a medium-sized dog on an examining table. The dog was squirming and growling, clearly unhappy.

"Fran," Mr. Lucas called to the volunteer coordinator, "do you think Chris could watch Dr. Madigan work? He seems interested."

Fran smiled. "I think that would be fine." She walked Chris to the examination room. "Dr. Madigan, this is Chris. He'd like to observe if that's alright."

The veterinarian looked up briefly, her hands busy restraining the dog. "Nice to meet you, Chris. I'm trying to clip this fellow's nails, but he's not cooperating."

Chris stepped closer. The dog's distress washed over him - not the chaotic tangle of human emotions that usually overwhelmed him, but something clearer. Simpler. He could feel the dog's fear, but also something underneath it. Without thinking, he reached out slowly and rested his hand on the dog's back.

The dog's head swiveled toward Chris. For a moment, nothing happened. Then the growling stopped. The dog's body relaxed, muscles loosening under Chris's palm. His brown eyes fixed on Chris with something that looked like trust.

Dr. Madigan paused, glancing between Chris and the dog. "Well. That's new." She studied Chris for a moment. "Would you mind staying close while I finish?"

Chris nodded, keeping his hand steady. The dog remained perfectly calm as Dr. Madigan clipped the nails and administered vaccinations. Chris felt something he'd never experienced before, like he was having a conversation without words, understanding what the animal needed and somehow providing it.

"Thank you," Dr. Madigan said when she finished. "That would normally have taken twice as long with a lot more stress for everyone involved."

Meanwhile, Mr. Lucas was walking Charlie down the main aisle to show him the feeding routine. As they moved through the kennel area, Charlie read each dog's name aloud, stopping to say hello. Most dogs were standing at their cage doors, tails wagging, hoping for attention. Charlie swore he could hear them saying 'adopt me, take me home.'

At the end of the row, Charlie spotted a small dog lying in the back corner of her pen, facing away.

"Mr. Lucas, why is that dog lying in the back? Is she sick?"

Fran, having left Chris with Dr. Madigan, joined them and shook her head. "She's been here for weeks. No one wants to adopt her because she shows no interest when people visit. She cowers if anyone gets too close." She pointed to faded scars visible through the dog's multicolored coat. "She was found on the roadside. Looks like she'd been beaten."

"How old is she?" Charlie asked quietly.

"About two, we think. Miniature Australian Shepherd."

Charlie could see the dog had one blue eye and one brown eye, but they both looked dull. Her normally fluffy coat was a patchwork of blue-gray, black, and white, but she was curled up as small as possible. A small sign on the cage door read, "Hope."

Without a word, Charlie walked to the pen and sat down cross-legged in front of the door.

Mr. Lucas started to speak, but Fran touched his arm and shook her head. They watched.

Hope lifted her head slightly, her mismatched eyes focusing on the boy. Charlie didn't move. Didn't speak. Just sat.

A minute passed. Two. Three.

Slowly, Hope uncurled herself. She stood, then padded toward the door. Her fluffy tail gave the slightest wag. She sat on her side of the gate, mirroring Charlie's position.

"That dog has never shown interest in anyone," Fran whispered. "Never."

Mr. Lucas moved quietly to the pen door. "Let's open it."

Charlie scooted back just enough for the gate to swing open. Hope stepped out carefully, sniffed the air once, then walked directly into Charlie's lap and curled up. She looked into his eyes with an expression that seemed to say, 'Now I'm home.'

Charlie's face transformed. "Can I give her a treat?"

Mr. Lucas handed him one from his pocket. Charlie held it flat in his palm. Hope's pink tongue gently licked it up.

Charlie stroked her soft merle coat, and Hope's tail began wagging in earnest.

*****

Back in the examination room, Dr. Madigan brought in an anxious cat that typically required sedation. Chris worked with her for about five minutes, moving slowly, keeping his voice low and steady. The cat eventually allowed the exam without incident.

Then a rabbit was brought in, having been found injured and terrified of human contact. Chris barely moved, projecting calm until the rabbit accepted his presence.

With each animal, Mr. Lucas watched from the doorway, seeing something remarkable unfold.

After the fourth successful interaction, Dr. Madigan set down her instruments and looked at Chris directly. "I've been doing this for fifteen years. I've never seen anything like what you do."

Chris looked thoughtful. "I've always been sensitive to emotions. It overwhelms me with people, but this feels different."

Dr. Madigan nodded slowly, clearly thinking about something.

Meanwhile, Charlie spent the next hour with Hope, learning where she liked to be petted, watching her slowly trust him completely. Then Mr. Lucas held up some cleaning supplies. "Think you can clean Hope's pen, then work your way down the line?"

Charlie nodded, gently coaxing Hope off his lap and back inside so he could clean thoroughly. She watched him the entire time, tail wagging whenever he looked her way.

Around noon, Mr. Lucas went out for sandwiches. When he returned, both boys were exactly where he left them - Chris with the animals, Charlie working his way through the pens with Hope watching his every move.

The afternoon continued. Chris worked with Dr. Madigan on several more cases, each one confirming what Mr. Lucas suspected - the empathic sensitivity that made Chris vulnerable around people was exactly what traumatized animals needed.

At 3:30, Dr. Madigan was finished for the day. As she packed her equipment, she turned to Chris.

"Chris, I'd like you to consider something." She paused. "I need someone at my veterinary clinic who can do what you do. We handle emergency cases evenings and weekends. Would you be interested in working there?"

Chris's eyes widened. "You want me to work there?"

"I've watched you all day. You have a gift." She handed him her business card. "Talk it over with your mother. Call me when you're ready."

"Thank you, Dr. Madigan." Chris carefully held the card, his hand quivering with awe.

Meanwhile, Charlie was kneeling by Hope's cage. "I'll come back," he whispered, pressing his hand against the door. Hope poked her nose through the mesh to touch his fingers.

On the drive home, the boys were quiet.

"You both seem thoughtful," Mr. Lucas observed.

"I'm sad," Charlie said. "I feel bad that Hope is alone."

"Yeah," Chris agreed. He pulled out his phone. "Mom? We're on our way home."

"Great, honey. How was your day?"

"Really good. We're going to stop and get food, so you don't have to worry about dinner."

"Perfect. See you soon."

They arrived home around 4:00. When Sharon walked in an hour later, McDonald's bags covered the kitchen table. Mr. Lucas stayed, and everyone began talking at once - Sharon about her first day with flowers, Chris about Dr. Madigan's offer, Charlie about Hope.

But Mr. Lucas noticed the moments between the words. The way Chris kept looking over at the business card on the table. How Charlie's voice changed whenever he said Hope's name. How Sharon's eyes filled with tears when she realized both her sons had found something that called to them.

"So what do you think, Mom?" Chris asked, holding the business card. "About the job?"

Sharon looked at her son - really looked at him. A week ago he was in the hospital. Now he was asking about working with animals, his face alive in a way she hadn't seen in years.

"I think," she said slowly, "that you should call Dr. Madigan on Tuesday and tell her yes."

Chris's smile could light the room.

"And Mom," Charlie said carefully. "I met this dog today. Her name is Hope." As Charlie described her - the mismatched eyes, how she came right to him - Sharon watched her son's face transform with the telling.

"She sounds special," Sharon said.

"Can we go back and see her tomorrow?" Charlie asked.

Sharon hesitated, but something in Charlie's expression made her nod. "I think we can do that."

Mr. Lucas said his goodbyes and stood to leave. Sharon walked him to the door.

"Thank you," she said. "For today. For showing them possibilities."

"They found those themselves," Mr. Lucas said. "I just drove."

But as he walked to his car, he thought about what he witnessed earlier - two boys discovering what called to them, a mother learning to say yes to her sons' joy. Sometimes people just needed someone to show them where the door was. They'd walk through it on their own.

Chapter 27: Hope and Love

Sunday morning, August 31

Hank arrived early to the Sunday school classroom, eager to share what he considered shocking news. When David entered, all eyes turned toward him.

Mr. Rigid, the Sunday School teacher, came in carrying his lesson materials and noticed the charged atmosphere. "Good morning, class. Let's open our Bibles to…"

"Mr. Rigid," Hank interrupted, his hand shooting up. "We need to talk about something important."

Mr. Rigid paused, clearly irritated by the interruption. "What is it, Hank?"

"David claimed God talks to him. Like, actually talks to him. And that he can see God, too."

The classroom erupted in murmurs. Mr. Rigid's jaw tightened. He looked at David. "Is that what you've been telling people?"

"Yes," David replied.

Mr. Rigid set his Bible down with deliberate care. "Well. That's… David, many people feel God's presence through prayer and scripture. That's different from claiming direct communication."

"But he says God answers his questions," Hank pressed. "Out loud."

Several students leaned forward, genuinely curious now. One girl asked, "What does God sound like, David?"

David considered. "Love speaks through my heart, not my head. It's more like knowing than hearing."

"See?" Mr. Rigid said, seizing on this. "That's called intuition, David. We all have that. Now, let's get back to today's lesson."

"But what does God look like?" another student asked.

"We really need to move on with…"

"Is it like a person? Or like a light?" The questions kept coming.

Mr. Rigid's face flushed. He was losing control of his classroom, and David was the reason. "Class, that's enough. David's experiences are his own. We're here to study Scripture, which is God's actual word to us. Now…"

"But if David can talk to God," a boy in the back piped up, "why do we need to study?"

"Because," Mr. Rigid said, his voice rising, "scripture is how God speaks to all of us. Not through…feelings or visions or whatever David thinks he's experiencing."

David spoke quietly. "I'm here for the experience and to play the Love Game."

"The what?" Mr. Rigid stared at him.

"The Love Game. It's about seeing Love in everything and everyone."

Mr. Rigid's patience snapped. "You're not here to learn how to live a better life? To overcome your sinful nature?"

"Love tells me I don't need to be better. I'm already perfect."

Several students laughed. Mr. Rigid's face went from red to almost purple.

"This is exactly the problem. You think you're perfect? None of us is perfect, David. We are all sinners. That's the fundamental truth of Christianity."

David remained calm. "Love tells me a different story."

"Your heart is unreliable," Mr. Rigid said sharply. "Feelings change. Scripture doesn't. That's why we study it."

"I respect that's what you believe," David said. "It's wonderful if it works for you. But when I tell Love's story, I feel perfect."

Something broke in Mr. Rigid. His lesson plan was abandoned. His authority was undermined. And this child was sitting there claiming to be perfect, claiming to hear from God directly, making Mr. Rigid's years of Bible study seem…unnecessary.

"David, I think it's best that you leave today." His voice shook with suppressed anger. "I'll talk to your father about this later."

The room went silent.

David's eyes filled with tears. "Are you…asking me to leave? You're kicking me out?"

"I think that would be best. Your presence is disruptive."

David stood slowly, his hands trembling. He walked toward the door in silence, tears streaming down his face.

After the door closed behind him, Mr. Rigid took a deep breath and opened his Bible with shaking hands. "Today we're going to talk about John 8:7. Hank, why don't you read the scripture for the class?"

Hank flipped through his Bible, found the passage, and read aloud, "He that is without sin among you, let him cast the first stone."

After leaving the class, David sat on a bench outside, wiping his face. "Angela, are you here?"

"*Always, Davidlove. I AM here.*"

"I feel bad. I feel unwanted." His voice broke. "It's like second grade when the teacher sent me to the principal's office for talking out of turn. She said I was disruptive and she didn't want me there. Or when Butch told me they didn't want me playing baseball because I was too small and wasn't good enough. I don't want to feel bad, but fear takes over and I forget all about the Love Game."

"*'There's value in feeling sad and afraid,'*" Angela said gently. "*It's another reminder that you're alive. It helps you redirect your focus to create a new reality. Let it be until you're ready to tell a new story.*" She paused. "*What do you want to feel right now?*"

"I want to feel better."

"Then what story can you tell? How can you see this situation in a way that will help you feel better?"

David thought, sniffling. "I could...I could see that Mr. Rigid was scared to have his beliefs challenged. He was probably just playing the survival game and didn't even know he was hurting me. I could remember that even though he asked me to leave, Love didn't leave. Love is still here. Even if he doesn't see it, I could also remember to see him as Love and perfect."

"*There you go, Davidlove.*"

The door to the Bible Study classroom opened. Jesse was talking with Mr. Brown when he noticed David on the bench, his face streaked with tears.

"Bye, Ken. See you later." Jesse walked quickly to David. "David, have you been crying?"

"Yes. Mr. Rigid asked me to leave class. He said I was disruptive and he didn't want me there."

Jesse felt heat rising, his face flushing red, his jaw clenching tight. He took a deep breath. Then another. He sat down beside David and wrapped his arms around him.

"Tell me exactly what happened."

David's restrained tears broke into sobbing as he relayed what happened, feeling safe in his father's arms.

Jesse held him tighter, his own anger carefully contained. "I hear you. I'm here." He took another slow breath. "This needs to be addressed, but not right now. Not when I'm this angry. Let's go home."

"What about church?"

"Not today, David. We're going home." As they walked to the car, Jesse's mind was already working. He would talk to Mr. Rigid. He would talk to the pastor. But he would do it when he could speak clearly and firmly without his anger taking over. David needed him to handle this right, not just as a reaction.

For now, his son needed to know he was believed, protected, and loved. The rest could wait.

*****

Crystal, anxious to know about Nathan, went to the hospital on her day off to check on him. She saw Rachel in the hall with her cleaning cart, her first day on the unit.

"Good morning, Rachel. I'm so glad to have you here. How's your day going so far?"

"Hi, Dr. Welling. I am happy to be here. My morning started off with a challenge, though. I was called to clean up some vomit when a couple of sick kids missed the emesis basins."

"Yeah, that happens around here. Have you seen Nathan yet?"

"I have. He looks so much better than yesterday. I also saw his parents, who kept thanking me. They asked me about the crystal and how it was working."

"What did you tell them?"

"They asked me if I cured him. I said no, I was just hoping he'd feel better. I don't see him as broken, just on a journey. I don't know where his road will take him."

Crystal nodded. "I'm going to go see him right now." She walked down the hall and, after a light tap on the door, entered Nathan's room. His parents were both there, and the mood in the room felt light. Nathan was sitting up with coloring books on the tray table.

"Good morning, everyone." Crystal smiled warmly. "How are you feeling, Nathan?"

"Good morning, Dr. Welling. I feel better today, not as sleepy. Look at the picture I colored."

Dr. Welling looked at the picture and smiled. "I see you put a lot of care into this, Nathan."

"I'm also hungry. Is it okay if my mom brings me some of my favorite foods?"

"As far as I'm concerned, you can have anything you want to eat. What do you like?"

"I really like the fish my dad catches in the stream. He covers them with breadcrumbs and fries them. I like to eat them with french fries and ketchup."

Dr. Welling laughed. "Sounds delicious. Have you been walking today?"

"Sure have. I walked down the hall once yesterday and twice today."

Nathan's dad, Dan, cleared his throat. "Can we talk with you outside?"

Dr. Welling paused thoughtfully. "We can, but I would rather not talk secretly, leaving it to Nathan's imagination. Secret conversations usually suggest something unwanted is happening."

Dan nodded. "I see your point. Well, does this improvement mean he's getting better? The cancer is going away? We want the truth, not false hope."

"I can't predict the future," Crystal said gently. "Nathan's liver and kidney function tests show improvement where they had been steadily declining. His blood count has also been improving. I don't have a medical explanation for this turnaround." She glanced at Nathan. "You can see for yourself how his mood and energy have changed."

"But is it false hope?" Dan asked.

"Hope doesn't predict the future," Crystal answered. "It's the desire for a favorable outcome combined with the feelings associated with that right now. The alternative is feeling hopeless and imagining an unfavorable outcome, which creates unwanted feelings. It's a choice." She paused. "Love appreciates this moment, and future outcomes will be what they will be."

Nathan's mother, Esther, looked between Crystal and Nathan. "I want to feel hopeful. I just...I don't know how when I'm so scared."

"That's understandable," Crystal said. "Ask Nathan to tell you about the Love Game. He can explain it better than I can."

"How would he know that?" Dan asked.

Nathan's face lit up. "Angela taught me."

Crystal continued, "If his labs continue to improve and he's eating and functioning well, we can consider discharging him to home. Currently we're just keeping him comfortable. If he's comfortable at home, we can follow him as an outpatient or arrange nurse visits for lab work."

"You mean he could come home?" Esther's voice broke.

"Possibly. Let's see how tomorrow's labs look."

"Sounds great to me," Nathan said. "I miss playing with my toys."

*****

Charlie was unusually quiet during breakfast, pushing his cereal around his bowl while Chris chatted excitedly about their visit to the Humane Society the day before.

"Mom?" Charlie finally spoke up, his voice tentative. "Could we just go and see Hope again? I know we can't adopt her, but I just want to see her."

Sharon looked at her son's hopeful face and felt her heart tug. "Charlie, honey, you know our situation. We're just getting back on our feet, and with everything that's happened..."

"I know," Charlie said quietly. "I just want to see her. Maybe pet her again?"

Sharon sighed, seeing the longing in his eyes. "Let me call Mr. Lucas and see if that would be okay."

She dialed Larry's number and he picked up on the second ring.

"Larry? It's Sharon. Charlie is asking if we can come back to the shelter today. He wants to show me Hope, the dog he connected with yesterday. I told him we can't adopt her right now, but he just wants to see her again."

"Of course," Larry's warm voice came through the phone. "I'll call ahead to let them know you're coming. How about I meet you there at eleven? I'd like to see how Hope is doing, too."

"That would be wonderful. Thank you, Larry."

Charlie's face brightened when she hung up. "Really? We can go see her?"

"Yes, but Charlie, remember what I said. We're just visiting. We can't bring her home."

"I know, Mom. I just want to see her."

At 11:00 sharp, Sharon pulled into the Humane Society parking lot with Charlie practically bouncing out of his seat. Larry waited by the entrance, greeting them with a smile.

"Ready to see your friend?" Larry asked Charlie, who nodded eagerly. Inside, they approached the front desk where Fran, the volunteer from the day before, sat.

"We're here to see Hope," Charlie said eagerly, his eyes bright with anticipation.

Fran looked up with a gentle smile. "Oh, honey, Hope is gone."

Charlie's face fell instantly. "Gone? What do you mean gone?"

Fran glanced at Larry, who gave her a small nod. "Well, let's just say Hope isn't here anymore. But we do have another dog named Love. Would you like to see her?"

Charlie shook his head, his voice small. "I really want to see Hope."

"Well," Fran said kindly, "why don't you just take a look anyway? Sometimes these things work out in ways we don't expect."

Charlie looked up at his mom, who nodded encouragingly. "Okay," he said sadly, "I guess we can look."

They walked down the aisle, Charlie's steps slow and reluctant. When they reached the cage where Hope was the day before, Charlie stopped abruptly.

There was a new sign on the door: "LOVE."

Inside the cage, the same beautiful miniature Australian Shepherd with the blue merle coat and mismatched eyes looked up and began wagging her tail furiously when she saw Charlie.

"It IS Hope!" Charlie cried out, his sadness instantly transforming into pure joy.

The dog pressed against the cage door, whimpering with excitement at seeing him again.

Mr. Lucas knelt down beside Charlie. "After you looked into Hope's eyes yesterday and said you saw Love, we felt we had to change her name. Hope is nice, but Love..." he paused, watching the connection between boy and dog, "Love is everything."

Fran joined them, watching as Charlie's fingers found the latch. "This dog transformed after being with you yesterday, Charlie. Gone was the fearful dog trembling in the corner. She started engaging with the staff after you left. It was like you flipped a switch in her."

The moment the door opened, Love bounded out and into Charlie's arms. Sharon watched in amazement as the dog wagged her tail in delight, wiggling her whole behind, then rolling over as Charlie rubbed her belly. The transformation was remarkable - this was not the cowering, fearful animal they first met yesterday.

"See, Mom?" Charlie looked up at Sharon with pleading eyes, his hands still gently stroking Love's soft merle coat. "We have to adopt her."

Sharon looked at her son, then at the dog gazing up at Charlie with complete adoration. She felt a familiar tightness in her chest - the fear of additional expenses, of one more thing to manage. She just started working. Money will be tight.

But then she saw Charlie's face, the pure joy radiating from him. After everything they'd been through - the fear, the legal uncertainty, the upheaval - here was something that made him light up. Something that could bring healing to all of them.

"How much does adoption cost?" Sharon asked Fran, the shelter director.

Fran looked at Charlie with Love in his arms, then back at Sharon. "Our normal fee is one hundred dollars. That includes spay surgery and first vaccinations." She paused, smiling. "But for you today, we'll do it for fifty."

Mr. Lucas spoke up quietly. "I'd be happy to help with supplies to get you started. And Dr. Madigan at the clinic where Chris will work is reasonable with her fees."

Sharon took a deep breath. The fear of being stressed with additional expenses weighed against the joy that this dog named Love would bring to the family. She followed her heart.

"I can't say no to Love," she said softly.

Charlie's face exploded into the biggest smile she'd seen in months. He threw his arms around her and Love barked once, tail wagging.

"I would appreciate that, Larry." Sharon met his eyes, grateful for his steady presence through all of this.

As they walked toward the front desk to complete the adoption paperwork, Love trotted next to Charlie, looking up at him every few steps as if to make sure he was still there. Sharon watched them, thinking "Maybe this is what healing looks like. One small choice at a time."

Chapter 28: Nature Walk and Talk

Sunday afternoon, August 31

Mark and Crystal decided to spend the afternoon hiking in a nearby state park. As they walked toward the trailhead, Mark got a call.

"It's Mom, wonder what she wants." He answered the phone, "Hi Mom, what's up?"

"How about coming over for a Labor Day cookout tomorrow afternoon? You can take care of the grill and maybe Crystal can bring the potato salad. I'll take care of the rest. Sarah is going to be here and wants to spend some time with us before she goes back to school."

Mark turned to Crystal. "Mom's inviting us to a cookout tomorrow. She wonders if you would bring the potato salad?"

"I'd love to."

"Mom, we'll see you tomorrow. Crystal will bring the potato salad. What time? Anything else you need?"

"Let's say around 4:00ish. I'll have iced tea, if you want something else to drink, you can bring it."

"Okay, mom. Thanks. Bye now."

After hanging up, Mark's expression grew thoughtful as they started down the trail. He was quiet for a while, and Crystal could sense something shifting in him.

"What is it?" she asked gently.

Mark inhaled deeply. "Sarah's going to be there tomorrow. She wants to spend time with me and her grandma before returning to college next week." He paused, trying to find the right words. "I'm feeling nervous about it."

"About me meeting her?"

"Yes. Sarah and I haven't always seen eye to eye about my personal life. When her mother and I divorced, she had strong opinions about that. I'm worried she'll think I'm moving too fast with you, that she'll judge our relationship."

Crystal felt her stomach tighten. "You think she won't accept us?"

Mark glanced at her, then back at the trail. "I don't know. And I've been thinking about things - about us - for a while now." He hesitated. "I've even been thinking about asking you to move in with me. But now with Sarah coming, I'm second-guessing everything. What if meeting my family makes you realize that my complications are too much? What if you change your mind about us?"

Crystal stopped walking. "Mark, that's a lot."

"I know. I'm sorry. The timing's terrible to bring this up."

"No, I mean we're doing it again." She looked around at the trees, the dappled sunlight. "We're creating all these disasters that haven't happened yet and may not happen at all."

Mark realized his shoulders were tight and his jaw clenched. "You're right. I can feel how closed off I've gotten."

"Me, too." Crystal started walking again, and Mark fell into step beside her. "This place, being in nature like this, it's supposed to help us open our hearts, not close them."

They walked in silence for a while, letting the rhythm of their steps, the rustling leaves, and the birdsong begin to shift something between them. Movement itself seemed to ease the urgency.

Mark asked quietly, "What am I actually afraid of?"

"That Sarah won't approve. That I'll leave." Crystal's voice was gentle. "And I'm afraid, too. Afraid of not being enough for your family, afraid of being the reason you and Sarah have tension between you."

The simple acknowledgments, spoken while walking among the trees, seemed to diffuse some of the anxiety.

They continued walking, and gradually Mark felt his breathing slow, his mind quiet. "You know what? I'm imagining the worst to try to prepare myself, but all it's doing is making me feel terrible right now."

"Same here," Crystal admitted. "I'm creating a whole story about Sarah rejecting me, and I haven't even met her yet."

Mark stopped at a clearing with a view of the valley below. "What if we tried something different? What if we imagine it going well?"

Crystal joined him, looking out at the vista. "What would that look like?"

Mark closed his eyes for a moment. "I imagine Sarah's face lighting up when she meets you. Her being excited that I'm happy. Her warmth, her acceptance." As he held that image, the tension in his face began to melt. "Ahhhh. That feels so much better."

"Let me try." Crystal took a slow breath. "I imagine tomorrow being easy. Natural. Sarah and I finding things to talk about. Her seeing how much I care about you. Me feeling welcomed." She opened her eyes. "Yes. That feels completely different."

They stood together in silence, absorbing the peace of the moment.

Mark reached for her hand. "I do want to talk about moving in together. But not from a place of fear, not because I'm afraid of losing you. When the time is right, we'll know."

"I'm open to the conversation," Crystal said. "Just maybe not today, when we're both spinning out about tomorrow."

Mark smiled. "Fair enough."

Crystal squeezed his hand. "So, what do we have right now? In this actual moment?"

"Right now, I love you," Mark said simply. "Right now, I'm excited for you to meet my daughter because she's important to me and so are you."

"Right now, I love you, too," Crystal responded. "And right now, I'm looking forward to meeting someone who is so important to this wonderful man I care about."

They continued walking, their earlier anxiety replaced by a quiet confidence. The movement, the conversation, and the natural beauty around them had all worked their own kind of magic.

"If we start spinning out in worry again?" Crystal asked.

"We come back to this," Mark responded, gesturing to the forest around them. "We remember what's actually happening in this moment, not what we're imagining might happen."

"Deal."

As they rounded a bend in the trail, Crystal laughed softly. "You know what's funny? We came out here to open our hearts, and we almost closed them completely first."

"But we didn't," Mark said. "We caught it. We talked it through."

"Walking and talking," Crystal mused. "There's something about moving our bodies and being in nature that makes it easier to work through things."

"Easier to let go of the fear and just be honest."

They walked on, connected not just to each other but to the peace they've rediscovered in the simple act of moving forward together.

Later, as they headed back to the parking lot, they noticed Jesse and David arriving.

"Mark! Crystal!" Jesse called as he and David got out of the car.

Mark turned with a smile. "Jesse! David! Just getting here?"

David rushed over and hugged them both. "I'm so glad to see you two. You look radiant."

Crystal smiled, returning the hug. "Thank you, David. It's been a beautiful afternoon."

"Yeah, thought we'd get outside and spend some time in nature," Jesse said.

"It's a beautiful day for it," Mark agreed. "This place has a way of opening hearts."

"Yep. That's what we're hoping for, too."

"Enjoy your hike," Mark said.

"You, too...I mean, enjoy your drive home," Jesse corrected himself with a chuckle.

As they parted ways, each of them carried a quiet understanding that they'd all come to the same place seeking the same thing.

*****

Just as Mark and Crystal decided to spend the afternoon hiking in nature at a nearby state park, Jesse and David's day unfolded and lead them there as well.

The phone rang as Jesse was settling into his Sunday afternoon routine. He glanced at the caller ID. It was Pastor Smith.

"Hello, Pastor."

"Jesse, I hope I'm not interrupting your Sunday rest. I had a conversation with Joe Rigid about David this morning after service."

Jesse's stomach tightened. He had been dreading this call ever since the incident at church. "I see."

"I'd like to talk with you about it, if you're willing. I could stop by around noon tomorrow if you're available."

"That would be fine, Pastor. I'll be here."

After disconnecting, Jesse sat staring at the phone. He knew this conversation was inevitable, but that didn't make it any easier. He needed to talk with David about what happened, hear his perspective, maybe gain some wisdom that would help him know what to say to Pastor Smith tomorrow.

He found David in his room, lying on his bed staring at the ceiling.

"David, can we talk?"

David sat up, his expression somewhat guarded. "Is this about what happened at church?"

Jesse nodded and sat on the edge of the bed. "Pastor Smith is coming over tomorrow. He talked with Mr. Rigid."

David stood up suddenly. "Let's take a walk, Dad. We can talk about this outside, surrounded by nature."

Jesse was relieved by the suggestion. "Yes, let's go. We can drive to the state park. It's only a thirty-minute drive."

Jesse found Vicki in the kitchen. "David and I are going to take a hike at the state park. I want to hang out with him for a while."

Vicki nodded, understanding. "That's a good idea. Take your time." She paused, then added, "Don't forget your water bottles."

No sooner did they leave than her phone rang. She picked up on the second ring.

"Hello?"

"Hi, this is Charlie. Can I speak to David?"

"David is out with his dad right now. Can I take a message?"

"When he gets home, would you tell him that I got a dog? Her name is Love."

"I don't know how long before they'll be back, but I'll give him your message. Are you having fun with Love?"

"Oh yes, Mrs. Walden. We are having a blast. She reminds me that unconditional love really exists."

*****

For the first few miles, they rode in comfortable silence, watching the suburban neighborhoods give way to rural farmland. Finally, David broke the quiet.

"Dad, what do you get out of going to church? I mean, what feelings do you have when you leave?"

Jesse considered the question carefully. "Most Sundays, I feel renewed. Like I've been reminded of what's important." He paused. "But I'll be honest, some Sundays I leave feeling frustrated or even angry."

David looked surprised. "Really?"

"When I see judgment instead of love. When people seem more concerned with being right than being kind." Jesse's grip tightened on the steering wheel. "Yesterday was one of those days."

They pulled into the trailhead parking lot and saw Mark and Crystal heading to their car. After a brief greeting and David's warm hug, Jesse and David started down the trail, the dappled sunlight filtering through the canopy above them.

David walked quietly for a few moments. "Do you talk to Jesus, and does he talk to you?"

"I do pray, yes. Sometimes it's formal prayers, but more often lately it's just conversations." Jesse stepped over a fallen branch. "As for him talking back...that's harder to explain. There's a peace that comes, especially when I'm struggling. Sometimes it feels like answers come, but not in words exactly."

"Usually? Not always?"

"I don't always feel better when I don't get an answer. Or if I get an answer that challenges me."

David kicked at a small stone on the path. "Before I got sick in June, I would talk to God and get angry when I didn't hear anything. I questioned God's existence. Two things I've learned since then. One, answers don't always come immediately. Love tells me I have to live into them. Second, my heart was not always open to receive. When I learned that, I realized I'd been receiving answers all along but just attributed them to my imagination."

They continued walking. Soon, a beautiful monarch butterfly landed on a bush next to them. They stopped and smiled. As they moved ahead, the butterfly caught up and landed on another bush beside the trail.

David held out his hand and a moment later the butterfly landed on it. "Hi butterfly, my name is David and this is my dad."

Jesse stepped closer and, surprising himself, said, "Hi, how are you? We're on a walk talking about church and how it makes us feel. Do you have anything you would like to share with us?"

David looked at his dad with a shocked expression. "Oh my gosh, I never expected that!" He turned back to the butterfly, waiting.

The butterfly responded, "*Everything is transforming, growing, learning and changing. As with each individual, a church or religion as an entity is also on their own journey - a reflection of the collective members. Some resist change, some welcome it, some embrace it. That offers a variety of contrasts, perfect opportunities for each of you to choose what you really want, if anything, from organized religions.*"

David nodded thoughtfully. "I've been feeling like I'm growing in a different direction, but I wasn't sure if that was okay."

"*You may be transforming at a rate or in a direction different than the church you are attending. If so, that particular church may no longer serve you in the way you desire. The experience has been a gift, but now you have to decide for yourself whether to stay in a place that doesn't serve you. That decision is an important part of your own journey.*"

Jesse spoke up. "What about loyalty to something that has served you in the past?"

"*Loyalty is an interesting concept, isn't it?*" the butterfly responded. "*It implies an indebtedness that may inhibit you from living your truth. Everyone has their own reason for being part of or avoiding organized religion, but at some level all want to feel better about their life. If you're not feeling better about yourself and all beings after worshipping the Divine, then consider looking in another direction. Whether you choose to or not, all is well. I AM here.*"

"Thank you so much for sharing your wisdom," David said. "I feel so much joy right now."

Jesse added, "Yes, I am so grateful."

As the butterfly fluttered off, they continued to walk in silence.

The trail forked ahead. One path descended through dense woods into a valley, the other climbed upward through thinning vegetation. David, without thinking, started to take the upper trail.

His dad stopped. "Wait, what led you to take that fork?"

"I don't know, I didn't think about it. I was just drawn, maybe out of curiosity, to go up." David paused. "Would you rather take the other trail?"

"I don't have a preference." Jesse replied, "I suppose if we had a destination in mind, then maybe one trail would be better than the other. Since we don't have a specific destination then it doesn't really matter, does it?" He looked at David thoughtfully, "What if the destination is the step we are standing on in this moment? How we appreciate where we are will determine the direction of our next step."

David smiled at his dad, "Then every step is a new destination."

"Exactly," agreed his dad as he thought to himself, *Where did that come from?* He put his hand on David's shoulder as they took the next step up the trail. It was strenuous in some spots, but when they reached the top, they found themselves standing at the edge of a ridge overlooking the whole valley below.

"Look how far we can see, Dad."

They stood together in silence, taking in the view and the feeling of connectedness.

After a while, David asked, "How are you feeling?"

"Out of breath and perfect," his dad responded.

They paused again, the quiet settling around them like the valley mist below.

"Are you concerned about the meeting with Pastor Smith tomorrow?"

"I was, but not anymore. I'm just absorbing the beauty, David."

"Dad, Love tells me that what you see as beautiful, what you appreciate, what opens your heart is just a mirror reflecting your true nature as Divine Love."

They sat down, sipping their water in the silence of awareness, seeing Love, knowing themselves.

The drive back was mostly quiet. David stared out the window but wasn't really seeing the landscape. He was feeling something he didn't have words for: being in nature with his dad, the two things he loved most, together for the first time. It was that Perfect feeling he got when his heart opened to Divine Love. Complete. Whole. Like everything was exactly as it should be.

Jesse glanced over and saw the expression on his son's face. He didn't interrupt the moment. Later they pulled into their driveway, feeling a quiet joy with smiles that came from opening a treasure chest.

David's mom greeted them, asking, "How was your hike?"

"Interesting, joyful, and inspiring," Jesse answered.

"We've never been on a hike together before. Being in nature with Dad..." David paused, trying to find the right words but nothing quite captured it. "It was Perfect. Today we met a butterfly. Next time I'm going to ask Jesus to walk with us."

"He was with me, but I didn't stop to talk to him," Dad offered.

Vicki relayed Charlie's message to David.

"Can I go over now? It's not too late, is it?"

"Dinner will be ready in about an hour and a half. Can you be home by then?"

"Yes, sure."

"OK, have fun."

David grabbed his helmet and tore out of the house to jump on his bike.

Chapter 29: North Star

Monday noon, September 1: Labor Day

The guest they'd been expecting arrived punctually at noon, when Pastor Smith knocked on the door. David answered, opening the door and saying, "Good afternoon, Pastor Smith. Please come on in. Mom and Dad will be with you in a couple of minutes. It's a nice day - would you like to sit on the patio in the backyard?"

"That would be fine, David."

Vicki came in from the kitchen. "Good afternoon, Pastor Smith. Can I get you some iced tea?"

"Sounds good."

"David, show Pastor Smith the way to the patio."

A few minutes later, Vicki emerged from the kitchen with a tray of iced tea and a plate of sandwiches cut in quarters. Jesse joined them shortly after and David pulled up a chair. The pastor shifted uncomfortably in his seat, his fingers drumming against his glass.

"Maybe we should have this conversation without David present," he said, glancing between the parents.

"I'm sure David can handle what we're going to be talking about," Jesse responded.

Vicki nodded. "I agree."

Pastor Smith cleared his throat. "Okay, I'll get started then. Mr. Rigid came to me after church yesterday and told me that he had asked David to leave class because he caused a disruption. David's classmates seemed to be more focused on David's claim that God talks to him than on listening to what Joe prepared for the lesson."

Jesse nodded thoughtfully. "So, it wasn't because David was being disrespectful or disruptive himself. It was because of how his classmates were reacting to him."

"That's right," Pastor Smith said, his voice careful. He paused, studying their faces. "Were you aware of David's claim?"

"Yes, we are aware," Jesse answered.

David spoke up. "I think of God as Love when we're having conversations. I see Love as well."

Pastor Smith's jaw tightened. He shifted in his seat again, directing his attention to Vicki and Jesse. "Mr. Rigid also said that David thinks of himself as perfect and doesn't believe in sin. Don't you think that's a little...crazy?"

David looked at him with wise, gentle eyes. "Crazy for seeing love and connection in everyone, Pastor?" He paused. "I see you and Mr. Rigid as perfect children of the Source of creation, just as I am."

"Perfect?" Pastor Smith's eyebrows rose. "David, we're all sinners. That's basic scripture."

"I respect that the scriptures may be working for you, but Love tells me a different story. Jesus saw life through the eyes of Love and that's what I am practicing. When I let go of judgments, my heart opens and I see the perfection of Divine..."

Pastor Smith leaned forward. "But how do you know that? How can you be sure what you're experiencing is actually God and not just...your imagination?"

"Because I am not separate from God or Love. I don't need to read it in a book when I can go to Love directly." David paused. "You say imagination like it's not real. But I know what I experience is true because of how it feels, that perfect combination of compassion, peace, joy, appreciation, unity. That's how I know I'm aligned with the Divine."

"That's quite a claim for someone your age." Pastor Smith's voice carried both concern and skepticism. "The Bible is God's word. Why wouldn't you trust it?"

"What you are asking me is not to trust the scripture but your interpretation of it. Pastor, wouldn't you agree that not all people interpret the scriptures the same way? So how do you know beyond your experience that your way is the right way?"

Pastor Smith's jaw tightened further. "We have two thousand years of church teaching, David. Theology isn't something you just make up as you go."

"I'm not making anything up," David said calmly. "I'm sharing what Love shows me directly."

Vicki spoke softly, her hand moving protectively toward David. "Pastor, I've watched David since he woke from his coma. The change in him isn't just philosophical - it's tangible. He radiates a peace I've never seen in a child."

Jesse added, "Pastor, I want you to know that I initially struggled with the same issues you're having right now. When David first started talking about Love and seeing God in everything, I was concerned. Skeptical, even." He paused, his voice growing thoughtful. "But through multiple experiences with David, playing the Love Game with him, my own spirit has been lifted. I've come to understand what it means to truly be 'of God.' It's been transformative."

Pastor Smith looked at Jesse with surprise. "You...you had doubts too?"

"Of course I did," Jesse answered. "I'm still learning. But I can tell you that what David experiences is real, and it's changed our whole family."

Pastor Smith looked back and forth between them, his expression troubled but perhaps slightly more open. "Peace is one thing, but claiming direct communication with God? That's different." He turned back to David. "What does this...Love...tell you that's different from what we teach in church?"

"Love doesn't reject me," David replied. "Love doesn't say that I don't belong. Love doesn't say I'm a sinner."

Pastor Smith's grip tightened on his glass. "But we are sinners, David. That's why we need Jesus."

"Does Love say one person is more valuable than another?" David asked.

"Well, no, but..."

"Does Love tell me I should be Christian rather than Muslim, Jewish, or Hindu?"

Pastor Smith hesitated. "God wants us to know the truth of Jesus Christ."

"Didn't Jesus teach unity? That he and God were one, and in a sense, we are all one?" David asked. "Love never says I am separate from God. I am of God. Like a wave is not the ocean but of the ocean."

Pastor Smith's mouth opened, then closed. His breathing grew slightly uneven. "That's...that's blasphemy, David."

Jesse spoke again, his voice calm but firm. "That's quite a judgmental accusation, Pastor. That puts David in the same company as Jesus when he claimed he and the Father were one."

Pastor Smith stared at Jesse, his face flushing. "Jesse, that was Jesus speaking."

"And David is speaking from his experience," Jesse said. "Pastor, just this morning David led me on a nature walk in the state park. I felt Jesus's presence in a way I never have before, seeing myself, others, and the natural world through the eyes of Divine Love that Jesus represents to me." His voice grew thoughtful. "It was life-altering."

Pastor Smith stared at Jesse. "You're saying you felt Jesus speak to you?"

"I'm saying I experienced something I never had before," Jesse responded. "Something that felt more real than anything I've encountered in church."

Pastor Smith shook his head slowly, rubbing his temples. "This is...I don't know what to make of this."

"What bothers you most about it?" David asked.

The pastor looked at him, startled by his directness. "I suppose...the idea that God speaks to you in a way that contradicts what we teach."

"What does it contradict?" David tilted his head to look at him.

"Well, the concept of sin, for one. Judgment. The need for salvation."

"Do you think God judges you, Pastor?"

Pastor Smith opened his mouth, then paused. "I...yes. God is righteous and just."

"When you feel judged, what does that feel like in your body?"

The pastor shifted uncomfortably. "I'm not sure what you mean."

"Fear? Tightness? Separation?" David's voice remained gentle.

Pastor Smith didn't answer, but his posture suggested that David had touched something.

Vicki interjected, "I used to feel that way too. Constant anxiety about whether I was good enough, whether God approved of me." She glanced at David. "Watching David, seeing how he experiences Love - it's shown me something different."

"Different how?" Pastor Smith asked, his voice quieter now.

"Love without conditions," she said. "Without the fear."

Pastor Smith looked down at his glass. "But doesn't that lead to...I don't know, moral relativism? If there's no judgment, no consequences..."

"I know God through the Love I see," David said. "I know it is Love because I feel a perfect mixture of joy, appreciation, compassion, peace, and unity." He paused. "Do you feel those things when you think about your god?"

Pastor Smith's knuckles whitened around his glass. The silence stretched.

"The god I've been taught about," David continued, "is a male fearsome god who advocates separating people into groups based on value, race, sexual orientation, gender identity, or birth location. A god who says you must believe a certain way to be saved from your sins, otherwise you will suffer for all eternity."

"That's...that's a harsh characterization," Pastor Smith said, but his voice lacked conviction.

"Is it inaccurate?" David asked.

Pastor Smith set his glass down carefully. "It's more nuanced than that."

"Perhaps," David said. "But does it feel like love to you?"

The pastor didn't answer. He looked troubled, wrestling with something internal.

"God taught me to play the Love Game as an alternative to the survival game - the kill or be eaten game," David said.

"The Love Game?" Pastor Smith asked.

"Seeing everyone and everything as expressions of Divine Love. Letting go of judgment. Choosing connection over separation."

Pastor Smith shook his head again. "David, this is a lot to process. I'm not sure..." He stopped. "What you're describing sounds beautiful, but it also sounds naive. The world isn't that simple."

"It's actually simpler than what we make it," David said. He glanced toward the edge of the yard. "Pastor, you never know when Love will show up to offer guidance." He pointed toward the edge of the woods.

The pastor looked but doesn't see anything. "What do you mean?"

"You'll see," David said quietly.

"It should be a relief for you to know I won't be coming back to Sunday School," David added matter-of-factly. "I'm not interested in learning about the Love of Christ from someone who wants to force his opinions on me and treats me with harsh judgment while holding a bible."

Pastor Smith winced.

"I would rather climb a tree or talk to the animals in the forest," David continued. "Whether you agree or not, I AM Love, and I see the Love that you are, just like the Love I see in that deer walking out of the woods."

A deer emerged silently from the woods, watching them with calm eyes. David stood slowly. "Excuse me."

Pastor Smith watched, his mouth slightly open, as David walked down to meet the deer. "David," he called out, "thank you for speaking your truth. I'm not sure I agree...or even if I need to agree."

Jesse and Vicki watched with familiar acceptance as their son approached the wild animal. The deer didn't startle or flee. Instead, it settled peacefully in the grass, and David sat beside it as if greeting an old friend.

"He speaks with more maturity than I expect for an eleven-year-old," Pastor Smith observed, his voice barely above a whisper.

"Much changed after David had his visions with God and awakened from his coma," Vicki explained.

Pastor Smith continued watching the scene, his internal struggle visible in the furrow of his brow. "Jesse, I've known you for years now, and I have never heard you talk this way. What's changed?"

"I'm learning to see through the eyes of Jesus," Jesse said simply. "And when I do, I'm able to see Divine love everywhere. I don't have to convince anyone to see what I see, and I especially don't reject people who see life differently."

Pastor Smith sat back in his chair. Something shifted in his expression - the defensiveness eased, replaced by genuine curiosity mixed with resistance. "That's...that's actually quite beautiful, Jesse. But surely you understand my concern. The congregation expects me to guide children toward a conservative faith. What would the parents think if I endorsed this kind of...individual spirituality?"

"We're not asking you to endorse anything," Vicki said. "Just consider that there might be more than one way to experience God."

Pastor Smith nodded slowly, his gaze drifting back to David and the deer. "If you were walking with Jesus when he was alive," Jesse asked, "would you have called him crazy or sick?"

The question landed like a stone in still water. Pastor Smith's expression once again grew troubled. "You know that's not the same. He was God's only son."

"Yes, I know because that's the story that I was told," Jesse said. "Yet many people were afraid of Jesus enough to want him dead."

"Jesse..." Pastor Smith's voice carried a note of warning but also indicated genuine internal wrestling. "You're not saying David is a modern-day Jesus."

"Of course not," Jesse replied. "David would probably disagree, though. He sees the oneness of existence. That means we are all connected to God or Love without exclusion."

Pastor Smith frowned, leaning forward despite himself. "What do you mean by that?"

"We're talking spirit. He is not separate from the spirit of God, Jesus, Joe Rigid, you or me. He sees the Love that Jesus is within you. You may walk, talk, and see life as Jesus does in those moments when you don't feel separate from anything. Jesus, according to David, was a master at playing the Love Game."

Pastor Smith sat with this for a long moment, his fingers loosening around his glass. When he spoke, his voice was softer, almost vulnerable. "That's...that's a profound way to think about it, Jesse. I'm not sure what to do with that understanding."

He fell silent, still watching the boy and the deer. The scene seemed to work on him in ways words could not. He couldn't hear their exchange, but something about the peaceful tableau held his attention

Finally, he spoke again, his voice subdued. "There is much to sit with here. I might need to have my own conversation with Jesus." He paused, his eyes still on David. "I appreciate you meeting with me and providing a background to David's experiences."

He set his glass down. "I need to have another talk with Joe about the way he handled the situation. Perhaps there was a better way to respond to what David shared." He stood slowly, as if his body was heavier than before. "Thank you - all of you, including David - for taking the time to talk with me, and thank you Vicki for the tea and sandwiches."

Jesse stood as well. "I'll show you out."

As Jesse guided him toward the door, Pastor Smith glanced back one more time at the boy sitting peacefully with the wild deer. Something in his expression suggested the image would stay with him for a long, long time.

*****

After leaving the conversation on the patio, David had approached the deer and gently touched her neck, feeling the warmth of her and the steady rhythm of her breathing. "Hi, old friend."

The deer responded, *"I AM here,"* then settled completely onto the ground. David sat beside her in the soft grass, cross-legged.

"How do you feel about your conversation with Pastor Smith?" the deer asked.

David considered. "In this moment, I feel perfect being with you."

"Okay, David. And in this moment, how do you feel about Mr. Rigid?"

David's face clouded slightly. "When I think about him now, the memory of him treating me unkindly and then rejecting me jumps up and I feel bad."

"Can you find a gift in that bad feeling? A way to feel even a little bit better?"

"I can't if I keep thinking the same way about him," David said, running his hand through the grass.

The deer's eyes held infinite patience. *"If you lived surrounded in nothing but pure light, you would be blinded just the way you would if you were engulfed in darkness."*

David looked up at her, listening intently. "What do you mean?"

"You need the inspiration of contrast. Have you ever seen the North Star in the middle of the day? It is the darkness of the night where this guiding light will be seen."

David tilted his head, beginning to understand. "So darkness helps us see the light?"

"Yes. Mr. Rigid's behavior is the perfect darkness for you to see your North Star - to know which way to move, to expand, to create, to find joy."

"Are you saying that unkindness is good?" David asked, his brow furrowed.

"I wouldn't say that. I would say unkindness is the perfect gift of darkness so people can refocus their attention to feeling better - not by going into battle to

eliminate the darkness, which only creates more darkness, but by choosing to shine their light of Love."

David nodded slowly, absorbing this. The midday sun warmed his back as he processed the teaching.

"*So often your world tries to control contrast,*" the deer continued, "*to exert power to make everything safe, for everyone to have the same values, the same interests, the same beliefs. In order to protect against experiencing contrasts, people build walls to maintain separation.*"

"But that's not what we're supposed to do?" David asked.

"*Your soul came specifically into this body on earth to expand through your experience with contrasts. Contrasts aren't problems to solve - they're essential for navigation and growth.*"

The wisdom hit David like a gentle wave of recognition. "Contrasts aren't problems to solve," he said slowly, feeling the truth of it settle into his bones. "They're essential for navigation and growth."

"*Yes,*" the deer said softly. "*So, David, embrace them as you would embrace me. When you shine your Light into the darkness, you become the North Star for others.*" She looked directly into his eyes, and in that gaze David felt the presence of something vast and eternal. "*Remember, Love is in all things, all beings, all situations - even darkness. Appreciate the darkness and you will know Love there too.*"

David reclined next to the deer in the green grass, looking up at the clear afternoon sky. A light breeze moved through the trees at the edge of the yard. The weight of understanding settled into him, not as a burden but as profound peace. He now understood how Mr. Rigid's harsh words weren't obstacles to his growth but the very contrast that illuminated his path forward. Just as the North Star can only be seen against the darkness of night, the light of Love became visible through the contrast of unkindness.

He reached out and rested his hand on the deer's warm side, feeling her steady breathing.

"All is well," he whispered to the sky, and meant it completely.

The deer remained with him a while longer in the grass, the two of them resting in perfect stillness under the midday sun, before she finally rose, touched her nose gently to David's shoulder, and disappeared back into the woods as silently as she had come.

Chapter 30: Revelations

Monday, September 1, late afternoon

Mark stood in front of Amma's house, holding a platter of marinated chicken breasts. He took a deep breath, then opened the door without knocking. "We're here!" he called out.

Crystal walked up carrying a large bowl of potato salad just as he stepped inside.

"Perfect timing," Mark said, holding the door open for her, though his voice carried a hint of nervousness.

"Are you as anxious as I am?" Crystal asked, adjusting her grip on the bowl.

"More, probably," Mark admitted with a small smile. "But we're doing this."

Amma appeared from the kitchen, her face lighting up with genuine warmth. "Mark! You look well," she said, touching his chin. "Crystal, dear, how are you?"

"I'm well, Amma. Thank you for having us," Crystal said, leaning in for a hug.

"Sarah! Your dad and Crystal are here," Amma called over her shoulder.

Twenty-one-year-old Sarah appeared from the kitchen, wiping her hands on a dish towel. Mark set the chicken platter on the table and opened his arms. "Come here, sweetheart."

The hug he gave her was unlike any she'd ever received from him. She felt herself surrendering into his arms, enwrapped in something warm and peaceful. Energy surged in gentle waves, and she felt goosebumps rise on her arms.

She looked straight into his eyes when they separated. "There's something different about you, Dad. What changed besides losing the beard?"

"Oh, so much, including having Crystal in my life," he said, gesturing toward Crystal.

Sarah studied Crystal with the measured gaze of a college senior meeting her father's serious girlfriend for the first time.

"Hi, Crystal," Sarah said, her tone polite but reserved.

"Hi, Sarah. I've been looking forward to meeting you," Crystal responded warmly.

"The backyard is all set up," Amma announced. "Mark, why don't you get the grill started? I've been looking forward to seeing if you remember how to cook those chicken breasts the way your father used to make them."

Mark headed out to the gas grill as Crystal asked, "Amma, where would you like the potato salad?"

"Let's put it on the kitchen counter. It's cooler in here and it will be a while before the chicken is ready."

"What can I do to help?" Crystal asked.

"Everything's set for now," Amma said. "There's iced tea and some vegetable hors d'oeuvres. Why don't you and Sarah get acquainted?"

Crystal and Sarah made their way to the patio table, settling into chairs with a view of Mark working at the grill. An awkward silence hung in the air between them for a moment.

Crystal broke it, saying, "Your dad talks about you all the time. He's so proud of you."

Sarah softened slightly. "He does?"

"Constantly. Your determination, your intelligence, your compassion." Crystal paused. "He mentioned you're in a pre-med program. What drew you to medicine?"

Sarah relaxed a bit more, sensing genuine interest rather than polite small talk. "I thought it was about helping people, easing suffering. But lately I'm not so sure. I've been so focused on grades and getting into medical school that I wonder if I've missed discovering what I'm actually passionate about." She looked down at her hands. "I say I want to help ease the suffering of others, but I've never really cared for the wellbeing of another person in that way. Waiting tables in the summer isn't the same as being a health caregiver."

Mark looked up from the grill as he arranged the chicken. "You wanted to be a doctor ever since you were a child. What changed?"

"Life, I suppose. School. Growing up." Sarah's voice carried something unspoken; a weight Crystal noticed but didn't pursue.

Crystal chose her words carefully. "You won't know anything about your future until you're there. The direction you take with each step will lead you to the perfect place for choosing your next step. Surprises happen all the time to make life interesting."

She paused, studying Sarah's face. "I've learned a lot in the last few months about living and dying, and especially how seeing my work through the eyes of Love makes a difference in how I show up with everything I do."

"Love?" Sarah asked, her scientific mind curious. "That's an interesting way to put it."

"I had a transformative experience with an angel," Crystal said simply. "She's someone I took care of before she passed and has been in my heart since."

Mark glanced over from the grill, watching Sarah's reaction carefully.

Sarah's eyebrows rose. "An angel? You mean...like a spiritual being?"

"She's had a profound effect on Mark too, but he can tell you about that. Amma knows Angela as well."

Amma heard them talking through the screen door. "Are you talking about Angela? Wait for me."

Sarah looked between them, her rational mind struggling with what she was hearing. "I never would have imagined in a million years that today's conversation would turn to angels."

Crystal smiled gently. "That's just the beginning."

"You and Dad are both so scientifically minded. We've never been a religious family either. I don't remember ever having talks about spirituality." Sarah's tone wasn't dismissive, just genuinely confused.

"It does challenge my understanding sometimes," Crystal admitted, "but then I witness things I can't explain any other way. Life is so much more than can be explained scientifically. It certainly expands the boundaries of what's possible."

Amma joined them at the table, settling into her chair with a knowing smile. She began telling the story of David and Angela, and how she met them in a dream.

Sarah interrupted, "Is David an angel too?"

"Yes, David is an angel, but he's still alive in physical form. I hope you get a chance to meet him," Amma continued. "I didn't know it was a dream at the time. We met in the park. Later I found out both Angela and David were patients in the hospital at the same time I had the dream. David was in a coma and Angela was being treated for cancer."

Sarah leaned forward, her curiosity piqued despite her skepticism.

"The remarkable thing," Amma continued, "is that when David woke from his coma, he told your dad about his dream and it was the same one I had. Exactly the same."

Sarah's eyes widened. "Wait, you and a boy in a coma had the same dream? That's...how is that even possible?"

"I don't know how it's possible," Amma said honestly. "I just know it happened."

"What was in the dream?" Sarah asked.

"We were in the park - David, Angela, and I - interacting with Love itself. What some people call God. They taught me the Love Game, which they had learned directly from Love." Amma's voice grew soft with wonder. "Nothing has been the same since."

Sarah's heart raced with an unexplainable feeling similar to joy but deeper, more expansive. She looked back and forth between her grandmother and Crystal, her logical mind wrestling with something her heart seemed to recognize.

"Amma," she said slowly, "you're telling me that you and a boy in a coma had identical dreams where you met God? And this actually happened?"

"I know how it sounds, sweetheart. If someone had told me this story six months ago, I would have thought they needed professional help." Amma reached across the table to touch Sarah's hand. "But I lived it. I felt it. And when your father confirmed David's experience matched mine exactly..." She shook her head. "Some things can't be explained, only experienced."

Sarah sat back in her chair, something shifting in her chest. "I feel like everything I thought I knew about reality just got turned upside down."

Mark called over, "Chicken's almost ready, ladies."

The three women brought the drinks, corn on the cob, green beans, and potato salad from the kitchen. As they were arranging everything on the outdoor table, Amma asked Sarah to set up five place settings.

"Is someone else coming?" Sarah asked, counting the four of them.

"The extra place setting is for Maggie - Mark's sister, your aunt," Amma replied casually.

Sarah paused, plate in hand. "But Aunt Maggie...I never even met Aunt Maggie. She died before I was born."

"I know, dear. Just trust me on this one."

As they settled around the table, Amma, Mark and Crystal sat still for a moment. They all heard a voice in their hearts: "*I AM here.*"

"Maggie is here," Amma said softly, looking at the empty chair. "Thank you for joining us."

Sarah looked around the table, then at the empty chair, then back at their faces. "You're joking, right? Is this some kind of test?"

"No," Mark said. "I heard her say she was here."

"Me, too," Crystal added.

Sarah's voice rose slightly. "Okay, I've been patient with the angel talk and the shared dreams, but this?" She looked at each of them in turn. "You're all in on this together, aren't you? Some kind of...I don't know, spiritual initiation or something?" Her rational mind pushed back hard. "I'm a science student. I deal in evidence, in things that can be measured and observed. You can't just tell me there's a dead person sitting at this table and expect me to..."

"Sarah," Mark interrupted gently. "No one expects you to believe anything. Maggie is present, but to know her, it's helpful to let go of judgments and expectations about what the presence of a spirit means."

He looked at his daughter with understanding. "You won't hear her voice through your ears. It will come from your heart - if and when you're ready. It will be like someone talking to you while you are dreaming. The voice comes without you controlling it. It's okay that you don't sense her presence in this moment. As you open your heart to even the possibility, she may let you know she's here at the perfect time."

Mark paused, choosing his words carefully. "Maggie helped a boy, a patient of mine, who attempted suicide after a lifetime of abuse. His recovery and turnaround were miraculous. You don't have to believe what we're saying - in fact, I don't want you to just believe us.

But our experiences, mine as well as Crystal's and Mom's, have transformed our lives in totally unexpected ways, and we have all witnessed healing that defies conventional explanation."

"I'm glad you're not pressuring me about this," Sarah said quietly, though her hand trembled a bit as she picked up her fork.

They began eating in contemplative silence. The tension gradually eased as the food and the evening air worked their subtle magic. After a few minutes, Mark turned toward the empty chair. "Maggie, what do you think about my desire to change my psychiatric practice?"

He grew still, his eyes softening as if listening to something only he could hear. After a long moment, he spoke, his voice carrying both his own warmth and something else - a wisdom flowing through him. *"I came to you in your dream to show you there is another way to treat individuals who are suffering emotionally and to support you. I wanted to show you what it looks like to see your patients through the eyes of love and then see how some will accept that energy and some will reject it. Your business is to shine the light of Love. It is not your business to take responsibility for the outcome."*

Mark returned fully to himself and continued in his own voice. "I want to create healing opportunities, teach the Love Game, incorporate inspirational nature experiences. I think I can make a difference in people's lives without trying to fix them. Instead of focusing on what's wrong with people, I want to help them discover what's right with them and help them remember who they really are beneath their pain."

"That sounds wonderful, Mark," Amma said warmly.

Sarah looked at her father with new eyes. "I'm not sure what the Love Game is all about, but I can see the joy in you as you talk about your new direction." She hesitated. "Aren't you afraid that you might fail? That your reputation might be challenged?"

"I would have been three months ago. Fear still comes up, but now I see it as a directional road sign, not a stop sign." Mark's voice strengthened. "There's another factor that's helping me stay aligned with this energy now more than any other time in my life. I am not alone. In addition to the spiritual support I have in Angela, Maggie, and Love itself, I have Mom, Crystal, David, Rachel, and Rachel's momma Nana. Fear doesn't last longer than a moment or two when you're surrounded by that much love."

Mark glanced at Crystal, then back at his daughter. "Everything has changed, Sarah. My whole understanding of healing, of what it means to serve people who are suffering. I've learned there's so much more to wellness than just treating symptoms or behaviors. I want to help people find their own inner healer, their own connection to Love."

Crystal added, "I've seen Mark's interactions with patients since his transformation. It's remarkable. People respond to him differently now. They feel seen, not just diagnosed."

As the evening air grew cooler, and after the dishes were cleared, Mark started a fire in the backyard fire pit. They gathered around with mugs of hot chocolate, the flames dancing between them, casting warm light on their faces.

Sarah asked more questions about their experiences. Crystal shared her recent experience with Nathan and how Angela continued to guide her work with families facing loss. Each answer opened new possibilities Sarah had never considered, slowly eroding the walls of her skepticism.

During a quiet lull in the conversation, as Sarah gazed into the flames, she became aware of a gentle presence - something warm and protective settling around her shoulders like an invisible embrace. Then she heard a voice clearly in her heart: "*I AM here. I am Maggie and I am here for you.*"

Sarah's head snapped up. She looked around the circle. No one else was reacting. "Did you hear that?" Sarah asked, her voice tremulous.

"What? I didn't hear anything," Amma said. Mark and Crystal shook their heads.

"What did you hear, Sarah?" Mark asked.

"It was nothing, probably my imagination. We've been talking about angels and spiritual stuff and I thought I heard..." She trailed off.

"*I AM and I did speak to you, Sarah,*" the voice came again, clearer this time.

Sarah's eyebrows furrowed as she scanned the space around her, her heart pounding.

Crystal noticed her confusion. "Is there something wrong, Sarah?"

"She spoke again." Sarah's voice was barely a whisper.

Mark leaned forward. "When someone or something is trying to get your attention and engage in conversation, the courteous thing to do is acknowledge them and show appreciation for their presence. That lets them know you're open to listen to what they want to share."

"Do I talk to them out loud?" Sarah asked, feeling slightly ridiculous.

"You can if you want, or you can send your thoughts to your heart. She will hear you," Amma offered.

Sarah took a deep breath, deciding to say it out loud. "Thanks for being here, Maggie. My heart is open to hear what you have to say."

Sarah looked to her family, waiting. Maggie said softly, "*Now is the perfect time.*"

"Time for what?" Mark asked, sensing a shift in the energy.

Sarah's face paled. "Maggie says now is the perfect moment to reveal my secret."

The silence around the fire was profound. Sarah started trembling.

Amma went to her side, kneeling beside her chair and putting her arm around her. "It's okay, child, there is only Love here."

Tears filled Sarah's eyes. "I'm pregnant."

Mark's mouth opened to say something but stopped when Crystal put her index finger up to her lips and shook her head. He nodded, understanding.

Amma whispered, "Sarah, breathe slow and deep. Let your body settle." She waited, holding Sarah as the young woman's breathing gradually slowed. "When you feel ready to talk, we would all be interested in how you feel about being pregnant."

Sarah took a moment to follow Amma's suggestion, drawing several deep breaths. "I'm scared. I didn't mean for this to happen. I was on birth control."

"Have you told your mother yet?" Amma asked quietly.

"No. I'm terrified about that too. She's going to freak out. I'm afraid I'm going to shatter her dreams for me to be a doctor." She looked toward her dad who was focused intently on her. "Are you going to say something, Dad?"

"My Sarah, I think it's best for me to listen right now," he replied. He reached for Crystal's hand in support as he observed a mixture of thoughts and feelings surging through him - old patterns of judgment rising and dissolving in the light of Love.

"I was seriously dating a boy at college. When I told him I was pregnant..." She paused, gathering herself. "He was terrified. He told me he wasn't ready to be a father and asked me to get an abortion. When I said I couldn't do that, he just...shut down. He said he didn't even know where his own life was going, that he couldn't handle this on top of everything else."

Her voice broke. "A week later he told me he was dropping out of school, moving to Hawaii to surf. He said he needed to figure out who he was before he could be responsible for anyone else. I understand he was overwhelmed, but it doesn't make me feel less abandoned. He just...retreated. And now I'm alone with this."

Maggie's voice came for everyone to hear: "*Sarah, you aren't alone and never will be. I AM here.*"

Sarah sobbed, her tears flowing freely. "I'm so sorry if I'm a disappointment."

Mark's eyes glistened with moisture. "A few months ago, I would probably have been disappointed. I would have lectured you about responsibility and consequences." His voice cracked. "Now, however, I see the Love you are and I feel perfect. Your pregnancy is a precious gift, as you are to me. Instead of bringing you down with the changes you might fear, it will take you to unimaginable heights."

"I keep thinking this baby will limit everything I can do with my life," Sarah admitted.

Mark leaned forward, his voice steady and sure. "Sarah, having a child doesn't diminish your possibilities - it expands them in ways you can't yet imagine. You can still become a doctor if that's what calls to you. This baby isn't an obstacle to your dreams; it might be the very thing that helps you discover what you truly want to create."

Crystal added gently, "Some of the most extraordinary people I know are mothers who refused to let anyone - including themselves - define their limitations. I work with families navigating unexpected situations all the time. There are more paths forward than you can see right now."

The fire crackled softly as they sat in contemplative silence. Finally, Amma spoke. "Sarah, would you like to take a walk with me tomorrow? I have a feeling the park might offer us some clarity as well as some peace."

Sarah nodded, wiping her eyes. "Yes. I'd like that."

Mark cleared his throat. "Let's get together for breakfast on Wednesday, all of us. We'll talk through the practical things. Doctor's appointments, living arrangements, how and when to tell your mother, what your options are for school."

"I'll be there too," Crystal said. "You don't have to figure this out alone, Sarah. We're all here."

Maggie's voice whispered in Sarah's heart: *"Your child will not limit your path, dear one. Love never limits; it only expands what's possible."*

As they prepared to leave, Sarah stood and looked at each of them in turn. "I came here tonight thinking this would be an awkward dinner with Dad's new girlfriend. I never imagined..." She shook her head in wonder. "Thank you. All of you. And you, Maggie. Thank you."

A warmth filled her chest, and she knew somehow that Maggie was smiling. Sarah realized that what she feared would be her greatest shame has become her entry point into a love she never knew existed - and possibly into a future more extraordinary than any she had previously imagined. As she hugged her father goodbye, she felt that same surge of peaceful energy she had when she first arrived, and now it felt like coming home.

Chapter 31: What do you want?

Tuesday Morning, September 2

Chris got up early, genuinely excited to have a job. Not just any job, but one working with animals. Dr. Madigan lit a fire in him he'd never felt before. Through his talks with Maggie, he'd started to understand that simply being who he was had value. And now he wanted more than just existing - he wanted his actions to make a positive difference in the world.

Maggie showed him that when he accepts Divine Love as the core of who he is, his actions will naturally reflect his passion to create a reality of love and kindness. He will attract the perfect situations to fulfill that desire.

Sharon dropped Chris off at the Madigan Veterinary Clinic before heading to the flower shop.

Dr. Madigan greeted Chris warmly, "I can see your excitement, Chris. We're glad to have you. Let's start slow though and introduce you to the office flow. The animals we board here aren't as healthy as the ones at the humane society. Some are recovering from surgery and need special care. Lisa is a vet technician. She'll show you around and point out what needs to be done."

Lisa, a woman in her thirties with kind eyes and efficient movements, extended her hand and shook Chris's in greeting. "First you need to change into scrubs. You can expect to get dirty." She led him to a cabinet. "Pick out your size and change in the bathroom. You can store your clothes in the locker."

Putting on the scrubs made Chris feel part of something bigger than just trying to survive - the focus of most of his life until now. It was a good feeling.

Lisa showed him where the sick and recovering animals were housed. As they walked down the hall, Chris stopped abruptly. In one of the larger kennels, a fox was lying with his leg wrapped in bandages.

"Is that the fox David found in the woods?" Chris asked, moving closer to the cage.

"Yes, it is," Lisa replied.

Chris's face lit up. "My brother Charlie told me about David's encounter while they were camping. I can't believe I get to see him."

"The fox is timid, and at times scared, but not aggressive. He seems to be recovering well," Lisa explained.

Chris knelt beside the cage and whispered something Lisa couldn't quite hear. The fox's ears immediately perked up, and his tail began to wag slightly. He moved toward the door of the cage, watching Chris with what almost looked like recognition.

Lisa's eyebrows rose. "Dr. Madigan told me you had a way with animals. What did you say to him?"

"I said, 'I see the love you are.'"

Lisa studied Chris for a moment, something shifting in her expression. "Well, whatever works. You definitely have a gift communicating with animals." She went on to explain his duties - cleaning kennels, helping feed the animals, and assisting when needed.

Throughout the morning, Chris found himself repeatedly called in when animals were distressed. A dog that wouldn't hold still for examination calmed immediately when Chris placed his hand on its back. A cat that had been hissing and biting at the staff purred contentedly in his arms. An elderly golden retriever recovering from surgery rested her head in his lap and closed her eyes peacefully.

Mid-afternoon, while cleaning the kennels, Chris forgot to properly latch a cage door. A small beagle managed to push it open and wandered down the hallway before Lisa gently coaxed him back.

The dog was safe, but Chris's hands began to tremble and his face drained of color as he waited for what he knew came next - the scolding, the putdown, the anger. His body tensed, preparing for impact. Years of harsh criticism and punishment had trained his system to shut down at the first sign of someone's displeasure.

Lisa noticed his reaction. "Hey, it happens to everyone, Chris. No harm done. Just remember to double-check next time, okay?" Her reassurance helped, but the knot in his stomach remained. His body hadn't caught up with his mind yet. The old fear still lived in his muscles, his breath, his racing heart.

Quietly, he called for Maggie's help. In his heart, he heard her gentle voice, *"There are no mistakes, Chris, just opportunities to learn how to adjust and refocus your thoughts toward the feeling you want to have in this moment. It may take longer for your body to stop reacting to the fear, but as you continue to practice focusing on appreciating all your experiences, your body's response will soften."*

She continued, *"In this moment, I see the Divine Love within your heart. There is nothing more powerful than that. Remember the Peace Pond? Let it handle the anger - even your own - while you focus on being kind to that beautiful soul of yours. As you continue focusing on appreciating your experiences, your body's response will soften."*

Chris took a slow, deep breath, remembering the still water of the Peace Pond, the way it reflected everything without judgment. Gradually, the knot in his stomach began to loosen, his hands steadied, and the tightness in his chest eased.

He returned to his work with renewed focus, checking each latch carefully, methodically. The animals seemed to sense his calm and responded in kind.

Dr. Madigan stopped by near the end of the day as Chris was giving fresh water to a recovering terrier. "Lisa tells me the fox responded to you beautifully today," she said with a warm smile. "I knew you had the gift when I met you at the humane society, but it's wonderful to see it in action here, too."

Chris felt warmth spreading through his body. "I just let them know I see them."

Dr. Madigan nodded thoughtfully. "That's exactly what they need. I'm very glad you're here, Chris."

As Chris changed out of his scrubs at the end of the day, he caught his reflection in the small bathroom mirror. The person looking back at him seemed different somehow - more solid, more present, more real. He felt something he'd never experienced before - the deep satisfaction of knowing his presence made a genuine difference. Not just to the animals, but to himself.

He pulled off the scrubs and placed them in the dirty linen hamper, already looking forward to Saturday when he'd be back.

When Sharon picked him up, Chris slid into the passenger seat with a tired smile.

"How was your first day?" she asked.

"I helped," he said simply. "I actually helped."

Sharon reached over and squeezed his hand, understanding everything those words meant.

*****

It was the last day before school started for David and Charlie. They decided to spend it at the park with Love. The park required dogs to be on a leash, but Love didn't seem to mind the restriction.

"Look at her," Charlie said, watching as a young couple stopped to pet Love. "She's a completely different dog."

David smiled, seeing how Love accepted treats from strangers with a wag of her tail, no longer the fearful, cowering animal first brought to the shelter. So much had changed in such a short time.

They were sitting on the bench beneath Chickadee's nest when they saw Mrs. Deera walking toward them with a young woman David had never seen before. He jumped up and ran to Mrs. Deera, giving her a long hug.

"I had a feeling you might be here," Mrs. Deera said, her eyes twinkling. "Hi, Charlie, nice to see you outside a dream."

"Hi, Mrs. Deera," Charlie responded.

The young woman beside Mrs. Deera looked confused. "Outside a dream?"

Mrs. Deera smiled. "Charlie and I shared a dream, Sarah. He was with his mother and brother by the Peace Pond during a gathering of mothers and their children talking about the guilt mothers carry. David and his mother were there as well."

Sarah's eyebrows rose slightly. After last night's dinner with its talk of angels and spiritual presences, apparently her grandmother's life had become even more extraordinary than she realized.

"Boys, this is my granddaughter, Sarah," Mrs. Deera continued. "Sarah, this is David and Charlie. We told you about David and Angela yesterday." She looked down at the dog. "And who is this friendly girl?"

"This is Love," Charlie said.

Mrs. Deera laughed. "Well, I can certainly see that. What a sweetheart." She scratched behind Love's ears. "I have something for you boys." She handed a bag to Charlie and one to David, then sat down on the bench with Sarah beside her.

Charlie looked in his bag and grinned. "Chocolate chip cookies! Mrs. Deera, thank you! Anyone want one?"

David raised his hand, "Me!"

"I made them fresh this morning. I had a feeling I might run into you."

David looked into his bag and found birdseed. "How perfect, Mrs. Deera. Thank you." He poured a few seeds into his palm and extended his hand toward the tree. "Hey, Chickadee, are you around?"

Chickadee flew down and landed in his hand. Sarah's eyes widened and she gasped softly.

"How are you, my friend?" David asked.

"Good! Good!" Chickadee chirped. *"Charlie here! Mrs. Deera too! New human? Teaching her the Love Game?"*

"Yes, this is Amma's granddaughter Sarah. We're just meeting her."

Chickadee took a seed and flew back up into the tree. David turned to Sarah. "Chickadee says it's nice to meet you and wants to know if we're teaching you the Love Game."

Sarah blinked, still processing the fact that a wild bird just ate from David's hand as casually as if he were a feeder.

David gave Sarah a few seeds. "Hold out your hand, palm flat."

Sarah did just that, her hand trembling slightly. A few moments later, Chickadee flew down and landed on her palm, her tiny feet tickling Sarah's skin. Before choosing a seed, the bird looked directly into Sarah's eyes.

Sarah felt a connection unlike anything she'd ever experienced. She'd never been this close to a wild animal before. Then, clear as her own thoughts, she heard the words: *"I AM here."*

She turned to her grandmother. "I know you're here, Grandma."

"I didn't say anything, dear," Amma said gently.

Sarah looked at David and Charlie, confused. "One of you said something, right?"

They shook their heads, smiling knowingly.

"That comes through your heart, Sarah," David said. "Chickadee spoke to you."

Sarah looked down at the small bird still perched on her palm, wonder spreading across her face. Chickadee took a seed and again flew off.

"When you're surrounded by Love," Amma said softly, "it's easier to open your heart to receive messages like that. The Love Game is a way of seeing and experiencing Divine Love everywhere - in birds, in people, in every moment. Love is what some call God. The key is letting go of judgments and expectations and appreciating what's present right now. That's what happened when you heard Chickadee."

Tears welled up in Sarah's eyes, joy flooding through her with unfamiliar intensity.

"When you're in this space, Sarah," David added, "it helps to get clear about what you really want. When you appreciate this moment and feel joy and know what you desire - that's when the universe responds."

Sarah nodded slowly, still processing everything.

"Let's go to the Peace Pond," Charlie suggested. "I always learn something about myself when I'm there."

Before they left, David poured more seeds for Chickadee onto the bench. Love led the way to the pond, staying one step ahead of Charlie.

They found a quiet spot by the water and settled onto the grass. Amma said, "Sarah, this is a special place. You can offer the pond a feeling you want to let go of, ask it questions, release judgments, and discover the Love that you are."

David added, "This is where I first understood that I was Love and everything everywhere is Love. To align with Love is to see everything through the eyes of unconditional Love in this present moment. The Pond reminded me that God and Love are one and the same."

"Are you ready, Sarah?" he asked. "Think of something you want to let go of or a question you want to ask. I like to put my feet in the water first to connect with the pond, but you don't have to. When you're ready to receive an answer, pick up a pebble representing what you're looking for and throw it into the water."

Sarah nodded and took off her socks and shoes, placing her feet in the cool water. The others did the same.

"One more thing," David offered. "The Pond doesn't tend to answer 'why' questions. It's better to ask 'what' or 'how.'"

"Let's all do this together," Amma suggested.

Sarah picked up a pebble and held it in her hand for several moments, her other hand resting on her still-flat belly - a gesture so subtle the others didn't notice. She closed her eyes, inhaled deeply, and threw the pebble into the water. Ripples spread to the edge of the shore then disappeared into stillness. One after another, more pebbles splashed quietly into the pond. They sat in silence, waiting.

After several minutes, David said softly, "When you feel complete with your answer, go ahead and open your eyes."

When all eyes were open, Amma asked gently, "Sarah, if you want to share, what question did you offer to the pond?"

Sarah shifted on the grass, considering how to share. "At first, I couldn't decide what to ask. So, I asked the pond, 'What question would best serve me right now?'"

She paused, looking at each of them. "The pond asked me, 'What do you really want in this present moment?'"

"I said, 'I want to not be scared.'"

"The pond asked again, deeper this time, 'What do you really want?'"

"I said, 'I want to be confident about my future.'"

Sarah's voice softened. "But the pond kept pressing: 'What do you want right now? Not later. Right now.'"

"I said, 'I want to trust that Love will guide me.'"

"The pond said, 'Trust looks to the future. What do you want now?'"

"Finally, I understood. I answered, 'I want to feel better right now.'"

"Then it asked, 'How can you create a better feeling in this moment?'"

David spoke up. "That's interesting, Sarah. My question was different, but I ended up at the same place - asking how to feel better."

"Me, too," Charlie nodded. "I asked about school starting tomorrow and feeling nervous about it."

"And I asked about supporting you through your changes, Sarah," Amma added quietly, reaching for her granddaughter's hand. "But we all ended up asking the same essential question."

Sarah looked between them, amazed. "What answer did you all receive?"

"Why don't we each share?" Amma suggested.

David went first. "The pond told me, 'See this moment through the eyes of Love.'"

"Same message for me," Charlie said.

"And for me," Amma added.

Sarah felt a chill run through her. "That's exactly what I heard too. Word for word."

Love chose that moment to come over and rest her head on Sarah's lap. Sarah couldn't help but laugh through sudden tears, stroking the dog's soft fur.

"The pond also reminded us," David continued, "that we often think of what we want as something in the future, something we have to work toward or wait for. But if we focus on the feeling of our desire being fulfilled right here in this moment, we create space for situations to appear that support our desire."

They sat quietly for a few more minutes, each absorbing the experience.

When they finally rose to leave, David reached out and took Sarah's hand. "Welcome to the Love Game."

Sarah squeezed his hand, then turned to embrace her grandmother. "Thank you for bringing me here, Grandma."

"Thank you for being open to it," Amma replied, holding her close.

After hugs all around, they prepared to part ways. Sarah and Amma continued their walk around the pond, Sarah looking back once to see David, Charlie, and Love heading toward the creek, the dog bounding ahead with unreserved joy.

"Grandma," Sarah said as they walked, "when the pond asked what I wanted right now, I kept thinking about the baby. About being a mother. About my whole life changing."

Amma squeezed her hand. "And what did you realize?"

"That I can't control the future. I can only choose how I feel about this moment." Sarah's voice grew stronger. "And in this moment, walking here with you, after what just happened, I feel loved. I feel held. I feel like maybe, just maybe, everything will be okay."

Amma stopped walking and pulled Sarah into another embrace. "More than okay, sweetheart. When you see through the eyes of Love, you'll see just how extraordinary your life is about to become."

*****

Sharon arrived at the flower shop with a flutter of nervous energy in her stomach. While Chris started his first day at the veterinary clinic and Charlie prepared for school to start tomorrow, she had her own milestone looming - hopefully her divorce would be finalized today.

Flora was already getting ready for the day, putting cash in the register. "Today I'll teach you how to use the register," Flora said. "Most people use credit cards now, so we don't need as much cash for change as we used to but we still ring up sales on the register."

She asked Sharon to unload some new vases from boxes in the storage room and put them on shelves to be ready for flower arranging.

As Sharon unpacked the vases, she mentioned she might need to leave around lunchtime to sign papers if her lawyer called. "I hope you'll understand if I need to take a break to talk to my lawyer."

"Of course, dear. You do what you need to do." Flora paused in her work, studying Sharon's face. "How are you feeling about it? Scared he'll fight you?"

"I've been practicing something different these last few days," Sharon said, carefully placing a crystal vase on the shelf. "Instead of imagining all the ways this could go wrong, I've been focusing on feeling good about whatever comes. Imagining the relief, the freedom - no matter what the terms are."

Flora's expression softened with approval. "That takes real courage, Sharon."

At 10:00, Sharon's phone rang. She glanced at the caller ID. It was Elin, her lawyer. Her heart jumped into her throat.

"I got a call from Les's lawyer," Elin said. "Seems those gentle suggestions we made about closer examination of his assets if this dragged on had an effect. Les spent the weekend thinking it over and has decided he wants the same thing you do - an uncontested divorce, no full disclosure. He agrees to stay away from you and the boys."

Sharon gripped the phone tighter, afraid to hope. "And the terms?"

"Better than expected. The house you're living in? It's paid off."

Sharon's knees went weak. She reached for the counter to steady herself. "What?"

"His real estate business has been more profitable than his tax returns suggested. He's been flipping properties. He's giving you the house and your car, free and clear. All debts stay in his name. Plus, he agreed to $1000 a month child support. He gave a little more than we expected, probably to make this go away quickly."

Sharon sank onto a nearby stool, the room tilting slightly. A paid-off house? No debt? She'd been prepared to negotiate for an apartment, for anything that would keep a roof over her boys' heads.

"His tax returns show he has significant income and assets," Elin continued. "Given what he's actually worth, this settlement is still low. Do you want to know the figures before you decide? We could push for more."

Sharon closed her eyes, thinking of Chris's haunted eyes when he talked about his father's rages. Charlie's nightmares. The years of walking on eggshells, of fear, of just surviving.

"No," she said, her voice steady. "I don't need to know and I don't want to counter his proposal. Let's finalize the paperwork so I can sign off on it today."

"Sharon, are you absolutely sure? You could..."

"I'm sure." Sharon opened her eyes, looking around the flower shop - at the beauty she'd been creating for three days now, at the peace she'd found, at her new life taking root. "Les probably thinks he won, and this deal confirms to him how stupid he thinks I am. And you know what, Elin? I'm completely at peace with that. I have what matters - safety for my boys and a fresh start."

Elin was quiet for a moment. "I've seen too many clients spend years in legal battles, trying to prove a point or punish their ex. It costs them everything - money, peace, years of their life. There's wisdom in knowing when you have enough."

"I have enough," Sharon said simply. "More than enough."

"There's absolutely nothing wrong with both of you walking away feeling like you got what you wanted. I'll file it with the court today. The house and car transfer will take a few weeks, but the divorce is done, Sharon. You're free."

After hanging up, Sharon sat perfectly still, phone in her hand, letting the reality sink in. Free. The word echoed in her mind like a bell ringing clear and true.

"Sharon?" Flora's voice cut through her thoughts. The older woman was standing in front of her, concern creasing her forehead. "Honey, you've gone white as a sheet. What happened?"

"It's over," Sharon whispered. Then louder, testing the truth of it on her tongue: "It's over! The divorce - Les agreed. The house is mine. Paid off. The car. Everything. He's staying away from us."

Her voice cracked on the last word, and suddenly tears were streaming down her face, not tears of sadness but of pure, overwhelming relief.

Flora's face transformed. "Oh, sweetheart!" She pulled Sharon into a tight embrace. "You're liberated. You and those boys are finally liberated."

Sharon buried her face in Flora's shoulder, her whole body shaking with sobs she'd been holding back for years. Flora just held her, one hand stroking her hair, murmuring, "It's okay, you're safe now, it's over."

When Sharon finally pulled back, wiping her eyes, she was laughing through her tears. "I'm sorry, I'm getting your shirt all wet."

"I don't care about the shirt." Flora cupped Sharon's face in both hands. "Look at you. You're glowing."

Around noon, Sharon headed out to meet Elin and sign the divorce papers. When she returned to the flower shop an hour later, there was a lightness to her step, a straightness to her spine that wasn't there before.

"How do you feel?" Flora asked gently.

"Liberated," Sharon said. "For the first time in years, completely liberated."

As the afternoon progressed, Sharon moved through the shop with renewed energy. She hummed while creating a bridal bouquet, her hands moving gracefully among the white roses and baby's breath.

Later, a woman came in looking worried and tired. "I need something cheerful," she said. "My friend just got out of surgery and she's pretty down."

Sharon felt her earlier joy bubble up again. "I'd love to help. Tell me about your friend. What are her favorite colors? Or what colors are in her home?"

The woman's face brightened slightly. "Oh, she loves yellow and orange. Her whole living room is decorated in warm colors like that."

"Perfect." Sharon moved to the vibrant blooms, selecting golden yellow gerbera daisies, orange Asiatic lilies, and deep purple statice for contrast. "These will feel right at home when she gets there."

As she worked, arranging each stem with care, the woman watched. "You really love this, don't you?"

Sharon paused, surprised by the observation. "I do. I really do."

"It shows." The woman's tired face softened into a smile. "You know what? She's going to love these. They make me feel better just looking at them."

After the woman left, Flora appeared at Sharon's shoulder. "You're different today. It's not just the divorce being final. There's something else."

Sharon considered this, looking down at her hands - hands that for so many years had trembled with fear, that had hidden bruises, that had held her boys when they cried. Now they're creating beauty.

"I feel like myself again, Flora. For the first time in so long, I feel completely unburdened and free to be who I really am."

"Well, if what I'm seeing today is what's to come, I see a beautiful future for us working together," Flora said with a warm smile.

Sharon opened her arms and Flora stepped into her hug. Sharon whispered, "I am forever grateful for your support."

As they prepared to close the shop that evening, Sharon looked around at the flowers, the peaceful atmosphere, the life she was building one arrangement at a time. "You know what, Flora? I think this is just the beginning."

Flora locked the door behind them. "Same time tomorrow?"

"Same time tomorrow," Sharon confirmed.

And for the first time in years, her future wasn't something to fear. It was full of possibility - wide open and full of light.

Chapter 32: Liberation

Tuesday evening, September 2

Sharon sat in her car outside the flower shop, phone in hand. She needed to make a call while she still had the courage. She dialed her sister.

"Hey, sis," Cindy answered warmly. "How are you holding up?"

"The divorce is final," Sharon responded.

"Oh, Sharon." Cindy's voice filled with emotion. "I'm so proud of you. I know it wasn't easy, but you did the right thing for you and the boys."

"Thanks, Cindy. That means everything to me." Sharon felt tears prick her eyes. She and Cindy had been close in their early years before each got married, but Les hated Cindy and got angry if Sharon even talked to her. Years of sisterhood lost to his control.

"You know," Cindy said, her voice taking on an edge, "just last week - before you filed - Les called me. He was going crazy trying to find you. Demanding to know where you were staying."

Sharon's chest tightened at the thought of Les hunting for her, desperate to maintain control. "What did you tell him?"

"I told him exactly what I thought of him and that he'd never get information from me. Sharon, I was so relieved when you left. I've been praying for this day for years."

Sharon closed her eyes, grateful. "Thank you for protecting us."

"Of course. You're my sister." Cindy paused. "Did you get a decent settlement?"

"The house, the car, no debts. And he's staying away from us. That's what matters. Now I can start fresh with my kids."

"That's wonderful, Sharon. Really wonderful." Cindy hesitated. "Listen, I need to ask - can I give your phone number to Mom and Dad? They've been asking about you."

Sharon took a deep breath, gripping the steering wheel. The lightness she'd felt all day - the relief of no longer fearing Les, no longer trying to keep herself and the boys safe from him - suddenly felt fragile. "Sure, go ahead. I don't expect them to be happy for me, but I'm not hiding anymore."

"Are you sure? You know how they are. Especially Dad..."

"I'm sure, Cindy."

They said goodbye, Sharon still sitting in the quiet car. She didn't have to wait long. Within ten minutes, her phone rang. Mom and Dad.

She answered, "Hello."

"I heard you left your husband." Her father's voice was hard, angry. "Abandoned your marriage vows. What the hell were you thinking?"

Sharon's chest immediately tightened. A familiar knot formed in her stomach - the same one she'd carried since childhood whenever she disappointed them. "I was thinking about protecting my children, Dad."

"Protecting them from their own father? You're being dramatic, Sharon. Making a mountain out of a molehill like you always do. A woman's place is to support her husband, work things out. Marriage takes commitment."

"Dad..."

"How will you even survive on your own? You've never been able to handle responsibility. You'll go crawling back within a month, mark my words."

"I have a job. I have a home. I'm taking care of my sons." Her voice sounded stronger than she felt.

Her mother's voice came on hesitantly. "Sharon, maybe if you just..."

"This is all your fault," her father cut her off. "You were never good enough. Never listened. Always causing problems."

Something shifted inside Sharon. Her breathing changed - not shallow with panic, but deep with purpose. Heat rose in her chest. Not fear this time. Anger. Fierce, protective, righteous anger.

"Chris tried to kill himself." The words came out quiet but hard as steel. "He was in the ICU. Les refused to let him see a psychiatrist. The doctor diagnosed him with PTSD from years of verbal abuse."

Silence on the line.

"Don't expect any help from us," her father said coldly. "You made your choice."

"I never expected help anyway, Dad." Sharon's voice was calm now, surprisingly steady.

The line went dead.

Sharon sat for a long moment, staring at the phone in her lap. Her hands were trembling, her whole body humming with adrenaline. But underneath the shaking, there was something else - something solid and unshakeable.

They'd said exactly what she knew they'd say. And she'd survived it. More than survived, she'd stood up to them. For Chris. For Charlie. For herself.

Her phone buzzed. A text from her mother: *I'm sorry. I wish I could help but you know how your father is. Please take care of yourself and the boys.*

Sharon stared at the message. Her mother, still trapped in the same pattern Sharon had just escaped. Still choosing peace over protection, submission over standing up. A wave of sadness washed over her - not for herself, but for the woman her mother could have been.

She typed back simply: *Thank you.*

Her phone buzzed again. This time it was a text from Rachel: *How did it go with the lawyer? Call me when you can.*

Sharon looked at the message, then at the flower shop behind her where Flora was probably still closing up. She thought of Nana's kitchen, always warm and welcoming. Of Vicki treating her boys like her own. Of Larry's quiet, steady kindness. Of Maggie's gentle guidance that helped her find the strength to leave.

She'd spent her whole life trying to earn love from people who only knew how to give it in tiny, conditional doses. But now? Now she was surrounded by people who chose to love her and her children, not because of biology or obligation, but because they wanted to. She remembered 'A house doesn't necessarily make a home. Biology doesn't necessarily make a family.'

For the first time in her life, she'd chosen her children over her parents' approval. It felt terrifying. It felt like grief. But more than anything, it felt like a door opening into a future she gets to choose.

Sharon started the car. She needed to get home to her boys. To tell them, face to face, that they were truly safe now. That the divorce was final. That they could stop looking over their shoulders.

As she pulled out of the parking lot, she realized the tightness in her chest was gone. The fear that had been her constant companion for years had lifted.

What remained was lighter than air - the unburdened feeling of a woman who was finally, truly free to build the life she and her sons deserved.

*****

When Sharon arrived home, both boys were waiting in the living room. They looked up as she entered, and she could see the question in their eyes.

"Chris, Charlie, come sit with me." She settled into the cushioned armchair, and they found places on the couch. "The divorce was finalized today."

A moment of silence. Charlie looked at his hands. Chris watched his mother's face.

"How are you feeling, Mom?" Chris asked.

She took a deep breath, feeling the lightness that had been with her all day. "Relieved. Really relieved. How are you both feeling?"

Chris shrugged, but there was something lighter in his posture. "I won't miss him. It's weird, but I feel calmer, like I can breathe better. It's only been two weeks, but everything feels different." He paused. "And the new job - I love it. I love working with the animals. It's the first time I've loved something like that." His voice dropped. "Maggie keeps reminding me that I am love and that I can accept that. Maybe someday I will."

Charlie sat quietly, picking at a thread on the couch cushion. Sharon watched him, waiting.

"Why doesn't he love me?" The words came out small, pained. "Maybe I'm just...maybe if I was better, he wouldn't have been so mad all the time. I always disappointed him."

Sharon's heart broke. She moved to sit beside Charlie on the couch, gently turning his face toward hers. "Charlie, honey, look at me."

He met her eyes, his own shining with unshed tears.

"Your father's anger was never about you. Not about Chris, not about me. He has issues about his own self-worth and need for power. You are not responsible for a grown man's problems." Her voice was thick with emotion. "You are kind and smart and funny and brave. If he couldn't see that, that's his loss, sweetheart. Not your fault."

Chris shifted on the couch closer to his brother. "Charlie, my brother, I'm here for you."

Charlie wiped his eyes with the back of his hand. "Really?"

"Really," Chris said firmly. "Always."

Sharon squeezed Charlie's shoulder. "You know what I'm grateful for? Not for what your father did to us - that was wrong and it hurt. But I'm grateful for the people who choose to be in our lives now. The people who actually see how wonderful you both are."

"David is my best friend," Charlie said, his voice gaining strength. "And Love is like my second-best friend." At the sound of his name, the dog trotted over and settled at Charlie's feet. "And Mr. Lucas is really nice to me. I feel good when I'm with him."

Sharon smiled. "I really like Larry too. I like the way he cares about you."

"What about you, Chris?" Sharon asked. "Who do you feel closest to?"

"I never thought I'd have friends," Chris admitted. "But at the clinic, Dr. Madigan and Lisa, they're really cool. They don't make me feel weird or broken." He glanced at his mom. "And Maggie, even though she's an angel, she's someone I can actually talk to." He paused. "And you, Mom. I feel like I can talk to you now. Like really talk."

Sharon's eyes welled up. "I feel that too, sweetheart. And I'm making friends too. Rachel, Nana, David's mom Vicki, and Flora at the flower shop has been wonderful this week."

They sat quietly for a moment, the weight of shared pain and new hope hanging between them.

Sharon spoke softly. "I know we've all been hurt by your dad. That pain is real." She looked at both boys. "It's okay to feel however you feel about it - sad, angry, scared. But when you get tired of feeling bad and you're ready for even a small shift, you can look for something to appreciate. Not about what he did, but anything else - about yourself, someone who cares about you, Love being here. Anything that helps you feel even a little bit better in that immediate moment."

Charlie suddenly perked up. "Mom, that's like the Peace Pond today! David and I went with Mrs. Deera and Sarah. We all asked how to feel better, and the pond told us the same thing, 'See this moment through the eyes of love.'"

"What does that mean to you, Charlie?" Sharon asked.

"David said appreciation helps you see through love's eyes. Like, I could keep thinking about Dad being mean, or I could think about Love being here with me. Both are true, but one feels way better."

Chris nodded. "Like at work. I could focus on being scared I'll mess up or focus on how the animals respond to me. Same moment, different feeling."

"Exactly!" Charlie said. "You can't judge and appreciate at the same time."

Sharon wiped her eyes. "When did you get so wise, Charlie?"

Charlie shrugged, smiling. "David taught me. And the Peace Pond."

Sharon inhaled deeply. "Here's what I'm learning. When we feel even a little bit better in each moment, we can start telling ourselves a different story about who we are." She looked at Charlie. "You're not a disappointment. That was the story you believed because of how your father treated you. But from a better-feeling place, we can see the truth: we're worthy of love, just as we are. Even feeling angry instead of hopeless is moving toward better," she continued. "Anger says 'I deserve better than this.' And that's true."

Charlie brightened. "So even when I'm mad at Dad, that's better than thinking I'm the problem?"

"Yes," Sharon said firmly. "Anger knows something is wrong with how you were treated, not something that was wrong with you."

Sharon pulled both boys close. "Tomorrow's your first day of school. New year, new start."

"I'm kind of nervous," Charlie admitted.

"Me too," Chris said quietly.

"Thanks for sharing your feelings, boys. I'm confident you'll find the best way to manage those feelings." She stood and pulled them up with her. "Come on, let's see what we can find to eat in the kitchen. I'm starving and I bet you are too."

As they rummaged through the freezer to find some ready-to-heat meals, Chris paused. "Mom?"

"Yeah, sweetheart?"

"Thanks. For leaving him. For keeping us safe."

Sharon's throat tightened. She put down the container she was holding and pulled him into another hug. "Always, Chris. I will always keep you safe."

Later, after they'd eaten and the boys headed to their rooms for the night, Sharon sat at the kitchen table with a cup of tea. She thought about her father's harsh words, her mother's fearful text, and Les's years of control. Then she thought about her boys: Charlie finding wisdom at the Peace Pond, Chris finding joy with animals, both of them learning to choose what felt better.

They were going to be okay. Better than okay.

*****

Sarah sat in Amma's living room, her laptop open on the coffee table, surrounded by pages of notes. After the Peace Pond experience that morning, she'd spent a couple of hours in the late afternoon researching. Something had clicked into place, and she couldn't stop exploring the possibilities.

Her hands trembled slightly as she dialed her father's number.

"Dad?" she said when Mark answered.

"Sarah! How was your day with Amma? Are you feeling better about things?"

"Actually, Dad, if Crystal's with you, can you put me on speaker? I'd like her to hear this if she's there."

"Of course, sweetheart. Crystal's right here with me. You're on speaker."

Sarah took a deep breath, feeling the same excitement bubbling up that had emerged by the pond. "I figured out what I really want."

"Tell us," Crystal's warm voice encouraged.

"I spent the afternoon asking myself what I'm actually excited about, what makes me feel alive. And you know what? I'm not excited about going back to school. I'm not excited about applying to medical school." She paused, expecting some pushback, but heard only patient silence. "But I am excited about being a mother. And I'm excited about something else."

"What's that, honey?" Mark asked gently.

Sarah's voice grew stronger, more animated. "I want to help you, Dad. You and Crystal and Rachel. Yesterday at the BBQ, you talked about creating a love-focused healing center for families dealing with childhood cancer - not just for medical treatment, but supporting the whole family with love and spiritual guidance. That vision stuck with me."

She began pacing in Amma's living room, her excitement building. "I don't want to be the doctor in the room. I want to be the person who helps make it happen - who figures out how to organize it, who builds the connections, who makes sure families know about what you're offering."

"Sarah..." Mark started, and she could hear something complex in his tone, wonder mixed with concern.

"Dad, I know what you're thinking. I'm pregnant, I'm not applying to medical school, this probably sounds impulsive." She paused, "But I've been questioning my direction for a while now. Finding out about this pregnancy three weeks ago was a huge wake-up call. And then having you and Crystal and Amma accept it and support me, then learning about this spiritual perspective I never had before - it all came together today at the pond."

"A few months ago, I would have been really disappointed to hear you wanted to give up on medical school," Mark admitted. "There might even be a little of that now. But Sarah, hearing the excitement in your voice, seeing you want to be part of what we're building, that eases any hesitation I have."

"What did you discover in your research?" Crystal asked, intrigued.

"I spent a couple hours this afternoon looking at healing centers, nonprofit models, funding approaches. There are places doing pieces of what you're envisioning, but nothing that combines medical care with spiritual healing the way you're describing. The closest models are places like Camp Sunshine for kids with cancer, but they're recreational, not integrated into treatment."

Mark's voice carried awe. "You've been researching all afternoon?"

"I couldn't stop. Once the vision became clear, I had to know if it was possible. And Dad, it is. More than possible, it's needed." Her excitement crescendoed again. "Maybe this baby I'm carrying is part of why this vision is coming to me now. Maybe becoming a mother will help me understand how to support other families."

She stopped pacing, her voice softening. "This is what I want, Dad. Not what I think I should want, but what actually makes my heart sing. Will you let me be part of what you're building?"

The silence on the other end stretched for a moment. Sarah's heart began to race.

Finally, she heard Crystal's voice, warm with emotion. "Sarah, the clarity in your voice, the excitement - this sounds like someone finding their true calling."

"But honey," Mark said gently, "are you sure about not applying to medical school? That's been your plan for years. What about finances, supporting yourself and the baby?"

"Dad, you've been supporting me through college. I'm not saying I have all the answers yet; that's part of what I want to figure out this week. I'm not saying we start this tomorrow. I'm saying I want to help build this, and I want to learn how to do it right."

"Tell us more about what you're seeing," Crystal encouraged.

Sarah's excitement returned. "I see families coming in scared and hopeless, then walking out with tools to find love even in the middle of their worst nightmare. I see children like Nathan - the one you told me about, Crystal - learning to play the Love Game while they're getting treatment."

She took another deep breath, her vision expanding. "I see parents learning that they can be part of their child's healing through opening their own hearts. And I see you, Dad, not just treating symptoms but helping families discover that love is the real medicine."

"Sarah," Mark said with amazement, "you're describing exactly what's been forming in my heart."

"The organizational piece, the outreach, the funding - that's exactly what we'd need to turn this dream into reality," Crystal added.

Sarah felt tears of joy on her face. "So you're not disappointed in me?"

"Disappointed?" Mark's voice cracked slightly. "Sarah, I'm watching you choose to follow love instead of fear. That takes courage."

"And you're going to be an incredible mother precisely because you're learning to trust love," Crystal added.

Sarah sank into Amma's armchair, overwhelmed with gratitude. "So, we're really going to explore this? We're going to build a love-focused healing center?"

"We're going to explore this," Mark said. "One step at a time."

Sarah's voice took on clearer determination. "Let me spend this week pulling together everything I found today. I want to show you not just the vision but some actual steps to make it happen. I want to dig deeper into the models I found, understand what the requirements might be, and look at funding possibilities." Her excitement continued building with each word. "I found some really helpful online resources like planning tools and case studies of successful centers. I'm finally using my research skills for something I actually care about."

"Sarah, I can hear it in your voice," Crystal said. "This is what passion sounds like."

"I haven't been this excited in a long time," Sarah continued. "And this feels right because I think we can create something amazing, something that could be there for my baby, for your grandchild, for so many families."

Mark's voice was thick with emotion. "Three weeks ago you found out you were pregnant and felt like your world was falling apart. Now I'm watching you turn what felt like a crisis into something that could touch thousands of families."

"That's the Love Game in action, right?" Sarah asked, surprising herself by using David's language. "Finding love in what seemed like a-disastrous, unwanted situation."

"Exactly that," Crystal agreed.

Sarah's mind was already working ahead. "Actually, there's one more thing. In the next week, I'd like to talk to each of you separately about your individual vision for this. Then we can all get together and I'll share everything I found."

"You said each of us," Mark noted. "You mean me, Crystal, and...?"

"And Rachel," Sarah responded. "From what you told me yesterday, she's the heart of the Love Game teaching. This wouldn't work without her."

"Of course," Crystal agreed.

"I want to understand what each person envisions," Sarah explained. "What this could mean to you, what possibilities you see. This would be new for all of us, and I think talking it through separately first will help us expand our thinking. Then when we come together, we can see how our visions connect."

Mark's voice carried something like relief mixed with pride. "Sarah, your enthusiasm for this, for doing the research, making the connections, organizing the pieces, that's exactly what will make something like this possible. Crystal and I have been focused on the healing work itself. Neither of us has the time or energy to spend on what you're doing."

"He's right," Crystal said. "I love working with families, supporting them through treatment. But the organizational side, the planning, the networking, that all takes a different kind of energy and focus. Your excitement about that part of it is invaluable."

"Actually, Crystal, do you know any parents who might have business or nonprofit experience? People who've been through treatment with their kids and might want to help?"

Crystal was quiet for a moment. "I know a few families. Some have nonprofit experience, others have business and fundraising backgrounds. Those are families who would understand the journey."

"Could you introduce me?" Sarah asked. "I'd love to learn from people who've walked this path."

"There's something beautiful about that," Mark added thoughtfully. "People who've been through it helping create something that could support others."

"I'll reach out to them this week," Crystal said. "When families see healing, even when outcomes weren't what they hoped, many may want to help other families going through the same thing."

"This is incredible," Sarah said. "Thank you both for believing in this and in me."

"We love you, Sarah," Mark said softly.

"Love you too, Dad. Crystal, thank you for everything. I'll call you both soon to set up those individual conversations."

"Can't wait," Crystal replied. "Take care of yourself, Sarah. And that baby."

"I will," Sarah promised, one hand unconsciously moving to her still-flat stomach. "I really will."

Chapter 33: The Beginning

Wednesday Morning, September 3

When Dr. Welling was making her rounds, she noticed Emily, a 10-year-old with cancer, holding something against her chest. "What do you have there?" she asked.

Emily held up a crystal.

"Where did you get that?" Dr. Welling asked.

"Nathan gave it to me before he left. He told me it represents Love and that it would help me feel better. He also told me that when I do feel better, it would be kind to pass it on to another child who was suffering."

Tears welled up in Dr. Welling's eyes.

"Why are you crying?" Emily asked.

"These are tears of joy. It was very nice of Nathan to give you this crystal so you would feel better the same way he did."

Dr. Welling, feeling her emotions rising, said, "Please excuse me, Emily. I'll be back in a little bit." She stepped into the hall and saw Rachel down the corridor.

Rachel immediately noticed that Dr. Welling had been crying and walked toward her.

"What's going on, Crystal?"

"Can we talk privately? Let's go to the consultation room." Dr. Welling told the ward secretary and Carolyn that she was taking Rachel from her duties for a few minutes.

Carolyn asked, "Is there something wrong?"

"On the contrary, Carolyn, everything is perfect."

In the consultation room, Crystal related the story of her experience with Emily and the crystal. "I see healing where I haven't seen it before. Not just physical healing, but something deeper."

Rachel touched Crystal's arm. "I'm here, Crystal."

"My heart is so full of love in this moment." Crystal took a deep breath. "I want to tell you something no one else knows yet. Mark intends to resign from his position as head of psychiatry department and focus on his private practice without the constraints of administrative bureaucracy. He wants to take more control over how he serves the emotional needs of his clients."

She paused, her excitement building. "We have a vision that I want to share with you because you're an integral part of this dream. Mark would have liked to be here when I presented this idea to you, but with the feelings I had after leaving Emily's room, I couldn't wait."

Rachel leaned forward, intrigued.

"We envision specializing in caring for children who have cancer and their families, providing emotional and spiritual support. I imagine this occurring on an individual level and extending to groups. Mark would like to write a book and give workshops to care providers about how they might better serve patients and their families. We would like to partner with you in this project."

Rachel sat quietly for a moment, overwhelmed. Finally, she spoke. "You want ME as a partner? I don't have any degrees or credentials..."

"Rachel, your journey from the darkest places to Love is your qualification," Crystal told her.

Rachel's eyes filled with tears, then she covered her face and sobbed. "I never imagined anyone wanting to include me in a vision like this. I feel the same way I did when Angela looked into my eyes and saw me as Love." She looked up through her tears. "I do know how to go into dark places, I've done it my whole life. But now I know how to bring Love with me. I would be honored to be part of your vision."

Crystal reached for Rachel's hand. "There's someone else who wants to be involved, Mark's daughter Sarah. You haven't met her yet, but she just found out she's pregnant and discovered this passion for helping organize something like this. She's excited to be part of the dream and is researching the practical details of how we can make this real."

Rachel looked surprised. "His daughter wants to help with this?"

"She called last night, full of ideas and enthusiasm. She's looking at the practical side - how to structure it, how to make it happen."

Crystal squeezed Rachel's hand. "For now, let's open our hearts to how each of us can contribute and what brings us joy in this creation."

"When will we all meet together?" Rachel asked.

"I'll talk to Mark and Sarah and get back to you so we can coordinate a time when we can all meet."

Rachel wiped her eyes and stood. "I should get back to the floor."

"And I have rounds to finish," Crystal said, also rising.

They embraced briefly at the door. When they stepped back into the hallway, everything looked the same - the nurses' station, the medicine carts, the fluorescent lights. But something had shifted. They were carrying a vision now, one that would transform how they show up for every patient, every family.

Crystal returned to her rounds, and Rachel headed back to her station. The work continued; the dream had begun.

*****

Wednesday Evening, September 3

Sharon dropped Chris off at the vet clinic, then took Charlie to his scout meeting. Chris had told her that Dr. Madigan wanted his help with an animal that Mr. Lucas had asked them to bring to the scout meeting that night.

At the scout meeting, Mr. Lucas approached Sharon before she could leave. For a moment they simply looked at each other, something unspoken passing between them. Sharon felt a flutter of connection but quickly dismissed it as just her imagination. Even if it wasn't, it was far too premature to make anything of it. She needed to learn how to take care of herself in a healthy way first.

"Please stay for a while. I have a surprise for you."

Sharon nodded, then Mr. Lucas spoke to the group. "May I have your attention? Please pull your chairs up and create a circle. Leave a path to the center. David, why don't you sit in the center? I have a surprise for everyone. Take your seats and be very quiet." After a couple of minutes, he said, "I'm going to ask Charlie to introduce our guests."

When Charlie stepped into the circle, Hank muttered, "Oh, this should be interesting."

Charlie started to speak, but his nervousness caused him to stutter. "I w-want to int-introduce..." He stopped, frustrated. Then he looked over at David, who was smiling and holding his hand over his heart. Charlie took a deep breath and started over, his voice clear and steady. "I want to introduce Dr. Madigan and my brother Chris, who works for her at the vet clinic. Let's welcome them." Charlie started clapping and the other boys followed.

Hank leaned toward another scout. "When did Charlie stop stuttering?"

The boys around him shrugged.

Sharon, standing off to the side, held her hand over her heart, knowing how much her boys had transformed over the last thirteen days. Her thoughts drifted to Les. Maybe someday he would find the way through his own darkness to see how wonderful his sons had blossomed. And this was just the beginning.

Dr. Madigan entered, followed by Chris carefully carrying the fox in his arms. As soon as the fox saw David, it started showing excitement, making soft whining sounds and wriggling in Chris's hold.

Chris walked to the center of the circle and kneeled, gently setting the fox down in front of David. The fox immediately nuzzled up to David's leg, tail wagging despite its slight limp. David reached down, scratching it behind its ear.

One of the boys said excitedly, "WOW! I've never seen a fox this close before."

Another one asked, "Why isn't it growling or acting afraid?"

Dr. Madigan explained, "David's compassion and calm presence helped the fox relax when he was hurt, and the fox remembers. He was fearful at the clinic but not aggressive after David left. We kept him a little longer than usual to make sure he was okay before sending him to rehab at the nature center."

She continued, "When Chris started working this week at the vet clinic, the fox relaxed every time Chris came close to him. Chris became his friend. Chris has the same calming presence that David has."

The boys, as well as Mr. Williams, the assistant scoutmaster, were stunned.

Mr. Lucas said, "Love creates miracles."

Dr. Madigan and Chris didn't stay more than fifteen minutes before gathering up the fox and leaving.

Hank said, "Maybe David isn't as crazy as we thought."

"Or maybe we're the crazy ones," said Jeremy.

*****

Wednesday Evening, September 3

Mrs. Deera's home felt warm and welcoming as Mark, Crystal, Rachel, and Sarah gathered in her living room. Coffee, tea, and slices of apple pie sat on the table, but the conversation had already moved beyond pleasantries and everyone was focused on the matter at hand.

"I'm so glad you could all come tonight," Mrs. Deera said, settling into her chair. "When Sarah called me this afternoon about wanting everyone to meet, I knew this house was the right place."

Sarah looked around the circle. Her father and Crystal sat on the couch, Rachel in the armchair, her grandmother across from her. "I've spent the day talking to each of you separately about your visions. And what I'm hearing is beautiful, but also...big. Maybe too big to hold in my head all at once."

Mark nodded. "I feel the same way. There's this sense of something wanting to emerge, but I can't quite grasp the whole of it."

"I keep seeing pieces," Crystal added. "Children healing, families finding hope. But how it all fits together..." She trailed off.

Rachel spoke quietly. "Angela used to tell me that some questions are too important to answer with just our thinking minds."

Mrs. Deera leaned forward. "The Peace Pond has been a place of clarity for many of us. What if we journey there together, not physically, but in meditation? We can each offer our questions to the pond and open ourselves to receive guidance."

Sarah's eyes lit up. "I was just there yesterday with you, Grandma, and David and Charlie."

"Then you know its power," Mrs. Deera said. "And you can help hold the space for the others."

"I've never done anything like this," Mark admitted.

"Neither have I," Crystal added.

Rachel smiled. "I have, with Angela. It's simpler than you think. You just need to be willing."

Mrs. Deera got up and dimmed the lights. "Let's move our chairs into a circle. Get comfortable. You can close your eyes or keep them soft. I'll guide us there."

They rearranged themselves, the pie forgotten. In the gentle lamplight, Mrs. Deera's voice became a steady anchor.

"Take a deep breath. Feel yourself here, in this room, safe and supported. Now imagine yourself walking a familiar path through the park. The evening air is cool. You can hear the rustle of leaves, the distant sound of water."

Sarah felt the Peace Pond and saw it appear in her mind's eye, vivid from yesterday's visit.

"You arrive at the Peace Pond," Mrs. Deera continued. "The water is still, reflecting the early stars. You're not alone. Look around the pond and see who else has arrived."

In the inner space of the meditation, they each sensed the others. Mark saw Crystal beside him. Sarah recognized Rachel across the water. They formed a circle at the pond's edge.

"And notice," Mrs. Deera's voice was soft now, "there are others here too. Angela. Maggie. They've come to hold this space with you."

Rachel's breath caught. Even in meditation, Angela's presence felt powerful and unmistakable.

"You're here to ask about your vision, your desire to serve Love by helping families whose children face illness, loss, and suffering. Feel that intention in your heart."

The pond's surface seemed to respond, becoming even more still, more reflective.

"Now, in the center of your circle, notice a presence. A warmth. A knowing. Love itself is here with you."

In the meditation, they each felt it differently. Mark as a gentle pressure in his chest, Crystal as warmth spreading through her body, Sarah as a sense of coming home, Rachel as the same recognition she felt when Angela first saw her.

Mrs. Deera's voice continued. "Love wants to speak to you. Open your heart and listen."

In the silence of the meditation, understanding bloomed:

What serves me is your Joy. Your open heart and creative intention to shine my light onto those who suffer - this serves me. Your choice to hold the hands of those walking through fear - this serves me.

Share the Love Game. Play together. How and where you focus your attention is part of your own journey. Start with one step. Let each step reveal the next.

You are working as One, honoring each soul's journey while staying true to your Loveself. This empowers your shared vision.

Sarah felt deep relief wash through her. One step at a time.

"Now," Mrs. Deera guided, "if you have a question about how to hold this vision, how to speak it, or how to begin, pick up a pebble from the pond's edge. Hold your question in your heart and offer the pebble to the water. Then open yourself to receive."

In the meditation, they each reached for a pebble. One by one, they released their questions to the pond. Ripples spread outward, then faded to stillness.

They sat in that stillness, waiting. Some received whispers of understanding. Others only felt the question settling deeper. The answers would come - perhaps not here, perhaps not now, but they would come.

"The pond has received your questions," Mrs. Deera said gently. "Trust that clarity will arrive in its own time. For now, express gratitude for this gathering, for Love's presence, for each other."

In the meditation space, they sensed Angela and Maggie's blessing, the pond's peace, Love's abiding presence.

"When you're ready, feel yourself walking back along the path. The park around you. This room. This circle of people who share your vision. Take a deep breath and, in your own time, open your eyes."

One by one, they returned. Mark opened his eyes first, looking slightly dazed. Crystal wiped tears from her cheeks. Rachel's face was radiant. Sarah met her grandmother's knowing gaze.

For a long moment, no one spoke.

Finally, Rachel broke the silence. "I felt Angela. She was there."

"Maggie too," Mark said, his voice thick with emotion.

Sarah leaned forward. "Did anyone else feel...I don't know how to describe it. Like Love was telling us we don't have to have all the answers right now?"

"Yes," Crystal agreed. "One step at a time. That's what I heard."

"I asked how to put words to this vision," Mark said. "But I didn't get words back. I got a feeling. Like the vision will speak itself as we move forward."

Mrs. Deera smiled. "The Peace Pond doesn't always answer immediately. Sometimes the answer unfolds over days, over weeks. But it always comes."

Sarah looked around the circle. "I know we just met, Rachel, but in that meditation...I could feel who you are. The Love Angela saw in you."

Rachel's eyes filled with tears. "I've never been part of something like this. Thank you for including me."

"We need you," Crystal said simply. "This won't work without all of us."

Mark reached for Crystal's hand. "So, what's our first step?"

Sarah pulled out her notebook. "I think our first step is to name what we experienced tonight. Not a mission statement - not yet. But our intention. What we felt in that meditation."

They spent the next hour talking, sharing what they sensed in the meditation, what resonated in their hearts. Mrs. Deera listened, occasionally offering a question that helped them go deeper.

By the time they were getting ready to leave, they hadn't solved everything. They didn't have a business plan or a budget or even a name. But they had something even more important: a shared spiritual foundation. A felt sense of being guided. And the knowledge that they were not alone in this work.

As Sarah hugged her grandmother goodbye, she whispered, "Thank you for bringing us together like this."

Mrs. Deera held her close. "Love brought you together, child. I just provided the space."

Walking to their cars under the stars, each carried the warmth of the meditation and the peace of the pond. The answers to their questions would come. The vision would clarify. For now, they had taken the first step.

And that was enough.

Epilogue: Nathan's Eighth Birthday

Saturday, October 25

The Johnson house buzzed with celebration as family and friends gathered for Nathan's eighth birthday. The dining room table overflowed with wrapping paper and opened gifts. Nathan sat in the middle of it all, his face radiant with good health that had seemed impossible just months ago. The shadow of illness that haunted his features through the summer was gone, replaced by bright eyes and rosy cheeks. His latest tests showed remission - not cured, Dr. Welling had cautioned, but remission. For now, that was everything.

The doorbell rang. Nathan looked up as his mother opened the door to reveal Rachel and Dr. Welling, both carrying beautifully wrapped gifts. They'd driven together, Dr. Welling had told Esther on the phone, wanting to arrive as a team.

Nathan immediately ran to Rachel, wrapping his arms around her with pure joy. The moment they embraced, he burst into laughter — the same miraculous, healing laughter that filled the hospital room months ago. He felt that wonderful tickling energy again, the sensation that bubbled up from somewhere deep inside whenever Rachel was near.

"I'm so glad you could come!" Nathan exclaimed. He released Rachel and turned to hug Dr. Welling warmly.

"We wouldn't miss this for anything," Rachel said, her voice thick with emotion.

Esther stepped forward. "Everyone, this is Dr. Crystal Welling, Nathan's oncologist." Dr. Welling waved to the gathered family and friends.

Esther's voice softened as she gestured to Rachel. "And this is Rachel. Her compassion and loving presence played an essential role in Nathan's healing." She paused, choosing her words carefully.

"Rachel is also Angela's mother. Angela passed away in August, but Nathan...Nathan talks with her still. She's been teaching him something she calls the Love Game."

A ripple moved through the room, some guests exchanging uncertain glances, others leaning forward with curiosity. Talking to someone who was dead?

The two women handed Nathan their gifts. He immediately sat down cross-legged on the floor, choosing Dr. Welling's package first. Inside was a beautiful crystal, clear and luminous, similar to the one he'd passed on to another child when he left the hospital.

"I thought you needed a Love crystal of your own," Dr. Welling said softly.

Nathan's eyes widened. "It's beautiful! I've missed having one."

"When you hold this crystal," Dr. Welling continued, "remember the Love that you are."

Nathan pressed the crystal against his heart and gave her another tight hug. "Thank you so much."

Dr. Welling's eyes glistened. "By the way, the little girl you gave your crystal to when you left the hospital? Emily is doing much better."

Tears appeared on faces around the room as everyone watched this exchange. Nathan turned to Rachel, his eyes bright with anticipation.

He carefully unwrapped her gift to reveal a drawing of a young boy holding a crystal, beautifully matted and framed. At the bottom, in careful handwriting, were the words, "Playing the Love Game."

Rachel's voice trembled as she explained. "Angela drew this before she got too sick to hold a pencil. This is David holding his crystal - David Walden, the boy who taught Angela the Love Game. She told me she wanted you to have it."

Nathan studied the picture quietly, his small fingers tracing the frame. "I feel happy looking at this." Then he turned and looked toward the corner of the room. "Thank you, Angela."

Rachel and Dr. Welling both turned their heads in the same direction.

"It's good to see you again, Angela," Dr. Welling said quietly.

The room fell silent. Joe Rigid, Esther's brother, stood frozen near the kitchen doorway, his coffee cup trembling in his hand. His wife Betty touched his arm, but he didn't seem to notice.

The doctor, a respected oncologist, was acknowledging the presence of a dead child as if it were perfectly natural. And there was his nephew, healthier than he'd been in over a year, talking to this invisible presence as easily as he breathed.

Betty broke the silence, her voice tentative. "Nathan, honey, can you explain the Love Game to us? I'd like to understand what Angela taught you."

Nathan sat up straighter, pleased to be asked. "You know when you're on a long drive and you play games like trying to find orange cars? The Love Game is kind of like that – only you try to find Love." He held up his new crystal, light dancing through it. "You know when you see it because of how you feel. It's a really wonderful feeling."

"But here's the thing," Nathan continued, his voice taking on the patient tone of someone sharing something important. "You can't see Love if you're wearing judgmental glasses. The best way to take off judgmental glasses is to appreciate whatever you see. Then you'll find Love everywhere."

His expression grew thoughtful. "It gets harder to play when something happens that makes you put your judgmental glasses back on and forget to appreciate things."

Several guests nodded slowly, processing this. One of Esther's friends wiped her eyes. "That's beautiful, Nathan," she whispered.

Joe's mind was still reeling from what Rachel had said moments before. David Walden. The name crashed through him like a wave. It had to be the same boy - the child he'd dismissed from Sunday school for claiming God spoke to him directly. The boy he'd called delusional, dangerous even.

And now that boy was somehow connected to his nephew's miracle.

His hands gripped the coffee cup tighter. Everything he thought he knew about what was proper and godly was crumbling. The child he'd rejected for hearing God had somehow helped save Nathan's life.

Joe's face paled as the full weight of this realization settled over him. He caught himself and glanced around at all the faces in the room. This was Nathan's birthday. He couldn't ruin it.

He took a large gulp of coffee, his hands shaking slightly.

"Isn't it time for Nathan to blow out the candles?" Joe asked, his voice a little too loud.

"Oh yes!" Esther said, sensing her brother's distress and grateful for the redirect. "Let's get the birthday cake!"

As the guests moved toward the kitchen, Joe stood rooted to the spot, staring at the drawing of David holding his crystal. The boy he'd dismissed. The boy who might have helped save his nephew's life.

Betty returned to his side. "Joe? Are you all right?"

He shook his head slowly. "I don't know, Betty. I really don't know."

*****

After saying goodbye to Nathan and his family, Rachel and Crystal drove to the park to meet Sarah and Mark at the Peace Pond. It had been seven weeks since their meditation gathering at Mrs. Deera's house, and this was their first time coming together since then to share what-had been unfolding.

They settled at the pond's edge, the October afternoon light golden on the water. Mark suggested they begin with a few moments of quiet, and they each closed their eyes, breathing in the peace of the pond. The presence of Angela and Maggie settled around them like a gentle embrace.

When they had all opened their eyes, Sarah pulled out a folder. "I have something to show you." She spread papers out on the grass between them. "These are the nonprofit filing documents for The Love Game Foundation. We're official. All four of us are listed as board members."

Mark leaned forward to look. "Sarah, this is incredible. How did you figure all this out?"

"Remember the family Crystal told me about? The parents who went through treatment with their daughter last year? The father's a nonprofit attorney, and the mother does fundraising." Sarah's face lit up. "They've been amazing. They understand what families go through and they wanted to help create something that could support others."

Crystal touched Sarah's arm. "I'm so glad you connected with them."

"There's something else," Sarah said. "I've decided to finish my senior year. I'd already paid for this semester, so I switched to business electives that include organizational development, nonprofit management, and fundraising. I have enough credits to graduate in

May." She glanced at her father. "And the light course load means I can keep working on the foundation. Plus, you know, prepare for the baby."

Mark's eyes glistened. "Sarah, I'm so proud of you. The way you've taken this vision and made it real..." His voice caught. "Your mom would be amazed."

Sarah wiped her eyes. "Thanks, Dad."

"I want to share what's happening on my end," Mark said. "Crystal's been referring families to me for support. Rachel and I are working with them together." He looked at Rachel with warmth and gratitude. "It's new and we're still learning, but it feels right. And something beautiful is happening - these families are telling other families about us."

Rachel's voice was soft. "I'm so grateful to be part of this. Working with Mark and these families..." She paused, her hands fidgeting with a blade of grass. "Sometimes I think I should say more in the sessions, contribute more. Mark keeps telling me I speak at exactly the right times, but..." She looked down. "I still have to remind myself that I deserve to be there."

Crystal reached over and took Rachel's hand. "Rachel, you do deserve to be there. What you offer these families - your presence, your compassion, the way you've walked through your own darkness - that's not something anyone can learn from a textbook."

Mark nodded. "When you speak, Rachel, it's always exactly what's needed. You have a gift for knowing when to be silent and when to share. Trust that."

Rachel squeezed Crystal's hand, tears on her cheeks. "Thank you. I'm learning to believe it."

"I've noticed something at the hospital," Crystal said, leaning forward with quiet excitement. "The patients whose parents have been meeting with you two - they're doing better. Their spirits are higher and they're engaging more with other kids. I think when parents carry hope and love instead of fear, their children feel it."

Sarah smiled. "That's the Love Game in action."

A gentle breeze moved across the pond. Sarah tilted her head slightly, as if listening. "Angela? Maggie? Are you here?"

The air seemed to shift, and they all felt it - that unmistakable presence.

Angela's voice came clearly to all of them, "*Sometimes when Rachel is at work, I visit the patient's rooms. I love when they can see me. They may not hear me say they are Love, but my presence brings smiles.*"

Rachel breathed, "Angela..."

Maggie's warmth surrounded them. "*I've been spending time with Sarah and Chris. I enjoy watching them discover joy, especially when they talk with me.*"

Sarah's hand moved unconsciously to her belly. "You're with us?"

"*Always,*" Maggie said.

Mark wiped his eyes. The presence of his sister, even in this form, always filled him with wonder.

Sarah opened her folder again and pulled out a single page. "I've been working on a mission statement. It's based on what we received in our meditation and on what we've all been experiencing." She looked around the circle. "Can I share it?"

"Please," Crystal encouraged.

Sarah read, "The Love Game Foundation is an organization of open hearts. We are committed to serving families whose children face life-threatening illness or families who have lost a child, regardless of their financial situation. We shine the light of Love on their suffering while holding their hands as they walk through the darkest hours of fear, grief, and despair. We teach and play the Love Game so Love can be seen and known as a way to nurture peace, joy and wellness."

The pond mirrored their faces, perfectly still. For a long moment, no one spoke.

Finally, Mark said, "It's perfect, Sarah. It captures everything."

Crystal nodded, her voice thick. "This is what we're here to do."

Rachel looked out at the water. "Do you remember what Love told us? That our joy serves Love? That we should take one step at a time?" She turned back to the group. "This is our first step. A real foundation. A mission. Families already finding us."

"What began with David," Sarah said softly, "was Love inviting a boy to play a game. And now it's grown into this."

Mark reached for Sarah's hand on one side, Crystal's on the other. His right hand trembled slightly, something he noticed happening more often lately, though he hadn't mentioned it to anyone yet. They formed a circle, hands joined, at the pond's edge.

"Love is truly the CEO," Rachel whispered, fresh tears flowing. "And we're honored to serve."

They sat in divine connection for several minutes, feeling the presence of Angela and Maggie, the peace of the pond, and something larger - the sense that this was just the beginning.

As the sun lowered toward the horizon, they gathered their papers. There was still so much to figure out - funding, space, reaching more families. But for now, they had this: a foundation built on Love, four hearts committed to service, and the guidance of something greater than themselves.

They walked back toward their cars together, carrying with them the certainty that what they were building would touch families they haven't even met yet, families walking through their darkest hours, about to discover that Love is always, always present.

About the Author

David Montgomery, M.D., is the author of *Loving to Heal: Easing the Way to Wellness* and *See Love ~ Know God.*

A board-certified physician specializing in obstetrics and gynecology, David now enjoys a more generalized practice that holistically assesses the health of men and women in the comfort of their own homes. Guided by his heart – whether in practicing medicine, painting, sculpting, writing, or even landscaping – he dedicates his life to healing and creativity. Embracing the spontaneous nature of inspiration, David allows insights to emerge in the present moment from his Divine Loveself, resulting in a process full of mystery. His art reflects his values and spiritual journey. He lives with his family amidst the expansive beauty of Arizona.

www.ingramcontent.com/pod-product-compliance
Lightning Source LLC
Chambersburg PA
CBHW071502110726
47908CB00003B/693